COURAGE & COMPROMISE

CROSSWAY BOOKS BY STEPHEN BLY

HOMESTEAD SERIES
BOOK TWO

COURAGE

&

COMPROMISE

STEPHEN BLY

CROSSWAY BOOKS

A DIVISION OF
GOOD NEWS PUBLISHERS
WHEATON, ILLINOIS

Courage & Compromise

Copyright © 2003 by Stephen Bly

Published by Crossway Books
A division of Good News Publishers
1300 Crescent Street
Wheaton, Illinois 60187

Cover design: Cindy Kiple

Cover illustration: Dan Brown

First printing, 2003

Printed in the United States of America

Library of Congress Cataloging-in-Publication Data
Bly, Stephen A., 1944-
    Courage and compromise / Stephen Bly.
       p. cm. — (Homestead series ; Bk. 2)
    ISBN 1-58134-433-3 (TPB)
    1. Rural families—Fiction. 2. Nebraska—Fiction. I. Title. II. Series.
PS3552.L93C68   2003
823'.54—dc21   2002156207

DP		13	12	11	10	09	08	07	06	05	04	03
15	14	13	12	11	10	9	8	7	6	5	4	3	2	1

For
the Erickson clan:
Nebraskans

There shall no evil befall thee,

neither shall any plague come nigh thy dwelling.

PSALM 91:10 (KJV)

One

"Jolie, did you feel something? Something dropped on me, right on my arm," Essie called out.

Jolie Bowers sat up in bed. For a moment she forgot where she was. She couldn't see the covers or her hands. The bedroom had a musty, sulfuric aroma. A flash of lightning bounced off the window pane and streaked through the thin cotton curtain, brightening Essie's round face and wide eyes. "What do you mean, you felt something?" Jolie asked.

"Like the ceiling leaking." The roar of wind and thunder mixed with driving rain muted Essie's words. "Look." She pointed. "It's right there on my arm."

Jolie flopped back down on her stomach and fluffed up her pillow. *There's no place I'd rather be in a storm than my nice, comfy bed.* She reached out and patted her sister. "We have rubber tarps on the sod roof, Essie. Not much can get past them. Let's snuggle up and sleep through the storm. We're safe in here. I do hope the corn is not damaged."

"My side of the bed is wet," Essie whined.

Jolie rolled over. *Lord, I wonder what it would be like to sleep in a bed all by myself?* An image of Tanner Wells darted into her mind. *I suppose I'll never know! I meant that in a pure way, Lord. Well, sort of a pure way.*

"It's really wet, Jolie. Feel over here."

Jolie propped herself up on one elbow and peeked out the window at the next flash of lightning. *Was that one of our rubber tarps blowing into the cornfield?*

She waited for more lightning to illuminate the room. A small drop of something splashed on the back of her hand. When the lightning hit again, she wiped mud off her hand. "I think you're right, sis. Let's get some pans to catch the drips." Jolie swung her feet to the side of the bed, strained to see in the dark, and waited for the dizziness in her head to clear.

When the lightning flashed again, she glanced straight above her at the underside of the sod roof.

"Ohhhhhhhhhhhhhhhhhhh!" she cried out.

Like a bucket of slop tossed at a hog, the mud, sticks, and straw of the sod roof slapped into Jolie's face.

She screamed as what felt like a wheelbarrow full of heavy, sticky, cold, wet mud plastered her and Essie. The bed straps broke, and they crashed to the floor.

"Jolie, where are you?" Essie hollered.

"Here! I'm here!" More mud plopped down on Jolie as she struggled to pull herself to her feet. This time when lightning flashed, she could see it right above their bed.

"The roof is gone," Essie sobbed. "And I'm all covered with mud."

"Jolie, what's happening?" Gibs hollered from the top bunk on the boys' side of the room. The blanket that divided the room crashed to the floor, the noise muted by the roar of the storm. Rain poured in through the opening. The boys' side of the roof gave way as Gibs vaulted to the floor.

With the next flash of lightning, Jolie spotted her mother at the doorway. "Come on," she hollered above the crash of the storm. "We've got to get to the barn."

"I'm covered with mud," Essie sobbed.

"We're all covered with mud," Lissa Bowers called out. "Come on! Hurry!"

"I can't see, Mama!" Essie wailed. "I can't see, and I'm freezin'."

"Hold my hand," Jolie called out as she sloshed and squished on her bare feet across the room.

"We will all hold hands," Lissa Bowers ordered. "Let's run out to the barn."

"The yard will be mud and standing water," Gibs protested.

Jolie and Essie inched toward their mother's voice.

"We don't have any choice. The house is melting," Lissa Bowers insisted.

"But our things, Mother—they'll all be ruined," Jolie cried.

"Darlin', we'll figure that out after daylight," Lissa Bowers said.

"But, Mama, I'm wearin' my nightshirt!" Essie cried.

"We're all wearing nightshirts. Now come on before the rafters crash down on our heads." With the next flash of lightning, Lissa Bowers reached for her youngest son's hand. Wearing only ducking trousers and mud on his head, Gibson Bowers shoved his hand into Essie's. She reached back for Jolie's.

Jolie could feel the mud and straw squish between her toes as they struggled to get to the front room. When it went pitch-black again, she hiked the sleeve of her nightshirt and tried to find a clean place to rub grime off her lips and eyes.

"Mama, I'm scared," Essie wailed.

"Hold tight, baby," Lissa Bowers called out. "Everyone hold tight."

"I wish Daddy were here," Essie called out.

"We all wish Daddy were here, but he isn't. We'll make do the best we can. Try not to step on anything sharp," Mrs. Bowers cautioned.

They slopped their way to the front door as thunder banged above the open roof. Lightning danced in the yard.

"What if the barn roof collapses?" Essie's voice quivered in near panic. "What will we do then?"

Jolie squeezed her younger sister's hand. "Daddy said it won't collapse. It has shingles. We'll be okay."

"But the barn only has three walls," Essie whimpered.

Jolie's toes felt numb. "It'll be fine, little sis. Grab my hand tighter."

"I can't see, Mama!" Essie hollered.

"The Lord will lead us." Lissa Bowers sucked in a deep breath. "Are you four ready to run for the barn?"

"Where's Lawson?" Jolie yelled.

"Isn't he with you?" Mrs. Bowers asked.

They heard more of the roof crash into the backroom.

"Lawson," Jolie screamed.

"You kids go to the barn. I'll get Lawson," Lissa ordered.

"No, Mama," Jolie shouted. "I'll grab him, and we'll be right there. You go on."

"Hurry, Jolie Lorita!" Lissa Bowers shouted.

Jolie's fingers felt along the cold, wet sod of the front room wall as she tried to find the doorway. This part of the floor was gritty between her almost numb toes. Her nightshirt hung heavy, wet on her shoulders, rubbing them raw. Her auburn hair plastered her cheeks and forehead. Rain and mud seeped across her cheeks. She pinched her lips tight and breathed through her nose. The odor of dirt and sulfur almost made her gag. She fought to keep from coughing.

Jolie paused in the wood-framed doorway between the two rooms of the house. When lightning flashed and thunder boomed at the same time, she hugged herself. Her knees and lips quivered. The boys' bunk beds lay in a broken pile of mattresses, mud, and splintered boards.

Then it was as dark as a mineshaft cave-in.

"Lawson," she screamed.

Jolie stumbled to the pile of rubble and mud. Rain beat against her face. She could feel mud up to her calves. *Oh, Lord . . . dear Lawson . . . please . . . We need him so. . . . I need him!*

She crammed her hands into the cold mud. Something hard cracked her knuckles. She tugged out Gibs's Winchester 1890 .22 rifle. "Lawson," she screamed again.

Jolie dug in the mud with the butt of the small rifle. Even though her hands had lost all feeling, she stuck them into the mud, no longer sure of what she hoped to find. "Lawson," she called again and again.

Lord, what am I going to do? He always sleeps so sound. He must be knocked out and covered with mud. He'll suffocate!

She dropped to her knees in the pitch-black room and stabbed her hands into the cold, sticky mud up to her elbows. The mud oozed around her knees. It felt like it was going to swallow her up. *Lord, I really need You right now! This can't be happening. It's a bad dream, and I want to wake up!*

Jolie tried to wipe her wet bangs off her eyes and smeared mud on her forehead. Mud dribbled into her mouth as she started to sob.

"Lawson Pritchett Bowers, you'd better be alive," she screamed.

"It's okay, Jolie. I'm over here. I ain't dead."

A wave of relief lifted her to her feet. Her chest heaved as she struggled to speak. "Where? I can't see you. Where are you?"

"I'm in the doorway, Jolie. Reach out your hand. Mama sent me back to get you. Come on, the barn is dry."

"Where were you?" she cried. Jolie used Gibs's rifle to push herself along in the mud. "I thought you were . . ."

"I woke up when I heard the horses bellowin' and went out to calm them."

"You never wake up early," she said.

"Yeah, I reckon that's a miracle. Here, grab my hand!"

Jolie held her free hand out in the dark ahead of her. "Then you weren't in here when the ceiling collapsed."

"No, it was all I could do to keep Stranger and Pilgrim from boltin' out into the night. They was tossin' me around on that lead rope like I was a tail on a big kite."

A strong hand gripped her arm. With the next flash of light, she spotted her sixteen-year-old brother, soaked and mud-splattered, in the doorway. Jolie threw her arms around his waist. He hugged her shoulders.

She hugged him tighter.

"I thought you were buried in the mud," she sobbed. "I thought you were dead."

He patted her mud-caked auburn hair. "It's okay, Jolie. . . . I'm okay. Ever'body is okay. We have to get to the barn."

"Don't turn loose of my hand," she pleaded.

Lawson laced his grimy fingers into hers. "Jolie, you've been raisin' all of us kids since you were nine. I don't reckon you ever needed me before."

"I need you now, Lawson Pritchett Bowers."

Lightning flashed and thunder clapped simultaneously above them. Cascades of mud dripped down everywhere from the sod ceiling of the front room. Jolie bolted toward the door. Lawson's strong arm yanked her back.

"Wait," he shouted. "Stay in the doorway." He threw his arms around her and squeezed so tightly she could barely breathe.

"Lawson, what are you . . ."

When the rafter cracked like a rifle shot, Jolie quit struggling. Lightning flashed just as the entire sod roof over the front room shattered, crashed, plopped, and splattered into everything in the room below.

Except the river rock fireplace.

And the two that huddled under the wooden doorframe.

"Now come on, Jolie." Lawson tugged her through the mud.

"We could have been under that. You saved my life."

"Maybe the Lord had something to do with it," he called out as he led her out onto the front porch.

Something down deep in her bones made Jolie feel warm. "God is good to us, Lawson."

"Even if we lost ever'thin'?"

Her muddy fingers squeezed her brother's hand. "No, we didn't lose everything, but for a minute I was scared I might have."

Lightning struck three times as they slipped and sloshed their way across the yard. Jolie couldn't keep her bottom lip from quivering in the cold. A dim light flickered from the corner of the barn near the stalls. Two horses and three people huddled near it. As Jolie scooted closer, she spotted the small barn lantern on a wooden bucket.

"The front room roof is gone too, Mama," Lawson reported.

Gibs jumped up and hugged Jolie around the waist. "I got the best big sister in the world. You found my model '90."

She shoved the gun at her fourteen-year-old brother.

The stunned family huddled around the dim lantern as if it were a campfire.

"You can let go of my hand if you want to," Lawson said.

"I don't want to," Jolie murmured. "Mama, Lawson saved my life when the roof gave way."

"And Jolie was down on her knees diggin' through the mud tryin' to save mine," he replied.

"That's why the Lord gives us family." Lissa Bowers surveyed the dim shadows of the barn.

"Mama, I'm freezing!" Essie wailed.

"Yes, baby, we're all freezing." Lissa scurried across the dirt floor of the barn and yanked down saddle blankets off the stall railing. "Everyone roll up in one of these and bury yourself in the haystack."

Essie stared at the small, square wool blanket. "This blanket is dirty, Mama."

"Not nearly as dirty as you, young lady."

"What're we going to do now?" Gibs asked. "Everything we own is covered with water and mud."

"We'll take one thing at a time," Lissa replied. "We'll stay out of the wind and rain and try to warm up and survive the night. Tomorrow we'll decide what to do next."

Jolie finally released her brother's hand but leaned her shoulder against his. "We'll simply clean up everything and build that cedar shingle roof. But I need to decide what to do about school tomorrow. How can I go with all my clothes muddy?"

Lissa Bowers handed canvas tarps to the boys. "You're the

teacher, Jolie Lorita. Just cancel school. There can't be many who can make it with the roads slicked up anyway. Boys, you roll up in these tarps and cover up with hay. It would be best to lay close to each other and share some warmth."

Before the kerosene lantern flickered and died, all five of them had buried themselves in saddle blankets, canvas tarps, and hay. Essie and Jolie huddled with their arms around each other.

"I never want to live in a sod house again," Essie whimpered.

Jolie rocked her sister back and forth. "If we had a cedar shingle roof, it would have been fine. It'll be okay once we get it all repaired."

"I wish Daddy was here," Essie mumbled.

Lissa Bowers flopped her arm across both of her daughters. "I'm glad someone in the family's getting a warm, dry night's sleep."

"Is he sleeping on the train?" Essie murmured.

Mrs. Bowers's voice softened to a sleepy whisper. "I imagine so."

"Why did he have to go to that ol' meeting in Lincoln?" Essie asked.

"Because they needed him," Jolie whispered.

"I need him worser."

"I wonder if other homes caved in like that?" Gibs rambled on in the dark.

"Will we build the cedar roof tomorrow?" Lawson asked.

"We'll probably have to shovel mud tomorrow," Jolie answered.

"If it ever stops rainin'," Essie added.

"Do you think the river will flood?" Gibs asked.

Essie sighed. "Will it come up this high again?"

"Our beds are ruined," Gibs said.

"I think I'll be able to clean up the stove," Jolie put in. "And dishes that aren't broken will clean. If it's clear, we'll haul everything out into the yard and let it dry. We'll wash the mud out of our clothes. And if we get the stove cleaned early, we can keep hot water boiling all day. A least we do have good well water."

Jolie stopped talking at the next flash of lightning.

A moment later thunder crashed.

"I counted to three. It's movin' away," Gibs announced.

"Mama, are you humming?" Jolie asked.

"Yes, I am, darlin'. My lips are shaking from the cold, and so I thought I might as well hum. Besides I'm counting my blessings."

Essie's voice was soft for the first time. "On a night like this?"

"Especially on a night like this, baby."

"I'm surely thankful that Jolie found my model '90. What blessings are you counting, Mama?" Gibs asked.

"For one, it's a blessing that your daddy isn't here. He would be so ashamed of not having the shingle roof installed that I believe he would have a heart attack."

"Mama, let's get it all cleaned up and rebuilt before Daddy comes home," Jolie suggested.

"Somehow, Miss Bowers, I knew you would say that."

"What other blessings, Mama?" Gibs pressed.

"It's a blessing that it didn't happen last month when Jeremiah, Bailey, and Leppy were all crammed into the front room with us."

"I wish Leppy had stayed," Essie said. "I don't know why he wanted to go back and clear things up in Colorado."

"It was the right thing to do," Mrs. Bowers said.

"What other blessings were you counting?" Essie asked.

Mrs. Bowers's voice sounded quiet, yet strong. "There is Jolie Lorita. No matter what I've gone through in the past ten years, I have always had her as a partner to work with me in everything. Right now she's layin' there, tryin' to figure out how to fix up her house again."

"It's your house, Mama," Jolie insisted.

"Darlin', I know most daughters live with their mothers until they marry. But I live with my daughter . . . until she gets married. I like it that way. And, sweet Jolie, I know how much your back hurts at night, and you never mention a word about it."

"I'm okay, Mama. Everybody gets tired."

"And most complain, but not you. More than Judge Pritchett himself, you have spoiled me. And another blessing is Lawson

Pritchett Bowers, who miraculously woke up in the storm and ran out and tied down Stranger and Pilgrim so they didn't run off. I suppose he's asleep by now. There is no sixteen-year-old in Nebraska that works as hard as that boy."

"Mudball ran off," Gibs mumbled.

"A pig won't go too far," Lissa consoled him. "He's smart. He'll be back when he misses breakfast."

"The food will be ruined," Essie added.

"I'll go huntin' first thing tomorrow, after I clean my gun, and find us some prairie chickens," Gibs offered.

"And I'm thanking the Lord for Gibson H. Bowers," Lissa continued. "He's the most optimistic hunter in the world and perhaps the bravest young boy in the West. Without batting his eye, he would go up against Mysterious Dave Mather armed with his .22."

"And my Henry, if I can find it in the mud," Gibs said.

"You girls have two of the finest brothers God ever created. They'll look after you until their last breath."

"How about me, Mama?" Essie called out. "Are you thankful for me?"

"Oh, baby, baby, baby, my cheeks hurt when I thank the Lord for you."

"They do?" Essie coughed.

"Yes, because I'm smiling so much. You're my joy and delight. Having you in my life makes every day fun. You make the sun shine way down deep inside of me, even when it's gloomy outside."

"It's gloomy now," Gibs observed.

"Does my voice sound gloomy?" Mrs. Bowers asked.

"I reckon it don't," he replied.

"That's because of my Estelle Cinnia."

"You make me feel good, Mama," Essie said.

"That's good, honey. That's what mamas are supposed to do on stormy nights when the ceiling falls down."

"I told Francis yesterday that my mother might be one of the two or three best mothers of all time," Essie announced.

"Two or three?" Gibs asked.

"Well, there was Jesus' mother . . . Mary. She rates up there," Essie declared.

"Oh my, now I'm not worthy to be in that category," Lissa Bowers protested.

"Who else?" Jolie asked.

"Mrs. Dufflemeyer."

"In Helena?" Jolie said.

"Yes, she made the twins' angel costumes the night before the school play, and Mr. Bowtie introduced her as the best mother in Montana."

"Mr. Bowton," Lissa Bowers corrected.

"Everyone called him Mr. Bowtie."

"So I'm right up there with Mary and Mrs. Dufflemeyer?" Lissa giggled.

"Yep. That's what I told . . ." Essie sat straight up. Straw tumbled on Jolie's face.

"Where is he?" Essie called out.

"Who?" Jolie asked.

"Francis. I didn't see Francis!"

Jolie tugged her back down. "I'm sure he's with his mother."

Essie squirmed, but Jolie held her down. "Where's Margaret?"

"She's in the rock corral. That much I know," Mrs. Bowers reported.

Essie propped herself up on her elbows. "Lawson, did you see Francis?"

"I told you he's asleep." Gibs yawned.

"I can't sleep, Mama," Essie said.

"Let's stop talking and see if that will help."

"I still won't be able to sleep," Essie whined.

Jolie felt the mud drying between her toes. Warmth returned to her bones, but her skin remained numb. "Maybe we can sing," she suggested.

"Sing?" Gibs moaned. "This ain't a time for singing."

"Sure it is," Lissa Bowers maintained. "Paul and Silas sang in the middle of the night in the Philippian jail even though they had been tortured."

"They wasn't tortured," Gibs argued. "They were just beat with a whip till nearly dead."

There was silence.

"I reckon that was sort of torture," he mumbled.

"We're much better off than Paul and Silas; so we can sing," Mrs. Bowers announced. "Big sis, you lead. You're the best singer."

"Only when Daddy is gone," Essie said.

By the time Jolie dozed off, only her mother's soft humming of "Oh, God Our Help in Ages Past" could be heard.

Lawson had water heating over a campfire in front of the barn by the time Jolie dragged herself out of the hay. She wrapped a dusty green canvas tarp around her shoulders and padded barefoot through the dirt, mud, and straw.

Lawson gazed east. "It's goin' to be clear today."

"Then we can get a lot of work done." Jolie squatted down. "The fire is nice, Lawson."

"I figured we might as well warm up before we start workin'." He nodded at the house. "Ain't that somethin', Jolie? The house is in worse shape than the day we arrived. I didn't figure anything could be worse than that."

"It looks like some of the rafters didn't break."

"Yeah, the sod and willows gave way and dropped down. I don't think the walls are too bad."

The outside of Jolie's fingers warmed over the campfire. "I can't comprehend why we aren't more devastated by it. Are we getting used to disaster?"

"Mama's even hummin' this mornin'."

"Where is she?" Jolie asked.

"Diggin' through our belongin's in the house. She's lookin' for clothes and things."

"Everything will be soiled or ruined."

Lawson stirred the fire. "She said she wanted to inspect her trunk."

"But those are her special dresses."

"That's what she said."

"I'm too dirty to put on anything clean."

"We drug the copper tub behind the canvas in that stall. You can have a bath. Mama already had one."

"She did?" Jolie asked.

"Yep. That water is for you and Essie. Me and Gibs get a fresh tub." Lawson smiled.

Jolie rubbed her hands over the flames. "Where's Gibs?"

"He went huntin' after he cleaned his gun. He said he had to shoot extra straight 'cause he's only got three cartridges."

"He went out barefooted?"

"And wearin' a saddle blanket for a shirt. Now go on. When you're done, I'll wake up Essie."

"But I don't have anything to change into."

"Mama will be here by the time you need to get out. Let me give you a pail of hot water to freshen it up. There's a bar of lye soap by the tub."

Jolie watched her brother pour the wooden pail full of boiling water. Some sloshed out, and steam rose from the cold ground. She clutched the canvas tarp to her shoulders. "But I don't have a towel. How will I dry off?"

Lawson glanced back at the roofless sod house. "Mama said she just got out of the water and shook like a duck." He tugged on his earlobe.

"But at least ducks have feathers," Jolie mumbled. She toted the steaming bucket into the barn and slid behind the canvas curtain to the thirty-gallon copper tub. She poured the water into the tub and tested it with a toe.

"Lawson?" she hollered over the six-foot-high solid wooden wall of the stall.

"What?" he called from the yard.

"Did Mama have clean clothes? What did she wear after she shook like a duck?"

"A tarp."

Jolie stuck her head out between the canvas and the stall wall. "Really?"

"Yep, she came out all wrapped up in a tarp and her wet hair hangin' down. She said she was goin' to the house to forage up somethin' to wear and then cook breakfast."

Jolie's back stiffened. "I'm cooking breakfast. That's my chore. I always cook breakfast. When Essie gets up, have her hunt for eggs. I'll milk Margaret."

She ducked back into the stall and stared at the small copper tub. She smelled old manure and new hay as she glanced around as if expecting someone to be peeking. *Lord, by faith I'm going to get in this tub. By faith Abraham went out . . . Well, by faith Jolie Lorita is going to get in this tub and scrub up, not knowing if she will have a towel or clothes to change into. I know that doesn't sound very profound, Lord, but it worries me.*

The water was tepid and clouded by the time she finished. There was no mud on her face or between her toes. Her auburn hair was squeaky clean. And there was no towel or clothes in sight.

Jolie stood in the tub, hugging herself and quivering. "Lawson, is Mama there?"

"No, but I'm here," Essie called out from the haystack.

"Where's Lawson?" Jolie's teeth chattered.

"He went to fetch Francis for me. Can I come in?"

Jolie splashed down into the water. "No, you may not."

"I just wanted to watch you shake like a duck. I ain't never shook like a duck before."

"Neither have I."

"Really?" Essie spouted. "I thought you'd done everything." She paused, then called out. "Did you find Francis?"

Jolie heard Lawson say, "I can't find him, Essie, but Margaret's fine. I'm sure he's around somewhere."

"Lawson!" Jolie stood back up in the tub and called over the railing. "Could you fetch Mama for me?"

"What do you mean, you can't find him?" Essie demanded.

"Lawson?" Jolie repeated as she hugged herself.

"He's not in the corral, Essie. But you taught him how to get out on his own. He must have wandered off to look at things after the storm."

"He can't wander off. He's too young," Essie wailed.

"Essie." Jolie clamped her knees together to keep them from shaking. "Go get Mama for me."

"I'm goin' to find him," Essie insisted. "Where all did you look for him?"

"Lawson!" Jolie hollered.

"Come on," he said, "I'll show you."

"Wait a minute," Jolie yelled. "Essie! Estelle Cinnia. Wait just a minute. I need some help here."

There was no reply.

"Lawson? Essie?"

Now what am I supposed to do? Get out and shake like a duck and wear a tarp all day? Mama, Mama, Mama . . . Melissa Pritchett Bowers can do that and look cute, but her oldest daughter can't. I knew I shouldn't have gotten in here without all my clothes laid out. Why don't I listen to me? I'm always better off when I listen to me.

Jolie sank back into the cool water.

Okay, Lord, You and I both know that's not true. I'm sorry. I'm always better off when I listen to You. Not me. She stared down at the dark green canvas tarp tossed on the dirt. *Now what exactly do You want me to do?*

Jolie sank down to her nose when the canvas flap flew open. "Mother! I'm taking a bath," she snapped.

Lissa Bowers marched in carrying several garments. "I should hope so. Are you clean yet?"

"Yes."

"Hop out of there, darlin'. Little sis will need a bath too."

"Mother, you're embarrassing me."

Lissa Bowers carefully laid the garments on the side of the stall and then stared at her daughter.

Jolie turned her eyes away. "Mother, don't look at me. I'm modest."

Mrs. Bowers shook her head. Her damp, long auburn braid flipped from side to side. "All I can see is a talking head and cloudy water. But modesty is a virtue. My father used to tell me that all the time with a certain sadness in his eyes. I think he knew it was something foreign to his only daughter."

Jolie looked at the clothes spread out on the stall. "Did you find some clothes that are dry and clean?"

Lissa Bowers paused at the canvas door. "Yes, all of those in my trunk were fine. Not a bit damp or dirty . . . yet."

Jolie sat up in the tub. "Did you find me a towel?"

"There are no clean towels, darlin'. Not even a flour sack. Perhaps you can turn your nightshirt inside out and pat yourself dry with some of the cleaner places. We'll start in washing things later."

Jolie stared at her mother's blue eyes and narrow face. "Mama, that's a pretty dress. I haven't seen you wear it since you were in Tabby McAlister's wedding."

Lissa spun around, and Jolie could hear the dress swish. "This is the dress I wore on my honeymoon. I know it's out of style, but it's clean. Well, sort of clean. And I can still wear it; so I slipped it on. I suppose it seems strange to have this fancy dress on and my hair in a braid."

"You look beautiful in a braid."

"Darlin', darlin', darlin'. Jolie Bowers is beautiful. Her mama is just an eccentric middle-aged lady with a braid. Now try on this gold dress. I know it's fancy, darlin', but today we don't have a choice. The green one is for little sis. It will be too big, but not much, I'm sure. I brought the red one, but we'd have to take it up a lot. That was the dress I wore when I carried Estelle."

"But, Mama, I can't wear your pretty gold dress."

"Jolie Lorita, we really don't have any choice. There is no reason to save that dress if not for a time like this. I didn't even know it was down there in the trunk. It needs to be pressed, but that will have to wait. You wear it."

Jolie bit her tongue. "No, Mama, I didn't mean that I don't want to wear it. I meant I'm too, eh, big to wear your clothes."

Lissa Bowers arched her thick brown eyebrows. "Yes, you are. And you are five inches taller, which means this dress will be several shocking inches above the dirt. We will wash this morning, and with a little wind, the clothes will be dry by noon. You can change back then. Until then we will make do with what's in the trunk. There's some give in that material. I'm sure you can button it. Use a hat pin if you need to. Now I'll slip out and stir up the fire. Do you know where Lawson and Essie went?"

"To look for Francis."

Mrs. Bowers darted out of the canvas-draped horse stall. Jolie eased out of the small copper tub and stood on the canvas tarp she had worn as a shawl. She shivered as she turned the nightshirt inside out.

Then she held it away from her body.

And shook.

"And one other thing." Lissa popped her head back inside.

Jolie clutched the nightshirt against her. "Mama, you did that on purpose."

"No, I didn't. But you do look nice in a blush, Jolie. I'm goin' to hook up Stranger and Pilgrim. They are the only team in fifty miles that can pull when the roads get slick. I believe you should drive down and post a note on the schoolhouse just in case some students actually show up today."

Jolie's hands and chin started to quiver in the cold. "I still say you did that on purpose."

Lissa Bowers grinned. "You're right, darlin'. Now put on that pretty gold dress."

The gold dress was so short Jolie's ankles showed. She tugged at the tiny abalone shell buttons down the front.

There's no way, Mother dear, that I can button this dress. It hardly covers up anything. I'll just wear my nightshirt. She glanced down at the crumpled, filthy beige nightshirt. *I can't wear that. I can't wear this!*

"Mother!" she whined.

Mrs. Bowers popped her head back inside. "Oh, my."

"It won't button."

"Yes, I can see that."

"I can't go around looking like this," Jolie moaned.

"I completely agree with you. Wait, I'll get you something else."

"Thank you."

Jolie combed her wet hair as she waited for her mother to return.

"Here." Lissa Bowers hiked into the stall and shoved a red plaid object at her.

Jolie's chin dropped. "What is it?"

"One of your father's old shirts from the trunk. It's too small for him."

"What am I supposed to do with it?"

"Wear it over your dress, darlin'. That way it doesn't matter if some of the buttons don't fasten."

"Wear it? Red plaid flannel with gold? Mother, that would look simply horrid!"

"Do you want to go around here all morning in a wet, dirty nightshirt? No one in this family will give it a second look."

Essie sprinted up to the campfire where Jolie had propped a black iron skillet on some rocks and squatted down to fry eggs.

"Francis ran off and drowned," Essie sobbed.

Jolie peered south toward the North Platte River. "Did you find his body?"

Essie's bottom lip curled and quivered. "No, but I just know he's drowned."

Jolie beat the eggs with a wire whip. "Did you find his tracks?"

Essie wiped her tears on her muddy dress sleeve. "No, but we found Mudball."

"Speaking of pigs, I could use some bacon this morning."

"Jolie, don't talk that way. He could hear you. Pigs are very sensitive."

"I didn't know that. Where did you find him?"

"He was fishin'."

"Fishin'?"

"He was standin' at the edge of the river snappin' at the water. Lawson said it looked like he was fishin'."

"Do you think Francis could have gone down there with Mudball?"

Essie warmed her dirty hands over the fire. "Not after that tiff they had last week."

"Tiff?" Jolie asked.

"You know, over who got the last piece of watermelon."

"You think that still bothers Mudball?"

"Pigs hold a grudge for a long, long time."

"Does that mean Francis avoided the river because he didn't want to be around Mudball?"

"Oh! Then Francis didn't drown," Essie shouted. "He wouldn't go with Mudball until Mudball apologized, and if the pig went to the river, Francis must have gone the opposite direction—to the railroad tracks. Thanks, Jolie. You're the smartest sister in the world."

"And your teacher."

Essie plucked up a short stick and poked at the fire. "But we don't have school today."

"No, I need to get that posted."

Essie stood up and pointed at the house. "I'm goin' to tell Mama that Francis didn't drown."

"Yes, and tell her that breakfast is ready."

Jolie paced around the fire, her arms folded across the flannel shirt. "Mother, I cannot drive to the schoolhouse looking like this."

Lissa Bowers scraped at the eggs on her plate. "Darlin', we don't have any other choice. You and I are the only ones who can control Pilgrim and Stranger on a muddy day. Besides, as soon as Gibs cleans the prairie chickens, I need him to help Lawson and me shovel the mud from the house."

"Why don't *you* go post a notice, and I'll shovel mud."

"Jolie Lorita, you're the schoolteacher. You need to take care of this little chore."

"But, Mama, look at this outfit. I like being tidy and matched."

"No one will be at the school. You know that. People stay off these roads when they slick up."

Jolie rolled her eyes at the light blue west Nebraska sky. "Mother, I can't let anyone see me like this!"

Lissa sipped on her coffee. "It's very modest, dear. Besides, you look fine. Doesn't she, boys?"

"It's really funny seein' Jolie in Daddy's old shirt!" Gibs laughed.

"Sort of humblin' to look like a girl from an orphanage." Lawson chuckled.

"You see?" Jolie triumphed.

"I don't know why you don't wear the dress without the shirt," Essie added. "I'm wearin' one of Mama's dresses, and I think it looks quite fetching."

Gibs shoved his plate at Essie. "In that case, why don't you go fetch me some more eggs."

Jolie clutched the lead lines as she waited for her sister. *Lord, I try very hard never to be in embarrassing situations, but it seems to do little good. I shall pull that canvas tarp over my head if anyone sees me. I like being neat. Today even with a bath and nice dress I feel untidy.*

She glanced down at her fingernails. "Oh, no!"

Essie climbed up in the wagon and plopped down. "What's wrong?"

"I forgot to brush the mud from under my fingernails."

Essie studied her own hands. "Gibs said he still had Montana mud under his nails. He said he reckoned he'd leave it there to remind him of all the places he's been."

Jolie glanced over her shoulder. "Perhaps I should go clean my nails."

"I think we should hurry to school so we can find Francis down at the railroad tracks," Essie declared.

Jolie wrapped the lead lines around her wrists. "Hang on, li'l sis."

Essie clutched the iron railing as Jolie slapped the lines. The big brown horses sprinted out of the yard, leaving parallel columns of flying mud.

Essie put one hand on top of her straw hat. "I thought Mama would be crying for sure this morning over the house."

Jolie didn't take her eyes off the galloping team. "Mama only cries over her man . . . and us kids. Nothing else."

The winding, muddy road north to the tracks ran fairly flat with just a slight grade. When they hit the weedy part, the mud stopped flying, and the wagon fishtailed, but Jolie kept it under control. The pastel blue sky and rising sun gave little hint of the torrents of rain and wind of the previous three days. Cool air whipped against Jolie's face. The flannel shirt felt comfortable.

"Jolie, I'm not going to marry any boy who wants to live in a house with a sod roof. Are you?" Essie blurted out.

Jolie licked her lips. They tasted salty. "I don't know. I hadn't thought about it, Essie."

"But you said last night was one of the worst nights in your life. You don't want to go through that again, do you?"

"Yes, it was. And, no, I never want to face that again. But when you said that, I thought about . . ."

"About Tanner?"

"Yes, and I realized that being with my husband would be the most important part. It won't matter where I am."

"Now you sound like Mama," Essie giggled. "But I'm goin' to put in the wedding vows that Leppy can never—I mean, that my future husband can never move me into a house with a sod roof."

"Estelle Cinnia, you aren't still pining for Leppy Verdue, are you?"

"Of course I am." Essie bit her lip. "He calls me his cutie."

"But he's—he's much older than you. Besides, you call Francis your cutie, and he's a calf."

Essie held her nose high. "And I like him very, very, very much."

"Leppy or Francis?"

"Both," Essie giggled. She scooted over next to Jolie as they bounced along. "When are you and Tanner getting married?"

"We've talked about the choices, but we haven't really set a date."

Essie clutched her sister's arm. "You'll tell me when you decide, won't you?"

"You'll be the first to know," Jolie announced.

"June 14," Essie blurted out.

"What?"

"You and Tanner are getting married on June 14 of next year."

"I told you, we haven't set a date yet."

"You also said that I'd be the first to know. Now if I'm really the first to know the date, that means I'll know it before you or Tanner. . . . So I'm tellin' you, June 14."

Jolie shook her head and grinned. "Why that date?"

"Because you said you were goin' to keep us in school until June 1. I heard you tell Daddy you didn't want to get married until school is out. So that gives you two weeks to get ready for the wedding. It doesn't take longer than two weeks to get ready for a wedding, does it?"

"I believe it takes your entire life," Jolie replied. "And you get high marks for logic today, but that date is still to be determined."

Essie waved her hand to the north. "I think there are some boys up there near the tracks."

Jolie sat straight up but kept the big horses racing. "I knew this would happen."

"It's only Theo, Greg, and him."

"Your friend Bullet?"

"Did you read his story about going hunting in the Rockies?" Essie asked.

"No, it's lying on my desk. I was going to read it today before school."

"Don't."

"Of course I will. I'm his teacher."

"Well, don't read the part about the grizzly bear attack when Gerrard gets his arm ripped off and keeps fighting until he blows the brains out of the bear and peers in the bear's ear and sees out the other side of his head, and then Gerrard sits down and cooks bear brains in his beans while he sews the arm back on."

"To himself or to the bear?"

"It's a horrible story," Essie groaned.

"Gruesome, perhaps, but creative."

When they reached Telegraph Road, Jolie wrapped the lead lines around her wrists and threw her weight toward the back of the wagon. They rumbled to a stop.

"Howdy, Miss Jolie. Are you cold?"

"Good mornin, Greg. It was just a little breezy; so I pulled on this old shirt, sort of like a light jacket."

"Is your good jacket dirty?" he asked.

"Yes, it is."

The smallest of the three boys trotted up to the other side of the wagon. "Hello, Estelle."

After an awkward pause, Jolie elbowed her sister.

"Good morning, Chester," Essie drawled.

"Are we havin' school today, Miss Jolie?" Greg Wells asked.

"No, I'm just headed down there to post a notice."

"It surely is muddy. I don't think any teams can make it except yours," Theo added.

"I reckon we can head home," Greg observed.

"Miss Jolie," Bullet asked, "can you give us a ride?"

"I'm not goin' that way, Bullet. I'm just goin' to school and back home."

Essie inched closer to her sister. "And we're goin' to find Francis."

"He's in our corral!" Theo exclaimed.

"He is?" Essie squealed.

"Yep," Greg said. "Tanner found him by the tracks this mornin'."

"Tanner's home?" Jolie gasped. Her stomach churned. *I will not have my sweetie looking at me dressed like this!*

"He bummed a ride on a handcar with the railroad inspection crew this mornin'. He was worried about how we made it through the storm. But there was no need to worry. We was warm and toasty all night."

"We weren't. Our roof caved in on us!" Essie announced.

"Oh, wow, that's a fine shinley," Bullet blurted out. "Can I come see?"

"It's a big mess—two feet of mud in our whole house and no roof at all left," Jolie said.

"Why doesn't something fun ever happen to us?" Bullet moaned. "Did I ever tell you about the time I slipped and fell in the privy behind the Panhandle Hotel? Now that was great."

Essie rolled her eyes at Jolie. "We have to go by the Wellses' house and get Francis."

"We do not have to go there," Jolie declared. "We can send Lawson down for him later when the roads dry out." *There's no way I'm going to see Tanner like this.*

"But Francis misses me," Essie insisted. "We have to get him now. He'll be very worried about me."

Greg scratched his shaggy brown hair. "Don't worry, Miss Jolie, Tanner won't be there. He headed back down the tracks with the inspection crew. He was just worried about us."

"Oh . . . well, in that case . . ."

"How come you don't want to see Tanner?" Bullet asked. "I thought you was his sweetie."

"She doesn't want him to see her dressed like this," Essie blurted out.

"Estelle!" Jolie scowled.

"Shoot, Miss Jolie, you'd look purdy no matter how funny-lookin' your clothes were!" Theo grinned.

"Yes, well, thank *you*, Theo."

"Think nothin' of it, Miss Jolie."

"Eh, since it looks like we'll be going to your house, you boys might as well ride with us," Jolie announced. "But we need to get to the schoolhouse first."

"I get to ride up front with Estelle," Bullet called out.

Essie's eyes showed panic.

"Actually I need all three of you to ride near the back of the wagon so that it doesn't fishtail on the slick road."

The boys piled in. Essie leaned over and whispered, "You're the very best sister in the entire state of Nebraska."

When they peaked the rise in the road before the school, the wagon slid sharply to the right. Jolie slapped the team to go faster to keep them on the road. She spotted several children on the front steps of the large sod building with tin roof.

"It's the Vockneys," Essie shouted.

April, May, and June Vockney sat on a bench, wearing matching green gingham dresses. Mary Vockney, in an oversized long beige dress, ran out to meet them.

"Hi, Miss Jolie," she shouted. "Can I use the swing first today?"

"Mary, what are you doing here so early?" Jolie asked.

"Mama and Daddy had to go up on the plateau to look for our cows, and so they brought us by. Why are you wearin' that funny shirt?"

Jolie glanced down at the flannel. "It's a long story. But we aren't having school today. The roads slicked up. I thought it safest to cancel school."

Mary mashed her round nose flat against her face. "They aren't slick to the north."

Jolie tied the lead lines to the brake handle. "I came down to post a 'no school' notice."

"What are they doin' with you?" She pointed at the Wells boys.

"I'm going to take them home and pick up Essie's calf Francis."

"Did he go visitin'?" Mary probed as her sisters ambled up to the wagon.

Essie raised her finger and mashed her own nose flat. "I think he got lost in the storm."

"Can you take us home too?" Mary asked.

"She can't do that," April declared. "Mama and Daddy are comin' back here to pick us up after school. They'll be mad if we aren't here waitin'."

"Maybe you should have school for all of us who showed up," Bullet suggested.

Jolie glanced back in time to catch him lift his eyelids with his fingers and roll his eyes until only the whites showed. *I don't think so, Bullet Wells.* "No school today."

"I don't want to sit on this porch all day," April lamented. "Miss Jolie, can we spend the day at your house? We won't bother you. Why, Lawson could give us a ride back to school in time to meet Mama and Daddy."

"Our roof collapsed. We really can't have company," Jolie informed her.

"You mean, it's sagging?" May asked.

"I mean, it melted and slopped all over the front and back rooms."

"Right on your beds?" June exclaimed.

"Right on everything."

"I still wish I could have seen that," Bullet called out. "Mama don't let me play in the mud since I lost the cat."

Jolie stared at Essie.

"Don't ask," Essie whispered.

"The Vockneys can stay with us," Theo offered.

May and June Vockney giggled.

Mary didn't. "I'm not going to stay at Chester's house. I have to help Essie settle in Francis."

"And I could help you wash and clean," April offered.

Jolie stared at the fifteen-year-old. *April Vockney, you want to tag along after Lawson Bowers. That's obvious.*

"Let me post a notice, and then I'll take you to the Wellses' place. After that we'll decide what to do," Jolie said.

April and Mary Vockney crowded into the seat next to Essie and Jolie. May and June lounged across from Greg and Theo, and Bullet Wells sulked, his arms and shoulders draped over the tailgate as they bounced up the road. When they reached the DeMarco homestead where the Wellses lived, Bullet scrambled out first.

"We'll go get your calf," Theo said.

Mary Vockney and Essie trailed after the boys while Jolie visited with Mrs. Wells. Soon they loaded Francis in the back with Essie.

Jolie looked down at Mrs. Wells. "Can the girls stay with you?"

"Certainly, but we have no way to get them back to school. Our horses won't pull on roads this slick."

Jolie sighed and glanced down at the girls. "Then you'll have to come with me. I trust you don't mind helping dig the mud out of our house. We'll bring you back to school in time to meet your parents."

April and Mary scampered into the wagon. May and June pouted but finally climbed in the back. The horses bolted back out onto the slick road, and Jolie worked to keep the wagon from slipping off. Essie hollered, "You might not have to wait long to see Tanner. I think that's him runnin' down the railroad tracks toward us."

Jolie yanked the leather ribbons, and the wagon slid to a stop. "Oh, no, this is terrible!" she moaned. "I knew this would happen!"

"What's wrong?" April asked.

"Jolie doesn't want her sweetie to see her like that."

"You mean with dirt under her fingernails?" Mary blurted out. "It happens to me all the time."

"Essie, give me the gray tarp," Jolie called out.

"Are you kidding?"

"No!" Jolie shouted.

Essie dragged the tarp to the front of the wagon. Jolie pulled it straight over her head. It draped down like a tent all around her.

She could hear Tanner jog up to the wagon. *Lord, I want this all to go away. I know he smells wonderful, and he's only a few feet away, but I will not let him see me like this.*

"Boy, am I glad to see you!" he puffed. "You're an answer to prayer."

"You can't see me. I'm hiding under a tarp," Jolie mumbled.

"He was talkin' to the horses," April informed her.

"The horses?" Jolie stuck her head out from under the tarp.

"Jolie, the rail gave way over at Bobcat Gulch, and the handcar tumbled into the rocks. A couple of the railroad men are hurt. You've got the only wagon that can reach them."

"But . . . but . . . I can't go there. I'm not dressed for it."

"There are injured men, Jolie Lorita. I don't reckon we have any choice." Tanner swung up on the seat beside her and April. "Why the tarp? Are you cold?"

Jolie shoved the canvas to the back of the wagon and slapped the lead lines. Stranger and Pilgrim bolted west along Telegraph Road.

He looked her up and down and then grinned.

"Tanner Wells, if you say one word about my attire or my fingernails, I will personally throw you off this moving wagon. Is that clear?"

Two

"Mash your hand right on top of the wound," Jolie shouted.

With eyes wild, like a cat falling off a cliff, June Vockney cried out, "But—but—I can't do it. I just can't, Miss Jolie!"

Stranger sensed tragedy and yanked to the left. "And I can't leave these horses. They're as nervous as we are and stand for no one but me and Mama." Jolie leaned back, the lines double-wrapped around her wrists. "You or May has to do it, June, or that man will bleed to death."

May Vockney covered her face and sobbed. Tears cascaded down her pointed chin and plummeted to her green gingham dress. "I can't. I just can't. Oh, Miss Jolie, don't make me. Please, please, please, don't make me do it."

Essie stuck her head out from under the canvas tarp where she and Mary Vockney had been hiding with Francis the calf since the wagon wheels locked and skidded to a halt at the bottom of Bobcat Gulch. "I'll do it, Jolie," she murmured. "I ain't never been around someone who died, and I don't reckon I want to start now. Can I close my eyes?"

"Hurry, Essie, press the palm of your hand against his arm."

Essie took a deep breath and blurted out, "Right where the blood is bubblin' out?"

"I'm goin' to throw up," May Vockney gurgled.

"Don't do it in the wagon," Jolie barked. "Essie, right on top of the wound. Quick. Do it! Clamp down and don't let up."

Essie slapped her right hand on the wound, then her left hand on top of the right, and pushed down, eyes squinted shut. "Like this?" she gasped.

Jolie wiped the sweat off her forehead on her daddy's flannel shirt. "That's it, Essie. You're doing great."

"Francis doesn't want to see this." Mary Vockney pulled the canvas back over her head.

Essie took deep breaths, her eyes still closed. "His blood is warm, Jolie. I didn't know blood was so warm."

Jolie tried to survey the wreck scene. "It should be around 98.6 degrees."

"I don't even know his name. And he's passed out; so I can't ask him." Essie sniffed. "Doesn't it seem strange that his blood is dripping through my fingers, and I don't even know his name?"

"I'm really, really going to be sick," May Vockney sobbed.

"You're saving his life, li'l sis. Don't back off. The Lord knows his name. And the Lord knows your name, Estelle Cinnia."

"He can call me Essie if He wants to," Essie said in a softer voice.

Mary Vockney crawled out from under the tarp, tugging Francis the calf with her. She refused to look at Essie and the wounded man. She peered down at the bottom of the railroad bridge. "Is the other one dead?"

May Vockney clutched June. "We should have stayed at the Wellses' house. I told you we should have stayed there. I don't want to be here," she whimpered. "I want to go home right now."

"None of us wants to be here," Mary said as she patted Francis on the head.

"It's all Miss Jolie's fault," June snapped. "It was her idea. We should be in the schoolroom havin' class. Then none of this would have happened."

"It would too have happened. Only there would be no one to help," Mary said.

"It's not Jolie's fault. It was just . . . ," Essie protested.

"It's okay, girls," Jolie responded. "May and June are just scared. There's nothing wrong with that. I'm scared too."

"Here come Tanner and April with another one," Mary shouted.

Essie's eyes were still shut, both hands covered with blood. "Is he bleedin'?"

"I don't know. He ain't movin'," Mary replied. "Tanner is carryin' him like a sack of taters."

June Vockney covered her ears. "I don't want to hear this."

"June, you and May move up to the front of the wagon so they can put him back there," Jolie ordered.

"No," May snapped, "we aren't movin'. Ever!"

The lead lines were so tight on Jolie's wrists that her fingers got puffed, red, and numb. "Mary, go back there and shove your sisters out of the wagon."

"What?" June gasped.

"Hurry. We need the space to save a life. You two can walk home."

June and May scooted forward.

"I would have done it, Miss Jolie," Mary declared.

"I know you would have, honey. And May and June knew you would."

With a wounded man in his arms, Tanner trudged to the back of the wagon. "I think this one injured his back on the rocks. I was scared to death to pick him up and scared to leave him."

"Is he bleedin'?" Essie asked again.

April Vockney scooted the man's feet into the wagon. "No," she said. "We didn't find a wound or blood. Maybe he's just knocked out."

Essie opened one eye to peek at the man in the torn brown suit and dark tie. "You think he'll be okay?" she asked a blood-smeared Tanner Wells.

Tanner rested his hands on his narrow hips. "Sometimes the wounds that don't show are the most serious," he replied. He glanced over at June. "Cover him to his chin with that tarp. He feels cold, which isn't good. So let's keep him warm until we get to town."

"I . . . I can't," she whimpered. "I can't do it."

Tanner leaned over the sideboard until his face was only inches from June's. "Darlin', I'm sure you can. Scoot over there and do it for me, okay?"

June wiped the tears on the back of her hand. "Okay." She crawled to the injured man and spread out the tarp like a blanket.

Tanner looked back down the draw. "I've got one more. He's not hurt bad but pinned under the wreckage. He's the boss. He wanted me to help the others first."

April scooted next to her sisters. "May and June, we need you to help down there. The timbers are too big for me. Tanner can lift one end, but I can't budge the other. Maybe all three of us together can do it. Get down and come help us."

"We can't," May sniveled. "We just can't."

Tanner reached in and hugged May's shoulder. "It's okay to be upset, darlin', but we need you now. So you and June come on down and help big sis and me. I'm countin' on you."

May whimpered, sniffed, then lifted her skirt and wiped her face. "Okay," she murmured and crawled off the wagon with June.

As Mary and Essie tended the two wounded men in the back, Jolie watched the Vockney sisters hike across the boulders to the bottom of the railroad bridge as Tanner held their hands. *Just a soft word and a hug from a handsome man, and they will do things they never dreamed they could do. It's something about Tanner's eyes and that deep voice of his. When he talks to me, I certainly want to do things . . . things I've dreamed of doing for a long, long time.*

The crew's boss wore a dark suit with torn pant legs. Mud smeared the coat and tie. His hat had a wide, floppy brim. Tanner carried him piggyback, then turned around and set him on the back of the wagon. With great care, he lifted the man's feet. "Mr. Culburtt, this is my fiancée, Jolie Bowers."

Even with pain in his eyes, the gray-headed man tipped his hat. "Miss Bowers, I must say when I saw you and Tanner drive up in this wagon, you were the prettiest angel I've ever seen. I didn't expect him to find a team that could pull with the road in this condition."

Jolie clutched the flannel shirt under her chin. "Normally I do dress better than this, Mr. Culburtt."

"And normally I'm not under a thousand-pound handcar with two busted ankles. This isn't a normal day, Miss Bowers. How's Trip Cleveland?"

Jolie looked at the two other injured men. "Which one is he?"

"The one who's bleeding on the little darlin' with her eyes closed," Culburtt replied.

"He's unconscious and lost a lot of blood. We have to get him to town in a hurry. That's my sister Estelle."

Essie peered out one eye and flashed a smile. "You can call me Essie."

Tanner helped the three Vockney girls into the back of the wagon and slid the tailgate into place.

"Can you get us to Dr. Fix's place in Gering in a hurry?" Culburtt asked.

"Yes, I can," Jolie said. "But you will need to hold on. These two horses like to run."

Tanner pulled up onto the seat beside her.

"Give 'em rein and let 'em run," Culburtt ordered.

Pilgrim and Stranger yanked the wagon up the grade and broke into a full gallop when they hit the flats. Culburtt's hat blew off, but he shouted, "Keep goin'! Hats are cheap."

Mud trailed from the iron rims of the wagon wheels as they raced west. All the way to the outskirts of Scottsbluff the storm-slick road was clear of traffic. Jolie didn't slow down in town. Her hat bounced on her back, held on by the yellow ribbon tied around her neck.

No one said a word.

Francis laid his head in Mary Vockney's lap.

Jolie hit the bridge at Gering at full speed. The timbers beneath them groaned and rattled as if surprised and terrified. Wagons and carriages pulled over as the big wagon roared down the middle of the muddy street. Storefronts emptied as people came out to watch them. Tanner leapt off before she had brought the team to a complete stop in front of Dr. Fix's office and hospital.

He packed the bleeding man through the door before Jolie set the handbrake. For several minutes there was noise and confusion as the other patients were toted inside. April helped Tanner carry the wounded in while the other Vockney girls waited with Jolie. Essie trailed in to wash the blood off her hands and dress.

With a damp towel in her hand, April returned by herself. "Miss Jolie," April asked as she handed the towel up, "how did you learn to drive so fast?"

Jolie wiped her face and hands and passed the towel to May Vockney. "I think it's a gift, April. It may sound funny. But just like the Lord gives some the ability to sing well, He sort of gives some a talent with horses. I just found one day I had a feel for what the team wanted to do. Once they knew that I knew, they seemed to respond. My mother's the same way."

April climbed up on the wagon beside her. "Daddy won't even let us drive. He says driving is for men."

Jolie studied the front door of the doctor's office, waiting for news. "You need to keep Daddy happy."

"Did you ever see Dr. Fix drive her buggy?" May asked.

Jolie glanced at the back of the wagon. "I don't think so."

"She drives as fast as you," June said. "Almost."

The sun moved slowly across the pale blue Nebraska sky, like a marble losing momentum rolling uphill. Jolie gazed at the other wagons and carriages as they rumbled by.

Lord, it seems strange that they pass by, not knowing that several men fight for their lives just inside that building. Maybe it's always that way. We go about our business, not knowing the tragedies and drama just a few steps away. I suppose we couldn't handle it if we knew everything. I'm glad You can handle it. I'm worn out from worry over the few things I do know.

Tanner led Mr. Culburtt out of the building. The railroad man sported two wrapped ankles and crutches. Essie skipped along beside them, hands and face clean, dress wet and streaked. She climbed up in the wagon. "Dr. Fix said I saved Trip's life. I've never saved anyone's life before."

Jolie hugged her sister. "I'm sure you did, Essie. I'm proud of you."

Essie leaned back and scratched Francis's head. "I did it with my eyes closed the whole time."

Tanner helped Mr. Culburtt climb in back with the girls.

"But your hands and your heart were open," Jolie remarked.

Essie's wet dress hung like a wrinkled sack. "Trip said he was goin' to buy me the best meal in Scottsbluff when he gets stronger."

"You got to talk to him?" Mary asked.

"Yes. He said he wanted to buy me a new dress to replace this one, but I told him I'd have to ask my daddy 'cause I don't think he would let some boy buy me a dress. And he laughed until Dr. Fix said he should stop laughing."

Tanner handed the crutches up to Mr. Culburtt. "I told Edward that we could drop him off over in Scottsbluff at the railroad yard on our way back."

For a while, Lord, I forgot how horrible I look. "Yes, of course. But I'm not, eh, prepared to stay in town long. How's the other man?"

Edward Culburtt rubbed his clean-shaven chin. "I'm worried about Ragsdale. He got knocked out crashing into the boulders, and he hasn't come to. He didn't even respond to Dr. Fix's smelling salts."

"I will hold him in my prayers until the Lord heals him or takes him home," Jolie offered.

Culburtt stared at her for a moment. "Thank you, Miss Bowers. That means a lot to me, and to Case Ragsdale. Sometimes I get the feelin' that everyone around here hates the railroads. It's nice to hear different."

"Who hates the railroads?" Jolie asked.

"There's a growing distrust," Culburtt murmured.

"We rode on the railroad all the way down from Montana," Essie blurted out.

"April rode on a street car in Denver almost eight blocks," Mary added.

"Everyone, hang on. These boys have been standing for almost two hours. They aren't used to this much self-control," Jolie warned.

Mary perched in the back of the wagon, holding Francis across her lap. This time Jolie's hat stayed on as they rumbled across the bridge over the North Platte River. They raced into the railroad yard and rolled up to the brick office. A man wearing a white shirt and tie stepped out.

Tanner helped Culburtt down.

"Willie," Culburtt hollered, "there was an accident out at Bobcat Gulch. Trip and Case are seriously injured. Gather up anyone left in the yard and meet in my office. I'll give 'em a report. Then we need to send some telegrams to stop the trains before they reach the point where the rails spread."

The man darted out the door toward the large tin-roofed shop.

"There's no way to thank you enough," Culburtt said.

"It was our Christian duty," Jolie said. "The Lord's pleasure will be thanks enough."

He stared at her again.

"What's the matter?" she asked.

"Miss Bowers, it's been years since I've been around a fine Christian lady like yourself. But I do remember. Indeed I remember. If you'd wait just a minute, I'd like Willie to draw you a bank check. Afraid we never have cash around here except on paydays. I certainly want to pay for the use of your team and time."

"Oh no, I couldn't take that," Jolie protested. "Mama and Daddy would pitch a fit if I took money. They would make me drive right back to town and return it."

He leaned forward on his crutches. "If I was them, I'd do the same. I understand. Miss Bowers, out of Christian charity you rushed to our side and drove us to the doctor on slick roads at danger to yourself and others. Your love of the Lord prompted you to give us something we needed. I'm a Christian man, Miss Bowers. It's been way too long since I've acknowledged that. And my love for the Lord is prompting me to give you something you need. Look around this railroad yard. What is it you need? Every homesteader needs something. Don't deny me the blessing of helpin' you out."

"You're very persuasive." Jolie studied the railroad yard cluttered with parts, ties, and rails.

"Mr. Culburtt, our sod roof caved in on us last night. We have shingles but no rafters or purling." She continued to survey the yard. "What is that lumber over there near the pile of railroad ties?"

Culburtt waved a crutch in the direction of the lumber. "That stack of gray, twisted boards? The company sent out precut lumber to build an office here and then changed their minds and used brick. It's all goin' to waste, bleached and dried by the sun and wind."

"May we have enough to make rafters and purling for our roof?" Jolie asked.

"I would greatly appreciate it if you would haul that entire stack off so we can clean up the yard. You might have to sort to find straight ones. The other you can use as kindling."

"The whole stack?" Essie asked. "We could make new beds and furniture and everything."

"But there's one catch," Culburtt added.

Jolie's heart sank. "Oh?"

"You have to haul off that keg of nails too. We've moved them time and time again. They're always in the way. They might be gettin' rusty by now."

A wide smile broke across Jolie's face. "Oh, thank you. That's quite generous. However, we wouldn't need the whole keg."

"Take them, Miss Bowers. You can sell them and . . . and buy some new clothes, for all I care. The Lord has taken care of us today, and I'm thankin' Him by giving to you."

Jolie clutched the flannel shirt. "If you put it that way, I'll take them."

"I trust we'll meet again. I would like to meet your parents some-day as well," Culburtt said, then hobbled into the brick office.

It took almost an hour to load the lumber. Jolie's hands felt dirty, splinter-pricked, and sweaty when they finished. Tanner stacked the lumber in such a way as to provide a makeshift bench behind the wagon seat. He tied the boards down as April, May, and June Vockney crawled up on the lumber. Essie and Mary crowded onto the wagon seat next to Jolie and held the complacent Francis in their laps.

Jolie watched as Tanner rolled his shirtsleeves down and but-toned them. "Hop on, and we'll give you a ride to the gun shop," she offered.

"I can walk on over from here," Tanner replied. "You have a very full load. You sure you will be all right going home?"

"Yes. The road is even drier now, and the horses are tired. Mama and the boys are at home to help unload the lumber. . . . I reckon it will take a week for my hands to heal."

"I told you I would do it all myself," he murmured.

"Why didn't I listen to you?" Jolie winced as she rubbed her hands.

"'Cause you're pigheaded and stubborn," Essie blurted out. "We all know that."

"Thank you, dear sister."

"You're welcome," Essie giggled.

Jolie glanced at the lumber behind her. "It's really wonderful how generous Mr. Culburtt was."

Tanner stepped closer to the wagon. "He's a grateful man, Jolie Bowers. Stranger and Pilgrim are the only horses in the county that can pull on that road when it's slick. Time was runnin' out for those two injured men."

"It seemed to be divine Providence." She watched him wipe his brow and set his hat. "I can't believe you weren't injured."

"Those two were workin' the handles. Me and Culburtt saw it comin' a second before they did and jumped. I was on the high side of the gulch; he was on the deep side. The Lord's grace, I reckon. The strange thing is, we made it over the tracks earlier today without any problem. They were lookin' for weakness. If it had happened then, there wouldn't have been any flannel-shirt-wearin' angel to rescue us."

"I know I look horrid. I trust you will eventually banish this image from your mind."

Tanner laughed. "Darlin', I'll remember this mornin' till the day I die. And probably tease you about it all those years in between."

"That's what I'm afraid of. All those years, huh?" Jolie winked. "I suppose I can live with it."

Tanner tipped his hat. "Good-bye, girls. Bye, Jolie. I'll see you Sunday, if not sooner."

"You're goin' to kiss her, ain't ya?" Mary Vockney blurted out. "Essie says she peeks, and you always kiss her good-bye."

"I don't always peek," Essie protested. "Just mostly peek."

"I didn't know if the schoolteacher was allowed to kiss in front of the students." Tanner grinned.

"There isn't any school today," April chided.

"I think, eh, Miss Jolie is a little bashful," Tanner mumbled.

"Oh, you do?" Jolie said. "Let's just see who's embarrassed, Mr. Tanner Wells."

Jolie pushed her hat back, leaned way off the wagon seat, closed her eyes, and puckered her lips.

June and May Vockney clapped their hands in delight.

Stranger and Pilgrim took that clap for a command and bolted forward.

The lead lines tumbled out of Jolie's hand. She grabbed at the side rail, missed it, and plunged off the wagon. Two massive, strong arms grabbed her and kept her from hitting the ground.

The girls screamed.

Mary and Francis tumbled back on May and June and were snagged by April.

Jolie hugged Tanner's neck as she watched Essie pounce on the lead lines, wrap them around her wrists, and throw her weight back, shouting, "Whoa, boys!"

To everyone's surprise, the two big brown horses slid to a halt.

Tanner jogged up to the wagon with Jolie still in his arms.

"I did it, Jolie!" Essie shouted. "I stopped 'em. Did you see that?"

"It was wonderful," Jolie laughed. "I'm proud of you. You learned something new today."

April Vockney stared at Tanner's strong arms and raised her eyebrows. "So did I, Miss Jolie!"

"Eh, yes, well, I fell out of the wagon, and Tanner kept me from hurting myself."

"You don't look hurt at all," June Vockney giggled.

"I've never seen a boy run down the street carryin' a girl like that before." May blushed.

"You may put me in the wagon now, Mr. Wells," Jolie instructed. "Like what, May?"

"Like you was just leavin' the church after your weddin'."

Tanner laughed.

"They were just practicing," Essie announced. "After all, they're getting married on June 14th of next year."

"We are?" Tanner turned to Jolie. "I didn't know we had agreed on a date."

"Essie's just teasing," Jolie explained.

"No, I'm not," Essie declared. "I think you'd better take the reins. Stranger and Pilgrim are getting embarrassed with all this talk about weddings."

Jolie retied her hat and took the lead lines.

"I'm still a little confused. Jolie, do you want to marry me on June 14?" Tanner asked.

"Is he proposin' to you, Miss Jolie?" May blurted out.

"No, we're merely—"

"It sounds like a proposal to me," May insisted.

Jolie could feel her face warm up. "We've already agreed to—"

"If a boy said to me, 'May Vockney, will you marry me on June 14?' I'd say he was proposin' to me."

"You'd say yes," April teased.

"Not for two more years. I promised Daddy I wouldn't get married until I'm sixteen," May replied.

"What I want to know, Miss Jolie," April said, "is, are you goin' to say yes or no?"

"What was the question?" Jolie laughed.

"Are you going to marry Tanner on June 14?" Essie prodded.

Jolie gazed into his eyes. *Oh, my . . . oh my.* "Yes, Tanner Wells, I will marry you on June 14."

The girls clapped.

Stranger and Pilgrim thundered out of town to the east. Essie leaned over toward her sister. "This may be the best day of my life!"

"Why is that?" Jolie asked.

"Because I saved a man's life, I stopped Stranger and Pilgrim all by myself, and I got to set the date for your wedding."

"Yes, it looks like you did. Isn't it strange that the best day of your life followed the worst night of your life?"

"I need to remember that . . . when the roof falls on my head again. Of course, I'll have better days, I bet," Essie giggled.

"Oh, what day do you have in mind?" Jolie probed.

"My wedding day."

"You're thinking about your wedding day?"

"Yes. It will be so wonderful. I'll get to take home all of the cake that's left over."

Jolie hugged her.

"Why did you do that?"

"Because twelve is a wonderful age."

"How is seventeen, almost eighteen?"

"It's nice too. But I've lost some things you still have."

"Yeah, and you've gained some things I don't have," Essie crowed.

"There are some men up there," April called out.

Essie rocked Francis back and forth. "I guess it's not too slick for their horses."

"Keep drivin', Miss Jolie," May called from the back. "They're Indians."

"No, I don't think so. I think it's Captain Richardson's vaqueros," Jolie replied.

"Are you really going to stop?" June called out.

"Just to say howdy. They have visited the homestead on occasion."

"We don't have to talk to them, do we?" May asked.

Jolie glared at the girls and yanked the team to a halt. All four sombrero-crested cowboys rode over to the wagon.

"¡Hola!, Jocko. ¿Cómo está usted hoy?" Jolie offered.

"Miss Jolie, it's good to see you. I thought it might be your mother at first, but I did not see a braid. I am doing fair, thank you."

The youngest of the vaqueros spoke rapidly in Spanish.

"What did he say?" Mary Vockney asked.

Jocko Martinez laughed. "Estaban thinks he has died and gone to heaven—to come across a wagon filled with six beautiful women."

"You tell Estaban he's very good at sweet-talking. He must have been hanging around Jocko too long," Jolie teased.

Martinez translated, and the cowboys laughed and jabbed their hats back on. Then the heaviest of the men spoke.

Martinez translated. "Tiny asked if the calf is your lunch."

"No," Essie insisted. "This is Francis."

A tall, thin vaquero said something and pointed at Jolie.

Jolie glanced at the man. "Camisa? Is he talking about my flannel shirt?"

"Berto said he used to have a shirt just like that, but he lost it in a poker game. He wanted to know if you won it at poker," Jocko said with a smile that flashed white teeth.

Jolie twisted the collar of the shirt. "Tell Berto if he bet a shirt like this in a poker game, he must have had a very poor hand."

When the words were translated, all the men roared, and the big one pointed at Jolie.

"Tiny asks if you will marry him, but take no offense. He is merely teasing. He says that to all the ladies."

"She's engaged to Tanner," Essie informed them.

Jocko leaned his hand back on the high cantle of his Visalia saddle. "Tanner is a very good gunsmith. The captain says he is as good as the Freund brothers in Cheyenne." Jocko pointed to the load. "Miss Jolie, it looks like you are building a room onto your house."

"We need to rebuild. Our sod roof caved in on us in that storm last night. We have no roof at all."

"Do you have the shingles?"

"Mama brought a load down from Carter Canyon a couple months ago."

"Do you need any help with the roofing?"

"Thank you, Jocko, but I'm afraid we couldn't pay you anything."

"Just some supper and pie would be enough, Miss Jolie. But first we have to go bail out the captain."

"From jail?" Essie asked.

"Yes, ma'am." Jocko tipped his big sombrero.

"What happened?" Jolie asked.

The vaquero shrugged. "He got in a fight, I think."

"The captain?" Essie's eyes got big. "Did anyone get shot?"

"No knives or guns. I think it was a fistfight."

"But the captain is an old man," Essie said.

Jocko translated for the others. They looked at each other and grinned.

"He can be quite *cabeza dura,* if you know what I mean."

"With whom did he fight?" Jolie asked.

"Some railroad *hombres.*" Jocko scratched his head. "I think they might have been drunk."

"I just can't believe the captain got in a fight," Jolie said.

"He was mad about the rate increase," Jocko reported.

"Rate increase?" Jolie queried.

"Haven't you heard? The railroad said in January to expect a modest rate increase. Then they announced last week that they would double the shipping rates."

"Double them?" Jolie gasped.

"The captain says it will put a lot of ranches in a position where they can't afford to sell their cattle. The homesteaders are mad, you know. What with prices down anyway, most of them were counting on eastern markets."

"Most of the homesteaders are barely surviving as it is," Jolie remarked.

"The captain heard that the farmers rioted in the streets over at that big meeting in Lincoln. That's when he went to town to find out for sure."

"The Young Farmers' Alliance meeting?" Jolie quizzed.

"I think that was it."

"Our daddy is there," Essie called out.

"I hope he didn't get hurt."

Jolie gripped the lead lines so tightly her fingers turned white. "Some got hurt?"

"Maybe it's just a rumor. I'll see what the captain says about helping you with the roof after we get him out of jail." He tipped his sombrero. "*Hasta luego, señoritas.*"

The youngest vaquero rode by the wagon and then called back to Jocko.

"What did he say?" April asked.

Jocko grinned. "He asked how old the shy one with the pretty, long black hair is."

"Me?" May gasped. "He asked about me?" She bit her lip and dropped her chin. "Tell him I'll be fifteen in December and that I'm not all that shy once you get to know me."

All four vaqueros whooped and shouted as they rode west toward Scottsbluff. Everyone clutched the wagon rail or a rope as Jolie slapped the lines. The wagon rumbled along in the slowly drying mud of Telegraph Road.

No activity stirred around the DeMarco homestead. Jolie let the horses run until they came to the corner where one road turned north toward the school and the other south to the river and the Bowerses' homestead. She slowed the horses and turned south.

Essie pulled her waist-length brunette hair around and let it drape down the front of her blood-stained dress. "Stranger and Pilgrim are gettin' tired now, aren't they?" she asked.

"Yes, they are. Do you want to drive them?" Jolie held out the lead lines to her sister.

Essie's mouth dropped open, her eyes widened, and she leaned away. "No, I don't think I'm ready for that."

"Okay, but you let me know when you want to try." Jolie leaned forward, her elbows on her knees. "You already taught them you mean business."

"I can't wait to tell Mama about the horses . . . and everything."

"I can't wait to get Francis off my lap," Mary puffed. "Did you know calves can be quite heavy and warm?"

Jolie sat up and threw her shoulders back. "Yes, I believe I've heard that."

The driveway down to the river was rutted and narrow, but the horses slowed to a trot, and the girls loosened their grips and retied their hats.

"Miss Jolie, does your mother like me?" April asked.

Jolie peered back at the girls. "Of course she does. Why do you ask?"

"I read in a Denver newspaper that sometimes the friendship between a bride and her mother-in-law can be quite strained."

"Mother-in-law?" Essie choked. "Are you and Lawson gettin' married?"

"Oh, yes." April dropped her chin. "Someday."

"Lawson never mentioned it to us," Essie commented.

"Of course not," April giggled. "He doesn't know it yet himself."

"He doesn't?" Essie reached over and scratched Francis's ear. "Isn't the boy supposed to know?"

April held her round nose high. "It's not that important."

"It isn't?" Essie said.

"No, but it will dawn on him someday. It's inevitable."

"Is that how it works?" Essie asked.

"Oh, yes."

Essie pulled a strand of her long hair across her upper lip, like a swooping mustache. "That means me and Leppy Verdue are goin' to get married someday 'cause he surely doesn't have any idea about it now."

As they rambled toward the sod house, Jolie slowed the team. She glanced up at the cloudless blue sky.

Last night brought the roof down. Now it's clear. Lord, I've never lived in such a fickle land. When it's quiet, it is so silent we hear the water drip in the well. And when it's wild, we can't hear a scream from three feet inside the house. The sun is past straight up, and so it's afternoon. Mama will be worried. I ran down to school at seven and was to be back by eight. Oh, dear, she will be beside herself.

"Look." Essie pointed. "They have everything dug out of the house and setting in the yard."

"Wow, you really did lose your roof!" Mary gasped.

"What's the big mud pile beside the house?" June asked.

"Our roof." Jolie pulled the team up to the open side of the barn.

"Where is everyone?" April asked. "I don't see Lawson."

"Maybe they're inside," Essie replied.

"I'll go check," April volunteered.

"We'll go with her," May and June chimed in.

"Me and Mary need to get Francis in the corral," Essie declared.

By the time Jolie climbed off the loaded wagon, she was alone with the team of horses. She took an old flour sack and rubbed their necks as she pulled off the rigging.

"Boys, you did a wonderful job today. I believe you might have saved a couple of men's lives. One, for sure. And you brought us back a load of boards. So you take the rest of the day off."

"There's no one in the house," April reported as she strolled back.

"Did they get the dirt and mud shoveled out?" Jolie asked.

"Most of it," May replied.

"The stove is still in there," June added.

April brushed her hands off. "It has a lot of dirt left on it."

"I'll clean it later." Jolie surveyed the homestead. "I wonder where Mama and the boys are?"

"Maybe they had to use the privy," June offered.

April glared at her younger sister.

"It was just an idea."

Essie hiked back around the barn. "Francis is very happy to be home," she announced.

"And Margaret bawled him out for runnin' off like that," Mary added.

"Essie, while I put the horses away, look around for Mama and the boys. They don't seem to be here," Jolie ordered.

"Where did they go?"

"I have no idea. They didn't have a team or wagon."

"Maybe they rode the pig," Mary blurted out.

"Mudball?" Essie laughed. "He doesn't do anything I tell him. He's very, very stubborn, you know."

"I can ride our pig," Mary bragged.

While Jolie turned the team out into the rock corral, Essie ran over to the house and buzzed through both rooms. Then she trooped to the shed, the well, the woodpile, and the privy. She circled back just as Jolie closed the gate behind Stranger and Pilgrim.

"No one's home, Jolie," Essie called out. "They're gone."

Jolie glanced around again. "They must have hiked off somewhere."

"Perhaps they've been kidnapped by Indians," May suggested.

Essie spun around. "What Indians? We haven't seen an Indian since we got to Nebraska."

"The Oglala Sioux." May shrugged her narrow shoulders. "I read that they lived around here."

"Not anymore," Jolie said. "They all got moved to Dakota. I think Wounded Knee ended any Indian threat around here."

May wrinkled her nose. "Maybe some of them hid out and didn't move to Dakota."

Essie stared off toward the river. "Maybe Mama and the boys went fishing. Or maybe Daddy came home in Mrs. DeMarco's rig, and they went to look for us."

Jolie untied the ropes on the wagon. "But we didn't pass them coming in. I don't believe they went that way."

"We didn't go all the way back down to the school," Essie reminded her.

Jolie coiled the rope and tossed it under the wagon seat. "But we haven't seen any other tracks. So I think we can eliminate the other-wagon theory." She handed Essie a ten-foot rough-cut one-by-four.

"What're we goin' to do, Jolie?" Essie sniffled.

"We're going to unload this lumber, boil water to wash clothes, and begin scrubbing up the things in the yard," Jolie announced. "We'll store the clean things in the barn until we get a roof on the house."

"No, I meant what're we goin' to do about Mama bein' gone?"

"I know exactly what you meant," Jolie returned.

"And I know what you meant," Essie mumbled.

For a while all the girls scurried around the yard with buckets of well water and muddy items.

"Miss Jolie," June called out as she approached, "here's another of your dresses."

Jolie studied the mud-encrusted burgundy dress with black lace. "That's Mama's dress."

June held it up and gasped. "It is? Our mama doesn't wear dresses like this."

"That's because our mama is twice as big as Mrs. Bowers," April reminded her.

"Stick it in the tub with the others. I'll try wringing some dirt out before I boil it," Jolie said.

"You surely are workin' up a sweat," May observed.

Jolie wiped her brow. "The fire's hot."

"You could take off that flannel shirt," April suggested.

"I've got a dress on the clothesline. As soon as it dries and I warm up an iron, I'll change. Until then the shirt stays on."

"I think we got all the clothes gathered. Can we eat our lunches now?" May inquired.

"I'm glad you brought your school lunches because we don't have much food left. After you eat, I'll hitch up the team and drive you to the schoolhouse. I expect your mother will be back by then."

"Did all your food get ruined?" June asked.

"We found the food box. Some of it survived. The things on shelves and in cupboards did much better than the beds and the things on the floor."

April pointed north. "Miss Jolie, someone's coming."

Jolie glanced down at the sweat-drenched flannel shirt. "This is not a good time, Lord," she murmured.

Essie ran to the edge of the house. "It's two men I never seen before."

Mary ran to the corner of the house and peered around with Essie. "They're wearin' guns! I think they're outlaws."

"Oh no," May moaned. "What'll we do?"

"Go about your business. Look busy," Jolie instructed. "Always let them come to you. Don't go running to them."

"Running to them? I think I'll clean the stalls at the back of the barn," June offered.

"I'll help her," May chimed in.

"But they don't need to be cleaned," Jolie said.

"That's okay. We don't mind." June scurried to the barn.

Mary and Essie huddled by the edge of the sod house and

watched the two men ride into the yard. Like curious puppies, they followed the men at a safe distance. As soon as the blond one tipped his hat, Jolie marched toward them. April stayed by the campfire where water boiled in a pot.

"Miss Jolie, I almost didn't recognize you," the blond man said.

"Mr. Maxwell Dix and Mr. Shakey Torrington." Jolie shaded her eyes. "I'm surprised to see you. It's been a couple months, I believe."

"You're lookin' just as purdy as ever!" Maxwell observed.

"Mr. Dix, I don't know whether to laugh or cry. I look simply horrid, and thank you for not mentioning it."

When he pulled his hat off, blond hair tumbled to his shoulders. "You're welcome, ma'am. It would certainly take more than an old, ill-fitting flannel shirt and a smudge on the end of your nose to detract from your purdiness."

Jolie wiped her nose on the sleeve of the flannel shirt.

"I see you got a corn crop comin' up," Dix remarked. "I didn't know you could grow corn out here."

"As long as the river is higher than the field, we can irrigate over the levee."

"I think it sent the last of the grasshoppers to perdition." He grinned.

"Yes, there's always a blessing in God's handiwork," she added.

"Miss Jolie, I see you redesigned your house," Shakey joshed. "The open-top look. I had me an open-top Winchester '76 for a while."

Jolie crossed her arms. "Last night's storm brought down our sod roof."

"Yes, ma'am." Shakey tipped his hat. "We can see that."

"What brings you boys back here?"

"We heard that Leppy was stayin' here with you. We wanted to talk to him. Is he around?"

"He went to Colorado," Essie blurted out.

"Colorado? Is he crazy?" Shakey huffed.

"He went to Placid City to make things right with the mayor," Essie continued.

Torrington glanced over at Dix. "They'll hang him for sure."

"No, they won't!" Essie mumbled. "If they hang my sweetie, they'll have to deal with me!"

Maxwell and Shakey stared at Essie.

"Eh, we're close friends." Essie's face colored.

"I can see that." Maxwell grinned.

"Max and Shakey, this is my sister Essie and her friend Mary."

Maxwell Dix nodded his head. "Mary, is that your purdy older sister over by the fire?"

She shook her head up and down. "That's April. The other two are in the barn hiding."

Dix threw his head back and laughed. Dimples romped across his face. "I love it. How old are they?"

"June is thirteen. May is fourteen. April is fifteen, but she belongs to Lawson Bowers."

"Shakey, this place is goin' to team with cowboys in a few years, mark my words."

"Did Chug go with Leppy?" Torrington asked.

"Chug went to Laramie," Jolie announced.

Torrington shook his head. "I just can't believe Leppy went back."

"I can," Essie said. "You must not know him like I do."

"I guess not, young lady," Dix said. "Do you expect him back anytime soon?"

Jolie frowned. "He doesn't live here."

Maxwell Dix raised his bushy blond eyebrows. "He doesn't? We heard he did."

"He and some others stayed with us until they settled legal matters, but we haven't seen him in several weeks."

"But he'll come visit me," Essie said. "I just know he will."

"Would you like to leave a message in case we see him?" Jolie asked.

"We'll be hangin' around Scottsbluff for a while," Maxwell replied. "So we'll find him if he comes to town. Just wanted to find out what side he was hirin' on with in this railroad fracas."

"What railroad fracas?" Jolie asked.

"The farmers and ranchers threatened to stop the train and hold it hostage until the company lowers its shipping fees. The railroad is hirin' men to protect its property. They said they would shoot anyone who tried to stop their trains."

Shakey Torrington yanked off his hat and scratched his neck. "We heard the ranchers might be willin' to pay more than the railroad to hire some men."

"So you two are going to hire on as mercenaries?" Jolie challenged.

"We thought we'd see who pays the best first," Torrington answered.

Jolie marched around their horses. "Why don't you figure out which side is right and support it?"

Torrington followed her with his eyes. "We don't care which side is right."

Maxwell shoved his hat back on his head but left his blond hair draped down. "We jist don't want to be fightin' against Leppy and Chug."

"Besides, times ain't too good for regular jobs. Ranches are goin' broke all over the plains," Torrington explained.

"What happened to your share of the cattle money?" Essie asked. "That must have been over eight hundred dollars apiece."

Maxwell Dix stared at her.

She covered her mouth with her hand. "I told you, me and Leppy was close."

"Miss Essie, a crooked roulette wheel in Hill City got most of mine," Maxwell Dix reported.

"Miss Faro stole mine," Torrington added. "I almost made a fortune except for that last card."

At the sound of a distant gunshot, both men drew their revolvers.

"Sounds like it was down by the river," Dix said.

"Small caliber," Torrington added.

"It was a Winchester model '90 .22," Jolie announced . "It's my brother."

"He's a very good shot," Essie added.

"How many brothers you got?" Maxwell Dix questioned.

"Two, and a mother and a father," Essie reported.

"We'll mosey on. If you see Leppy or Chug, tell them we'll be campin' at the usual place. We'll wait until we see how this conflict develops."

"Are either of you carpenters?" Jolie blurted out. *Lord, I'm not sure why I said that.*

Dix rode over to the house. "You wantin' us to build your roof?"

"You're goin' to camp out somewhere. You could camp here today and build a roof."

"You fixin' to pay us cash dollars?" Torrington hooted.

"No," she admitted. "But we'd feed you."

"Have we got any food? I thought most of it was muddy," Essie commented. "You said we could face a famine."

Maxwell Dix laughed. "This could be interesting, Shakey. They got no food, and they want us to work for meals."

"Reminds me of Ol' Chad Walker down in Texas," Shakey Torrington guffawed. "That was about the way he paid us."

"And we worked for him for six months before we were smart enough to quit." Dix stood up on the saddle horse and inspected what beams were left in the roof. "Shoot, I'd just as soon spend the night here as go ridin' off. Besides, we got some chuck in our saddlebags."

"So we're goin' to stay here, build a roof, and help feed 'em for free?"

Dix dropped down in the saddle. "Sounds like a good deal, don't it?"

Torrington shook his head. "You're crazy, Maxwell."

"Besides," Dix winked, "those girls in the barn will have to come out sooner or later."

Mary Vockney rubbed her nose on the back of her hand. "They are very, very shy."

Brushing back the blond hair that hung down to his shoulders, Maxwell Dix studied the three-sided barn. "Yep, I can see that."

A voice wafted from the open side of the barn. "We aren't shy after you get to know us."

Within thirty minutes Dix and Torrington were hanging on the center beam of the sod house nailing replacement rafters. Jolie pulled her dress off the line and hiked back to the barn where May and June clustered.

"Go back out, girls. Let's finish cleaning the pans in the yard. I'm going to change my dress and then cook us something. It looks like potato soup today. I'll need to get you back to school after that."

"We can't go out there," May protested.

"Why not?"

"They might see us."

"Did you see Maxwell's dimples when he smiles?" Jolie offered. "It's like someone is tickling his chin with a feather."

By the time Jolie had changed into the still damp but comfortable-fitting clean dress, May and June Vockney were back out in the yard washing dishes with April.

At the sound of a holler, Essie and Mary ran to the edge of the cornfield. "It's Gibs and Lawson. They're chasin' somethin'!"

Jolie scooted over next to them. "Whatever it is, they're scaring it to death."

"I think it's a calf," Mary observed.

"We don't have another calf, and Francis is over there with his mother," Essie reported.

"Maybe it's a big dog," Mary suggested.

Essie clapped her hands. "It's a deer. A fawn!"

"Catch it, Jolie," Gibs yelled. "Don't let it get by. Tackle it!"

Jolie glanced at Essie. "Catch it? How do you catch a fawn that doesn't want to be caught?"

"Stop him!" Gibson hollered again.

Lawson caught up with him, but stopped running when he spotted the Vockney girls. He packed his brother's rifle and two dead prairie chickens.

"I didn't have any bullets left," Gibs yelled. "Grab him!"

Mary Vockney dove at the panicked spotted fawn. She grabbed him by one hind leg and his tiny tail.

"I got him!" she shouted.

The fawn kicked loose and darted to the right. Maxwell Dix stood by the pile of lumber and yelled at the fleeing fawn. The little deer ducked through the open front door of the house.

"He went in the house!" Gibs shouted. He ran to the doorway and slammed the door. "Now we got him."

Shakey Torrington looked down from the rafters. "What're you goin' to do with him?"

Gibs looked up at the man and then over at Dix. "Who are you guys?"

Maxwell Dix winked. "Roofers. Your sis hired us."

Gibs looked around. "Where did we get these boards, Jolie?"

"The railroad gave them to us," she replied.

"For free?" Gibs asked.

"They had surplus to get rid of and asked if we would haul them off."

"Isn't that a fine shinley?" He turned back to Dix. "But roofers don't carry single-action Colt revolvers in their holsters, with a bullet belt that don't show green on the brass. How come you're wearin' a gun, mister?"

"Woodpeckers," Dix replied.

"Really?"

"Sometimes they become such a nuisance we have to plug 'em just to get the job done."

"But our house is made of sod, not wood," Gibs remarked.

"That's what makes them really testy, son."

"What're you goin' to do with this little guy?" Shakey called down.

"He's an orphan," Gibs announced. "His mama drowned in the river, and he was stuck. Must have took us two hours to get him out of the bog. Have you got any .22 WCF bullets? I'll plug him, and we'll have him for supper."

"Eat him!" Essie cried out. "You can't eat him. He ain't big enough to eat."

"He's goin' to mess up this backroom if you don't do somethin'," Shakey called down.

Maxwell stepped over to his horse and tugged off his rope. "Open the door, son. Shakey, you drop down and chase him out."

Torrington lowered himself into the backroom.

Gibs threw open the front door.

The fawn darted into the yard.

Maxwell Dix circled the sisal rope over his head once and then tossed the loop over the fleeing deer. When the little brown-and-white-speckled fawn hit the end of the rope, he flipped straight up in the air and crashed down on his back.

"You killed him!" Mary shouted.

"No. He's gettin' up." Essie ran toward the fawn.

Dix shoved the rope into Gibs's hand. "Here you are, son. Bring my rope back when you're done with it."

"Did you see that, Jolie? He roped him just like that," Gibs called out.

"Mr. Dix is very talented. He's a friend of Leppy's, you know."

"You are?" Gibs exclaimed. "Did you help him pull down Placid City?"

Dix chuckled. "So he told you about that?"

"Yeah. I wish I could have been there." The fawn jerked Gibs several steps forward. "Whoa, he's strong."

"His name is Max," Essie announced.

"It is?" Gibs stumbled after the bounding fawn.

"I named him after Mr. Dix."

Shakey Torrington hooted. "There you go, Maxwell. You're such a deer."

"Keep that up, and there'll be a tombstone named after you, Torrington." Dix's grin showed his dimples.

"I shot them two prairie chickens," Gibs hollered as he and the fawn played tug-of-war. "I would have had three, but the bullet wouldn't fire. Grab the rope with me, Lawson."

Lawson released April Vockney's hand and chased after his brother.

"Dally around that snubbin' post," Shakey suggested.

The boys wrapped the rope around the post. When the fawn yanked the line taut, he stopped pulling and stood shaking and panting.

"You should turn him loose," May Vockney advised. "He's scared."

"He won't live until dark. He ain't got a mama. The coyotes will pull him down before the sun disappears," Dix warned.

"What're we goin' to do?" Essie howled.

"Either shoot him or bottle-feed him," Dix suggested.

"Can I borrow your gun?" Gibs hollered.

"Gibson Hunter Bowers, we are *not* goin' to shoot him," Essie cried.

"Then you better find a way to feed him some of Margaret's milk," Jolie replied.

Gibs inspected the fawn while Mary and Essie ran to the barn.

Torrington and Dix crawled back onto the roof and resumed hammering.

Jolie retrieved the two game birds. "Looks like we'll be having prairie chicken stew today. Maybe the famine is over."

"Did you really hire them men, Jolie?"

"Yes. They wanted to camp. I said they could stay here. They were the ones that stopped by and left the cattle money for Leppy and Chug."

"She sweet-talked them into helpin' with the roof," April revealed.

"It was nice of them to agree. I can't believe you got a whole load of boards for free," Lawson said.

"It's kind of a long story." Jolie stared back at the river. "When Mama gets here, I'll tell all of you at once."

"Where did Mama go?" Lawson asked.

"What do you mean, where did she go? Wasn't she with you?" Jolie demanded.

"She wasn't with us. After we got the house shoveled out and you weren't back, she said you must have gotten stuck, and she hiked out the drive to look for you."

"But we didn't see her."

"Where did you go?"

"Scottsbluff."

"You went all the way to town?"

"When did Mama leave?"

"Several hours ago," Lawson reported.

Three

As the big wagon rolled out of the yard, Lawson and Gibs helped Maxwell Dix and Shakey Torrington nail purling boards to the rafters. May and June Vockney scooted next to Jolie on the wagon seat. April, Mary, and Essie stood behind them.

The mud on the driveway down to the homestead had firmed up enough to no longer stream behind the iron rims of the wagon wheels. Stranger and Pilgrim thundered north in unison as the passengers clung to the wagon.

Essie's waist-length hair flagged behind her, held in place by a crooked yellow bow. "Where do you think Mama is?"

Jolie let the breeze flip her bangs back out of her eyes. "Perhaps she went over to visit the Wellses since she was at the tracks. If she did, then she knows about our delay."

"She could have been at Chester's house when we came back from town." Essie held her mouth wide open to catch the wind.

Jolie watched the two dirt tracks that wound ahead of the rig through the dry summer weeds. "I suppose so."

"We should have stopped at the Wellses' house," May Vockney offered, one hand on top of her straw hat.

"That's just 'cause you want to see Greg Wells." Mary Vockney yawned, her mouth wide like Essie's.

"I do not!" May paused. "I want to see Theo."

"I don't want to see Chester," Mary declared. "At least not for ten or twenty years."

Short prairie grass that had faded from light green to brown stretched to the horizon as they reached the top of the rise. When the sod schoolhouse came into view, Jolie pulled the wagon over.

"Why are we stopping?" April asked.

"There are some men up there." Jolie studied the horizon.

Essie shaded her eyes with her hands. "Are they Captain Richardson's vaqueros?"

Jolie fingered the top button of the high collar of her dress. "I don't think so, but they're cowboys."

"They've got a woman with them!" April exclaimed.

Essie grabbed her sister's shoulder. "That's Mama! They have Mama, Jolie!"

Jolie's eyes strained as her heart leapt. *They have her surrounded. One is trying to put his arm around her . . . or pat her on the back. This isn't good, Lord. We have to . . . I need to . . . I wish Daddy were here, or Tanner, or Lawson, or Gibs, or Maxwell and Shakey.*

Essie's grip caused Jolie to flinch. "What're we goin' to do, Jolie?"

"I'm going to let the horses run, Essie. Girls, hang on."

"Are you goin' to run over them, Miss Jolie?" April called.

"I will if they don't back away from Mama." Jolie leaned forward and slapped the lines so hard they sounded like a bullwhip when they cracked on the big brown horse's rump.

Stranger and Pilgrim flew down the road as if chased by shadowy demons. The grade was downhill, and the rear wheels barely kept to the ground as they roared at the six men bunched around Lissa Bowers. All of them turned to stare at the approaching wagon.

Jolie kept the team at a full gallop. The girls clutched each other, the wagon, and their hats. Horses and men scattered in every direction. Several men dove into the mud beside the road. Only Lissa Bowers stood and waited at the side of the road.

Jolie wrapped the lines around her wrists, threw herself back into

Essie's arms, and shouted, "Whoa, boys! Whoa!" Stranger and Pilgrim slid to a noisy stop three feet from Mrs. Bowers.

"Nice stop, honey," Lissa called out. "It was rather humorous to see grown men panic like that."

"Are you all right, Mama?" Essie hollered.

Mrs. Bowers glanced back at the men, who now led their horses back to the wagon. "Yes, thank you, darlin'. I take it they have never seen how the Bowers ladies drive. These boys and I just concluded some business."

"Who are they, Mama?" Jolie asked as she watched them brush dirt from their duckings and jam hats back on.

"She done tried to run us down," one of them grumbled.

"Nonsense. She missed you by inches," Lissa said.

"I ain't never seen a girl drive like that before," another groused.

"You learned a lot this afternoon about ladies." Lissa Bowers grinned. "This is Galen, and I don't remember all of their names, but they are from west Texas and came up here to work. Boys, I want to introduce my daughters."

A man with a black vest and long mustache whistled. "You have a family of six girls?"

Lissa Bowers studied the man's unshaven face. "I didn't say all my family was on the wagon."

"You got more at home?" he asked.

"Our brothers are at home," Essie informed him.

"Well, darlin'," the mustached man said, "just how many boys are at your house now?"

"Right now?"

"Yep, right now."

Essie searched Jolie's eyes. "There's, eh, four at home now," she replied.

"Four and your daddy?" Galen prodded.

"Oh, Daddy's been gone a long time," Essie responded.

Several of the cowboys mounted. A big man in a brown vest

slapped his black beaver felt hat at Galen. "You know how to pick 'em all right, Faxon. A grass widow with ten kids."

"A purdy grass widow with ten kids," Galen Faxon corrected him as he mounted. "Come on, we have to go talk to the railroad man." He turned to Lissa Bowers and tipped his hat. "Ma'am, it was nice to visit with you. Thanks for bein' a good sport and lettin' us josh and jaw. I hope to see you again."

She nodded. "Mr. Faxon, boys, thank you for your generosity."

Each of the six tipped his hat, then rode west.

"They thought we were your daughters," April laughed.

"Yes, they did. I didn't say that, of course." Lissa Bowers flipped her auburn braid over her shoulder and climbed up into the wagon. "But I didn't try to clear it up either. They were a rather arrogant pack when they first rode up." She patted Jolie's knee. "Mrs. Wells said there was a handcar accident. Now tell me all about it."

"Mama, tell us what you did first," Essie begged.

"I was worried that Stranger and Pilgrim might get stuck. So after we got the house shoveled out, I hiked to the school. When no one was there, I walked back to the Wellses'. DeLila told me of the wreck and about you and Tanner going off to take care of the wounded. That was quite Samaritan of you, dressed as you were."

"After a while I could almost—," Jolie began.

"We were all with them, Mrs. Bowers. And I helped bring out the wounded," April blurted out. She clamped her hand over her mouth. "Sorry, I didn't mean to interrupt."

Lissa Bowers reached back and put her arm around April's shoulder. "You will all need to give me a full report. Yes, I knew you were at home. DeLila said she saw you return from town and head to the homestead. But Mr. Wells and I got to visiting about case-hardened plow tips, and time zipped by. I knew you would be bringing the girls back."

It took the distance to the schoolhouse for Jolie and the girls to explain the day to Lissa Bowers. With no trees at the sod building,

Jolie parked in the shade of the east side of the school as they waited for Mr. and Mrs. Vockney to return.

Mary and Essie ran for the swing.

May and June skipped toward the privy.

April sat on the front seat of the wagon next to Mrs. Bowers. Jolie clutched the lead lines taut in her hands.

"Mama, you have to tell us about those men now," Jolie stated.

"I was hiking back to the school to wait for you. Mr. Wells couldn't give me a ride because of the slick roads. I knew you'd bring April and her sisters back—that is, I hoped Lawson would turn loose of her long enough to let her return."

April Vockney blushed and covered her mouth with her hand. "I'm sorry, Mrs. Bowers, it was all my fault."

"What was all your fault?"

"Eh . . . nothing." April blushed again.

"Young lady, I know my son. He's very enthusiastic about holdin' Miss April's hand. Anyway, as I crested the hill, the cowboys were riding west. They trotted up, thinking they'd discovered a young lady. I reckon the braid and no hat fooled them, at least from a distance."

"Mrs. Bowers, I don't think you look a day over forty," April blurted out.

Lissa Bowers chuckled.

"Mama's only thirty-eight," Jolie informed an embarrassed April Vockney.

"She is? Oh, no." April slapped her hand against her flat chest. "I'm goin' to die. I meant to say thirty. Really. My mama's forty-four, and I . . . I'm goin' to wait with the others." April started to climb down off the wagon. "I can't believe I said that."

Lissa Bowers laced her arm into April's. "Now, sweetie, you stay here. If my oldest son has anything to do with it, he's plannin' on you being a part of this family someday. I'd like that."

"You would?"

"Yes, and you might want to hear this story."

April sat back down.

"When the men rode up, we began to visit. Galen Faxon asked if I needed a ride somewhere. Then he suggested that maybe I didn't like riding horses."

"He assumed you couldn't ride?" Jolie said. "That was a serious mistake."

Lissa Bowers grinned. "Yes, you're quite right about that."

"What did you tell him?" Jolie probed.

"I said I only liked riding fast horses. He told me I should 'climb aboard' because his was the fastest of the lot. I told him I could out-race him on the red roan mare. They laughed and declared she was the slowest of the lot."

"Oh, no," Jolie gasped. "You didn't challenge him to a race."

"I told him I would take the roan mare and race him down around the schoolhouse and back."

"Did you straddle the horse, Mrs. Bowers?" April asked, eyes wide.

"Yes, very discreetly, of course."

"And you won," Jolie said as a matter of fact.

"$4.25."

"You bet on a race?" April gasped. "Mama don't let us bet on anything."

"No betting. Betting assumes risk. There was no risk in this," Lissa assured them.

"But what if you had lost, Mama?" Jolie asked.

Lissa Bowers patted Jolie's knee. "The thought of losing never entered my head."

Essie rounded the corner of the building. "Mama, here come Mr. and Mrs. Vockney."

Jolie drove the wagon back to the front of the school where the girls waited.

"All the Bowers ladies at one time," Mrs. Vockney remarked. "It's a rare sight for such an active family, and on another day it would be delightful."

Lissa Bowers studied the husky woman. "Is this a bad day?"

"Didn't you find your livestock, Mrs. Vockney?" Jolie asked.

"Ernest is sure the steers are up on the plateau somewhere, but no one was at Captain Richardson's ranch except for one of the vaqueros. We looked all day for the steers but couldn't find them."

"The captain and his men are in Scottsbluff," Jolie said.

"You saw them?" Mrs. Vockney asked.

"We saw his foreman, Jocko Martinez, and three of the others," Jolie reported. "They were on their way to get the captain."

"Yes, while we were at the ranch, the vaquero told us the captain went to talk to the railroad." Mrs. Vockney waved her rather large hands as she spoke. "Did you hear they're goin' to double shipping costs?"

"That will break us." Mr. Vockney stared down at the ground. "How can they do this? How can a company just change the rates and put farmers off their homesteads? That's not fair. The prices are down, production is down, and shipping is up. I think the railroad wants us to go broke so they can buy our places."

"I hadn't heard anything about it," Lissa replied. "But I've been so busy getting our homestead fixed up. Are you sure they're going to double shipping rates?"

"That's the talk."

"Maxwell and Shakey say there are farmers' riots in Lincoln, and both the railroad and cattlemen are hirin' gunmen to shoot it out," Essie offered.

"Gunmen?" Mrs. Vockney gasped. "But . . . but . . . that's a thing of the past. These are modern times."

"Who in the world are Maxwell and Shakey?" Lissa Bowers asked.

Essie lifted her long hair high above her head. "Those are the gunmen Jolie sweet-talked into roofin' our house for a bowl of potato stew," she announced.

"You said something about visitors, but I didn't hear that you had hired them," Lissa said.

Jolie grimaced. "I hadn't gotten to that part."

"You're putting on the cedar shingles?" Mrs. Vockney asked.

"Yes," Jolie answered. "We had to. Our sod roof caved in during the storm last night."

"Oh, my. Was everything ruined? You should have called off school."

"I did. I took the girls home, and they helped us a lot. I think we'll salvage most things except the beds and mattresses."

Mrs. Vockney glanced at her husband. "One of these days we'll get a cedar roof."

He shook his head. "If the railroad doubles the rates, we won't have a house to roof, Mama. I don't know what we'll do. I don't want my girls to starve, and I don't want to be part of a gunfight."

"The Lord will provide," Jolie reminded him.

He stared at her for a moment. "I was your age once," he murmured.

"Are you saying it's only the young who are foolish enough to trust the Lord?" Lissa Bowers challenged.

"I'm sayin' the young haven't failed enough to be terrified of failin' again," Ernest Vockney answered.

"Now, Ernest, that's no way to talk in front of the girls."

"I won't lie to them, Mama."

"Daddy is at the Farmers' Alliance meetings in Lincoln. When he comes home, he'll help us figure it out," Jolie commented.

"In the meantime, we all need to grow some good crops. It won't matter what the shipping costs are if the crops are terrible," Lissa Bowers said.

Mrs. Vockney twisted her bonnet strings and scowled. "A gunfight? I can't believe that. Oh, my . . . we should never have left New Mexico."

"There was nothin' but rattlesnakes and rocks on our place in New Mexico," April remarked. "Now let's go home. There are chores to do and a homestead to look after."

Mr. Vockney studied his oldest, then shook his head. "I really was young once. Some days I miss it more than others."

When the Vockneys rolled east, Jolie turned the wagon west.

"Are we ready to go home?" Mrs. Bowers asked.

"I hope so. I left potato-and-prairie-chicken stew in the pot," Jolie said. "I told the men to help themselves, but they don't always mind me."

"Since when?" Lissa Bowers laughed.

They crested the hill, crossed the tracks, and then turned off on the long drive back to their place.

"That's funny," Essie said.

"What, baby?" Lissa Bowers asked.

"I thought I saw a westbound train way down the tracks when we crossed them."

Lissa Bowers unfastened the top button on her high collar and fanned herself. "What's so unusual about that?"

"The tracks are out at Bobcat Gulch," Jolie shouted. "Mr. Culburtt telegraphed for the trains to be stopped."

Lissa Bowers glanced back at the tracks. "Perhaps they repaired them by now."

"I heard Mr. Culburtt tell them to shut down all trains in western Nebraska for twelve hours," Jolie insisted.

"Circle the wagon around, Jolie," Lissa Bowers called out. "We'll flag them down and warn them."

"It looks muddy out there," Jolie cautioned. "The road is firm but not that field. I think we'll get stuck."

"Here, give me the lines." Lissa turned Stranger and Pilgrim out into the abandoned field. "I'm sure they can make it."

"Hurry, Mama," Essie urged. "The train is getting closer."

Halfway into the circle, the big horses slowed as the heavy wagon sank into the mud of the once-plowed field. Lissa Bowers slapped the lines and hollered, but the two big brown horses labored to a standstill.

"What're we goin' to do?" Essie called out.

Lissa Bowers shoved the lead lines into Jolie's hands and stood up in the wagon. "I'll go wave down the train."

Jolie glanced down at the mud. "Mama, you stay here and try to get them out of the bog. I'll never be able to do that. I'll go signal the train."

Lissa Bowers brushed her auburn braid back. "Go on, darlin'. Little sis and I will get the boys out of the mud as quick as we can."

The mud oozed up past the ankles on Jolie's lace-up shoes. She held her dress up as she slopped, mucked, and waded her way back to the driveway. Still holding her dress above her ankles, she trotted to the tracks. Out of the corner of her eye she spied her mother in front of Stranger and Pilgrim, tugging them forward one step at a time.

A hundred-pound lady leading a ton and a half of horseflesh—nothing stops Mama. She glanced at the tracks. They hummed a prelude. *How do I stop a train?*

When she reached the crossing, the train was still a mile to the east. Jolie sucked in air and scanned the countryside.

In Ambush Along the Santa Fe, Stuart Brannon stood on the trestle 140 feet above the rocky floor of Dead Man Canyon and pointed his gun at the oncoming train until it stopped just two inches from where he stood. But I don't have the nerve to do that.

Jolie glanced back over her shoulder and spotted her mother leading the horses out of the mud. Essie held the lead lines. Both shouted at the struggling animals.

Lord, I have never done this before. Show me how.

Jolie stepped back about four feet from the edge of the south rail and waited as the train roared toward her. The sound multiplied until her mother's shouts were drowned out. Steam rolled out of the straight stack and hung in the air, leaving a river of white mist in the air parallel to the tracks.

When the train was about two hundred feet away, Jolie waved her hands over her head. "Stop . . . stop!" she screamed.

At fifty feet she bounced on her toes and waved. She no longer could hear her own shouts.

With the train almost even, Jolie jumped up and down, scream-ing and waving.

The engineer blew his horn.

The fireman tipped his hat.

They both grinned and waved.

As they barreled past.

A little blond-haired boy waved from the first Pullman car, as did a man in the shadows behind the boy.

With chin dropped and mouth open, Jolie waved back. "No . . . NO! They didn't stop." Her mumble never reached her ears.

Jolie spun around and sprinted back to where her mother had finally yanked the horses and wagon back up to the road.

"Mama, they wouldn't stop!" she yelled.

"Jump in, darlin'," Lissa Bowers shouted as she pulled herself back into the wagon and plucked the lead lines from Essie's hands. The wagon started rolling west even before Jolie was seated. Essie yanked her down.

"What're we going to do, Mama?" Jolie asked.

"We'll race up there and signal the engineer to stop."

"Can we outrun a train?" Essie asked.

"We have to, baby."

"Mama, they wouldn't stop for me," Jolie fumed.

"I noticed."

"I prayed and prayed, Mama," Jolie yelled.

"Good. Maybe now it's time to do what the Lord's telling us to do," Lissa yelled back.

"What's He telling us?" Essie hollered.

"To keep that train from plunging into Bobcat Gulch."

Stranger and Pilgrim lathered at the pace but didn't weaken. Jolie felt the heavy slap of the wagon seat on her backside as they bounced along. She glanced at Essie.

"It's like gettin' a whippin'." Essie grimaced as she clung wide-eyed to the railing. "A whippin' from Mama," she added. "Daddy don't whip this hard."

The train was half a mile ahead of them at the crossing. By the time they passed the Wells homestead, it was only a quarter mile away.

"Did someone just throw something at us?" Lissa Bowers called out.

Essie looked back. "It was Chester. There's a big ol' squash in the back of the wagon."

"Mama, hurry," Jolie urged. "There are passengers on that train."

"Darlin', I'll push these boys to the limit, but they can't go any faster. It's in the Lord's hands and these two sets of hooves now."

"We aren't goin' to make it to the next crossing," Essie bellowed.

They reached the crossing west of the Wells homestead just even with the caboose. Two wheels left the ground as Lissa Bowers swerved over the tracks and back west, this time on the north side.

"I don't think there's another crossing before the gulch, Mama," Jolie yelled.

"We'll find one or make one," Mrs. Bowers declared, never taking her eyes off the horses and the road ahead.

"Then what do we do?" Jolie pressed.

"I have no idea, darlin'."

They slowly gained on the train. Every time they waved at the passengers, the passengers waved back.

Jolie clutched the wagon seat with both hands. *Lord, we don't know what we're doing. We're just about to wreck the wagon and kill ourselves, and yet it's so exciting it's almost sinful. Sometimes I'm confused about what's sinful and what isn't. Someday when it's peaceful, I'd appreciate You explaining it to me.*

"Mama, they aren't stopping," Essie yelled.

"Girls, when we draw even with them, wave at the engineer. He can stop it."

Jolie and Essie waved and shouted.

The engineer blew his steam whistle.

"No!" Jolie yelled. "Don't wave at us. Stop the train!"

"Mama, they ain't even slowin' down," Essie wailed.

"I know, baby. We'll have to outrun them."

When Pilgrim and Stranger felt the line slap, they sprinted faster. The wagon wheels bounced along, off the ground half of the time.

"Mama, we're goin' to wreck," Essie whimpered. "I'm scared."

"Hang onto Jolie, baby."

"Mama, the train is speedin' up," Jolie declared. "They think we want to race."

Lissa Bowers leaned back. "This is stupid. I don't know if it's worth killing us just to try to stop them."

"It's worth it, Mama," Jolie pleaded as she grabbed her mother's arm. "There are little children on the train. I saw a cute little blond boy and others."

"You're right, Jolie Lorita!" Lissa Bowers stood up and urged the team on.

When they hit the gradual incline, the train slowed, and the wagon gained ground. By the time they reached the top of the grade, they were a hundred yards ahead of the train.

"Where's a crossing?" Lissa Bowers yelled.

"I think that's sort of one at the dry creek bed . . . either that or just silt that's washed up near the tracks," Jolie replied.

"Are there any rocks in the wagon to throw at the horses to make them run faster?"

"No rocks—just a long green squash!" Essie hollered.

"Then we'll just have to make do with this speed."

"What're we goin' to do?" Jolie yelled.

"Park across the tracks."

"But—but—," Essie stammered.

Lissa Bowers spun the team to the left. The left wheels raised a foot off the ground. Essie and Jolie grabbed for each other.

Lissa threw herself back and yanked the lines as the horses climbed the muddy train track embankment. The front wheels dropped between the tracks, but at the slap of the lines, the big horses jerked the front wheels out from the track and plopped the back ones down.

"Get out, girls!" Lissa ordered.

"What're you going to do?" Jolie stood beside her mother.

"Stay here until they put on the brakes. Then I'll drive off the tracks."

"What if he doesn't put on the brakes, Mama?" Essie sobbed.

"He will."

"I'm not leaving, Mama!" Jolie called out. "Go on, Essie; jump out."

"I'm too scared to get down," Essie yelled. "I want to stay."

"Lord, take care of us," Lissa Bowers prayed.

"Take care of us now!" Essie added.

Jolie stood on the wagon seat and held her hands up at the roaring train.

Eight engine wheels locked.

Steel slid on steel.

The whistle blew.

Lissa Bowers slapped the lead lines.

The wagon lurched forward.

Jolie tumbled into the back of the wagon.

The train screeched closer.

Essie pulled her dress over her head.

The iron rims of the back wagon wheels caught on the rail.

Lissa screamed at the horses.

"We're stuck," Essie shrieked.

Jolie found herself on her hands and knees in the back of the wagon with a long green squash in her hand. She hurled it at the horses. When it smacked into Pilgrim's rump, the startled horse lunged forward. Stranger jumped in empathy, and the wheels popped over the rail and rolled forward just as the engine skidded by. Jolie felt the steam and sparks.

"We did it," Essie shouted as she flopped her dress down. "I just knew we would be in heaven by now."

Lissa pulled the wagon forward and parked it parallel to the stopping train.

"We did it, Mama," Jolie called out.

"You and that squash did it. We'll have to thank Bullet Wells for that."

"No, you did it, Mama. You out-drove the train and made your stand," Jolie insisted.

"I've stopped a few trains in my day, Jolie Lorita . . . but never one quite like this!" Mrs. Bowers grinned as she hugged her daughters.

The first man out of the train was an angry engineer waving his fist.

The second one out was a man wearing a badge and waving a single-action Colt revolver.

"Check the draw, boys. Don't wander into an ambush," the man with the badge shouted as he sprinted to the wagon. A dozen armed men leapt out of the train and scattered up and down the railroad tracks.

Lissa Bowers stayed in the driver's seat. "I'm glad you're—"

"Get down out of the wagon. You're all under arrest!" the man shouted.

Lissa Bowers glanced at her daughters' startled faces. "Arrest? For what?"

"Attempted ambush of a train," the man said. "We know what you're up to."

Jolie saw her mother's neck turn red.

"What did you say?" Lissa Bowers snapped.

"I said, get down out of the wagon. Now!" he ordered.

Essie started to climb off.

"Sit down, baby," Mrs. Bowers barked. "We're not turning these horses loose, and we have no intentions of getting down."

"Woman, you don't understand. I could shoot you for ambushin' a train."

Jolie felt emboldened by her mother's resolve. "Then shoot us," Jolie called out. "Let that little blond-haired boy and a hundred other passengers watch you shoot unarmed women and a child."

The man glanced back at those watching from the train. "I didn't mean I would really shoot you," he mumbled. "Where are the others?"

"What others?"

"Your *compadres*. Lady, I won't shoot you. That's right. But I'll crawl up there and toss you out on your ear. You can count on that."

"You'd better get help then," Lissa challenged.

"Lady, we're trying to prevent a tragedy."

"So are we. That's why we stopped the train."

The man shoved his hat back with the barrel of his revolver. "What do you mean?"

"The bridge is weakened and the rails spread apart at Bobcat Gulch," Jolie explained. "They lost a handcar and seriously injured two men there this morning. I hauled the two men to town. The railroad said they were stopping all trains for at least twelve hours. Didn't they telegraph you?"

"We, eh, didn't stop at Antelope to check," the engineer admitted. "We were tryin' to make up for lost time."

A couple of other men with guns drawn approached the wagon. "How do we know you're tellin' the truth?" one of them asked.

"Hike down to Bobcat Gulch and check yourself," Jolie challenged. "You'll see rails spread, a handcar wrecked on the rocks, and blood all over."

The man with the badge rubbed his unshaven chin. "It could be a trap."

"Do you honestly think I would park my beautiful daughters on the track just to ambush a train?" Lissa Bowers scoffed. "I'd have to be crazy."

"You're their mama?" the man with the badge replied. "You don't look, eh . . . well, no matter what your age, I figure you're crazy to pull that stunt. I'll give you credit for courage, but you're with the cattlemen, aren't you?"

"We're homesteaders," Jolie insisted.

"Oh, that's your scheme." He studied the wheat fields to the south of the tracks. "Where are the others?"

Lissa Bowers closed her eyes and rubbed her temples. "Why do you keep saying that?"

"We heard the ranchers were hirin' gunmen from all over the West to attack the railroads until they reverse the shipping increase. Now with the farmers' strike in Lincoln, the homesteaders are joinin' up with the ranchers," the man explained.

"People are really taking sides?" Lissa asked.

"Yes, ma'am. Just like you. They are taking sides. They say there's goin' to be a war. If so, we're ready. We got armed guards on every train. Now I'm goin' to have to arrest you."

"That's absurd. Our story is easy to verify. Go check the track at Bobcat Gulch."

"I'll go," the engineer said. "It felt soft last time I crossed it."

"You ain't goin' by yourself. It still could be an ambush." The man with the badge grabbed one of the others. "We'll go with you." The three marched west along the tracks.

Jolie climbed off the wagon.

"Where are you going?" Essie asked.

"To retrieve my squash. I want it in my stew."

Many of the passengers had poured off the train despite the conductor's insistence that they remain on board. Others opened windows and leaned out. A couple dozen ventured over near the guards and the wagon.

"It's okay, folks," one of the train guards called out. "We're just checkin' for weak rails. Stick close to the train."

A little blond-headed boy trotted up to the wagon. "I'm Landen Yarrow, and I saw you back at the crossing!" he shouted.

"Yes, you did, Landen," Jolie replied. "You waved at me."

"And you waved at me."

"Yes, I did. And my name is Jolie Bowers."

He pulled off his wool cap. "Have you got a boyfriend?"

Jolie laughed. "How old are you, Landen?"

"Eight." His grin revealed two missing lower teeth.

"She's going to be married next June 14," Essie announced.

"She is?" Lissa Bowers winked at Jolie. "You didn't tell me that you and Tanner had set the date already."

"They didn't set it. I did," Essie declared.

"Well . . . well," the boy stammered and then looked at Lissa Bowers. "Do *you* have a boyfriend?"

"Oh, my, honey, you're a busy young man."

"She's my mother, and she's married to my daddy," Essie fumed.

"She's a mama?"

"I'm afraid so," Lissa admitted.

"I ain't havin' a very good trip," he mumbled.

"Sorry about that." Lissa Bowers rubbed her temples again. "It's been hectic for all of us."

The boy turned to Essie and shrugged. "Well, how about you? Do you have a boyfriend?"

"Whether I do or not is of no interest to you," Essie giggled. "I don't intend on bein' anyone's third choice."

"Landen!" a man shouted.

The boy peered through the milling crowd at a well-dressed man in suit and tie who looked about thirty.

"Don't you bother those ladies," the man called out as he approached.

"They're all spoken for, Strath, except her." He pointed at Essie. "And she's rather snippy."

The man ambled up to the wagon and tipped his hat. "Ladies, please excuse my son. He's rather precocious."

"Your son?" Jolie gasped. "I mean . . . I thought . . ."

"I believe my stammering Jolie thought you to be a bit younger and perhaps brothers." Lissa grinned.

"That's all right. Landen and I have been special pals ever since my wife . . . his mama died." The man leaned down to the boy, their faces only inches apart. Except for age and hair color, they looked identical. "We've been through a lot, haven't we, partner?"

"Strath is a lawyer."

"My, I am impressed," Lissa said. "I'm Lissa Bowers, and these are my daughters, Jolie and Essie."

"I'm Strath Yarrow, and you know Landen." He pulled off his wide-brimmed hat to reveal thick, wavy dark brown hair. "I'm a retired lawyer. I retired right after my wife died."

"A career change, Mr. Yarrow?" Lissa Bowers asked.

"I was in Chicago in court defending a company I didn't want to defend when my wife died, Mrs. Bowers. I wasn't with her or Landen. He tried to take care of her the best he could. I let them both down that day. I decided that any job that took me away from my family was the wrong one for me." He glanced across at the wheat fields and rubbed the corners of his eyes with his fingertips. "Excuse me for sounding melancholy. I had no intention of mentioning those things to strangers."

"That's quite all right, Mr. Yarrow," Lissa said. "Some sorrow cannot be contained."

"When did your wife die?" Essie blurted out.

Yarrow sighed and shook his head. "A year ago last month. Doctor said it was a hemorrhage in the brain."

"Are you coming west for a new start?" Jolie asked. *Lord, I don't think I've ever seen such hurting eyes in anyone. Have mercy on his crushed spirit.*

Yarrow took a big, deep breath, then let it out slowly. "Yes, we are. We bought ourselves a proved-up homestead and are goin' to live in a sod house and be farmers. I don't know anything about farming. We might not be too successful, but we'll be in it together," Strath said. "And right now that seems to be most important to both of us."

"We're homesteading too." Essie pointed in the direction of the North Platte River. "Just south of here."

"We haven't seen our place yet," Landen piped up. "But I think it must be the best homestead in the world."

"Is it in Nebraska?" Jolie asked.

"Yes, just out of Scottsbluff to the west, I believe," Strath Yarrow replied.

"Perhaps we'll see each other again in town," Lissa Bowers remarked.

"That would be nice." He put his hand on his son's shoulder. "I think we should get back to the train. Again I'm sorry for any annoyance he caused."

"He's a delightful young man," Lissa Bowers assured him.

"He wanted to know if we had boyfriends," Essie called out.

Yarrow laughed and then scratched the back of his neck. "Yes, he's had it on his mind all summer that he needs to find me a wife. He's afraid we'll starve on my cooking."

"A wife for you?" Essie gulped.

"Strath saw Jolie through the train window too," Landen blurted out. "And he said—"

Strath's hand dropped down over his son's mouth. "Now, ladies, Landen and I will excuse ourselves before I die of embarrassment."

Jolie watched him wend through the crowd at the train door, leading Landen by the hand.

"My, that was a whirlwind conversation," Lissa Bowers commented.

"I didn't know he was askin' about a wife for his father!" Essie exclaimed.

"Would it have made a difference?" Lissa smiled.

"Maybe," Essie mumbled.

"And what about poor Leppy Verdue?" Jolie reminded her.

"Oh, yeah, I forgot about him." Essie sighed. "Sometimes life gets complicated, don't it?"

Jolie nodded her head and refused to look back at the train.

When the train guards and engineer came tramping back up the tracks, most of the passengers rushed toward them.

"The ladies are right, boys," the badged man hollered. "The tracks at Bobcat Gulch washed out in the storm. There's a crew up there now . . . and two rails pulled off. If we had plowed ahead, we could have killed them and lots of us too."

The badged man looked up at Lissa Bowers and pulled off his

hat. "Ma'am, please accept my apologies. This talk about a railroad war has got us jumpy."

She studied his face as he surveyed her. "Your apology is accepted," she replied.

A tight smile broke across his face as he said, "Ma'am, what's your name? I'd like to put it in the report."

"Her name is Lissa Bowers. I'm Essie. And this is Jolie."

"You can put in your report Mrs. Matthew Bowers," Jolie added.

Her mother glanced at her and nodded. Then she flipped her long braid back over her shoulder. "And put in there that I'm a homesteader."

"Yes, ma'am, I'll do that." He tipped his hat.

"What're we goin' to do now?" one of the passengers asked.

"We'll wait until those rails get laid." He called to the other guards. "Boys, circle the train and stand guard. Just because these purdy ladies ain't bushwhackers don't mean there ain't some around."

"If you men will excuse us, we have a lot of chores to do before dark," Lissa Bowers said.

"You three saved a lot of lives today," he commented.

"I trust you all to make good use of your extra years," Jolie called out.

Lissa Bowers turned the wagon around. "Would you like to drive, Jolie Lorita?"

"By the looks of how tired Pilgrim and Stranger are, I think Estelle Cinnia should drive them." Jolie handed the lead lines to her sister.

"Me? But what if I do somethin' wrong? Everyone is watching."

"What if you do it right? Everyone will be impressed," Jolie encouraged.

"Is he watching me?" Essie whispered.

"Which he?" Jolie asked.

"You know which he."

"I'm not going to look over there."

"Mama," Essie asked, "is he watching me?"

Lissa Bowers laughed. "As a matter of fact, he is."

Essie let off the tension on the lines and slapped them on the horses' rumps. The wagon wheels creaked as the big horses plodded away from the train.

"And his father is watching too," Mrs. Bowers added.

Essie didn't take her eyes off the horses' ears. "That's who I meant, Mama."

"I know exactly who both of you meant," Mrs. Bowers said.

Jolie retied her hat string under her chin. "His was certainly a sad story, Mama."

"Yes, it was. There are many tragedies in this world. I'm glad that hasn't happened to us."

"It seemed a little awkward that he would tell us such things— to strangers," Jolie continued.

"Perhaps it's easier to talk about pain to those you'll never see again," Lissa Bowers offered.

"We might see him again," Essie murmured.

Lissa glanced at both of her daughters. "You're right, baby. I think we might see him again."

The horses plodded east until they came back to Telegraph Road. Then they sped up to a slow trot. Essie rolled up to the Wells place, still at the lines, with her nose held high. They stayed long enough for Mrs. Bowers to describe the train chase to Mr. and Mrs. Wells. Then they drove toward home. Lissa Bowers held the lines when they pulled into the yard.

"Which one is Dix?" she asked, looking at the two men hammering on the rafters.

"The blond one," Jolie offered.

"The other one is Shakey," Essie added. "I wonder why they call him Shakey? I've never seen him shake."

Lissa Bowers drove the rig up next to the house. "Hello," she called out. "I appreciate your helping with the roof."

Maxwell Dix shoved his long blond hair behind his ears and

wiped his forehead on his shirtsleeve. "We were made an offer we couldn't refuse—a place to camp and prairie chicken stew."

"It's mighty good stew," Shakey called out.

"Where have you been?" Gibs asked. "It's getting late, and me and Lawson was worried. Lawson kept the stew warm, but we already ate . . . a long time ago."

"Mama stopped a train," Essie blurted out.

Maxwell rubbed his chin. "That ain't hard to believe."

"No, a real train."

"Really, Mama?" Lawson asked.

"Come on, I'll tell you about it as we rub down these horses. They had a rough day even for their standards."

Jolie and Essie hiked across the dried-mud yard. Lissa Bowers stopped the wagon halfway to the barn and twisted around toward the sod house. "Do either of you know a Galen Faxon from west Texas?"

Both Maxwell and Shakey dropped their hands on their holstered revolvers.

She nodded. "That's what I suspected."

"Where did you see Faxon?" Maxwell Dix called out.

"On Telegraph Road headed to Scottsbluff."

"If they're bringin' in Faxon and that west Texas gang of his, it looks like someone's gettin' real serious," Shakey Torrington mumbled.

"Perhaps someone is just tryin' to bluff the other side by a show of force," Jolie suggested.

Shakey slammed down his hammer. "I can tell you one thing, Galen Faxon didn't ride all the way up here from Texas for a bluff."

The sun had set somewhere on the distant Wyoming mountains by the time they gathered for supper at the campfire near the barn. The stew had been expanded to include more potatoes and chunks of squash.

"I apologize for the bread," Jolie explained. "Most of the flour got wet."

"It's quite tasty, Miss Jolie," Shakey said. "It's certainly better than Maxwell's cookin'."

Dix waved a fork-stabbed piece of potato at Torrington. "You can cook anytime you want, Shakey."

"I ain't that desperate," Torrington laughed. "Besides it ain't exactly a famine."

"Well, it's a long way from a feast," Jolie sighed.

"Mama, I don't think that storm beat down the corn too bad. It's so short that it weathered better than some other people's," Lawson said.

"I think you're right," Lissa Bowers replied. "Must be some advantage to a late crop."

"Me and Lawson was wantin' to sleep in our room tonight. You reckon that's all right?" Gibs asked.

Mrs. Bowers studied the gray twilight sky. "I don't think we'll have a storm. But if we do, you come over to the barn."

"If we have another storm like last night, I think the walls will give out," Jolie observed.

Lissa took a deep breath and shook her head. "I know, I know. . . . I wish your father would come home."

"Little brother said Mr. Bowers was at that farmers' meeting in Lincoln," Maxwell commented.

"Yes, the folks around here took up a collection and paid his way. He felt obligated to go."

"They must think highly of him," Maxwell said.

"Daddy is really good at speakin', especially when nobody knows what to say," Essie explained.

"It might be his best talent," Jolie added.

"No, it's not his best talent," Mrs. Bowers murmured.

"I'd like to meet him someday. He's got himself a nice family," Dix remarked. He squatted next to the campfire and shoved a log in.

Lissa Bowers cleared her throat. "What will you do, Mr. Dix, if my husband is on one side of the railroad confrontation and you are on the other? Will you be happy to meet him then? Or will you shoot him?"

"Mama!" Jolie gasped.

No one said a word for a moment.

"Ma'am, I've been ponderin' the same thing. I suppose I'll make that decision when it comes. I reckon I think of it as a show of force rather than a gunfight."

"Daddy don't pack a gun," Gibs replied. "That is, most times he don't."

"That's good to know, little brother, 'cause I surely ain't goin' to aim at an unarmed man."

"I might shoot Galen Faxon, armed or not," Shakey Torrington growled. "I knew a cowboy who was on the Pecos River south of ol' John Chisum's place pushin' steers when Faxon gunned down Harold Kinney over an unbranded yearlin' that wasn't worth a dollar. Ain't no man should lose his life over a dollar."

Jolie stared at the fire. *Lord, this kind of talk scares me more than a speeding train. It might not be Daddy . . . or Maxwell Dix . . . but it could be someone like Daddy and Maxwell. But perhaps it's not this complex. Maybe Daddy will come home and tell us it's all settled.*

When the dishes were washed and dried, Gibs and Lawson took the smallest lantern and blankets and disappeared into the unroofed house. Dix and Torrington unrolled their bedrolls near the campfire. Mrs. Bowers and the girls headed to the barn.

With the largest lantern setting on a barrel, they used the stall with the copper tub and canvas curtain for a dressing room.

"It feels nice to have a clean nightshirt," Essie declared as she emerged barefoot. Her waist-length brown hair flowed around her shoulders like a shawl.

"I'm surprised at how well most of the clothes cleaned up." Jolie took her turn behind the canvas curtain.

"The mud was coarse, and we got to it before it dried." In her long flannel nightgown, Lissa Bowers lounged on the nail keg and combed out her auburn braid. "It wasn't the fine silt of a flood or that horrible musty smell. My gown smells quite nice."

"Does it smell like lilacs?" Jolie called out.

"Should it, darlin'?"

Jolie peeked out. "I added my lilac water to the final rinse."

Mrs. Bowers shook her head and grinned. "Oh, my, that's how you do it."

"I read it in the *Prairie Almanac*, but I'm afraid most of my copies got ruined."

Essie pulled a quilt on top of the stack of hay. "I'm sleepy. I've had a very busy day."

"Considering that we woke up covered with mud, I believe we have all had a long day." Lissa Bowers unfolded another quilt next to her youngest daughter. "I'm surprised these blankets dried so quickly."

"There was a breeze all day," Jolie said.

"Will you turn off the lantern, darlin'? I think I'm too tired to stand up anymore." Lissa turned to the open side of the barn. "Good night, boys," she called out into the darkness across the yard.

"Night, Mama," Gibs shouted back.

Two other voices filtered in from the dying firelight. "G'night, Mrs. Bowers."

"G'night, ma'am."

Jolie spread her blanket next to her mother's and then turned out the lantern. She made it to the hay before the light died out. From the covers she could look out at the fire embers. Stars sprinkled the Nebraska sky.

The quilt was soft and cool on her toes. She folded her arms under her head for a pillow. The flannel sleeves of her nightgown hinted of lilac. "It's been a good day, Mama. It was a horrible night and a good day."

"Do you know what I liked best about this day?" Essie blurted out.

"Why don't you tell me."

"I liked holdin' my hand on Trip Cleveland's wound until we got him to the doctor. I think it's the first time I made a difference in anyone's life. I ain't ever goin' to forget how that felt."

"That's very noble of you, Estelle Cinnia. I'm proud of my girls. This has been a day for heroics. Perhaps tomorrow will be a day of peace."

"How about you, Mama? What did you like best about this day? Was it when you outraced Galen Faxon?" Essie asked.

"Oh, that was fun, but what I liked best was Jolie Lorita standing up in the wagon seat holdin' out her hands to stop the train. I don't think I will ever forget that image. She looked like Joan of Arc."

"It was foolish," Jolie admitted. "I just didn't know what else to do."

"I thought I was goin' to wet myself," Essie giggled. "But I got too scared to. How about you, Jolie? What will you remember most from this day?"

There was a long pause.

"Oh . . . oh, there were so many things I can't—"

"I know what she'll remember," Lissa declared.

"Mama, you do not."

"She'll remember the sadness in Strath Yarrow's eyes."

"Mother!"

"Am I right?"

Even in the dark Jolie pulled the blanket over her face. "Yes, Mama. Did I do something wrong?"

"I didn't see any wrong behavior."

"Did I think the wrong thoughts?"

"Darlin', I don't know what kind of thoughts you had . . . but I can guess."

Jolie had almost drifted into sleep when she felt her mother turn over on her side.

"Mama, are you awake?"

"Yes, darlin'."

"How can I know for sure that Tanner is the one and that some other man won't tempt me?"

"Were you tempted today?" Lissa Bowers asked.

"A little," Jolie admitted.

"And what did you do with those thoughts?"

"I chased them out of my mind."

"I suppose you'll have to do that for the rest of your life."

"Really? You never have to do that, do you?"

Lissa Bowers chuckled. "Yes, I do, darlin', but I must admit, some temptations get easier to chase over the years."

"But how I can I be sure it's Tanner?"

"Is he the last one you think about before you go to sleep?"

"Yes, and the first one I think about in the morning."

"Do all your dreams about the future include images of Tanner?"

"Yes, they do, Mama."

"Do you sometimes hurt all over because you want him to hold you and touch you?"

"Oh, yes, Mama."

"I'm not listenin' to this," Essie mumbled.

"When you talk to the Lord about Tanner, do you have a peaceful time?"

"Yes, I do, Mama."

"Do you want to have children with Tanner?"

"Mama, now I'm getting embarrassed," Jolie objected.

"You didn't answer me."

"More than anything I can think of."

"Is he perfect, darlin'?"

Another pause.

"Is Tanner Wells perfect, Jolie Lorita?"

"No, Mama. He can be bullheaded, unreasonable, and condescending at times. Is that bad?"

"It's good, darlin'. There are no perfect people this side of heaven. What if Tanner Wells spent the next fifty years bullheaded, unreasonable, and condescending at times? Could you live with that the rest of your life?"

"I think I can."

"Then, Jolie Lorita Bowers, every day for the rest of your life I want you to wake up and say to yourself, 'Tanner Wells, I have decided to love you today. There's nothing you can do about it.' You have to choose to love someone every day of your life."

"Did you choose to love Daddy today, Mama?" Essie piped up.

"Oh, my, yes. Over and over and over today. And I'm choosing him right now. Are you choosing Tanner, Jolie?"

"Yes, Mama."

"So there you have it. He's the one."

"Just like that?"

"It wasn't easy, was it?"

"No, Mama. But I know you're right."

"Everyone knows you're right," Essie complained.

Jolie stared out of the barn at the fire. "Did I talk too loud?"

Lissa Bowers cleared her throat. "Maxwell and Shakey, did we talk too loud?"

The reply was deep, slow, plaintive. "No, ma'am, it was just about right. I surely wish I had been told all that when I was a pup."

"We'll go to sleep now. Good night, boys."

"Good night, Mama," Shakey Torrington replied.

Four

"Tanner, you stop that!" Jolie blinked her eyes open and sat straight up.

"Were you dreamin' about him?" Essie giggled.

Jolie stared around as daylight broke into the barn. "Something was tickling me."

"I was."

"You were?"

"With this straw. It's time to get up."

"I slept in. I guess I was tired."

Essie struggled to tie a yellow ribbon on her brown hair. "Do you always dream about Tanner, Jolie?"

Jolie took a deep breath. The barn air tasted like stale hay, leather, and manure. "No." She reached her hand out to Essie.

"What other boys do you dream about?" Essie pulled her sister to her feet.

"I don't dream of any others." Jolie retied the yellow ribbon on Essie's hair.

"Not even Strath Yarrow?"

"No." Jolie glanced around. "Hand me my stockings and shoes, li'l sis."

"Are you goin' to put them on before you put on your dress?" Essie fetched the shoes and handed them to her.

"Yes, I am this morning. I don't like goin' barefoot in the barn."

"But there ain't no sticks or rocks. It's soft and squishy."

"Yes, it's the soft and squishy part I try to avoid." Jolie sat on the nail barrel and pulled on her socks.

"Sometimes I dream of Chester," Essie confessed.

"You do?" Jolie rubbed a cramp out of her toes before she pulled on the sock. "Is that good or bad?"

"Oh, they're usually happy dreams."

When Jolie pulled on her shoes, her toes warmed. She leaned over to lace them up. "That's very mature of you."

"Thank you," Essie giggled. "I'm happily pushin' him over a cliff. Or happily tossing a rattlesnake down his duckings. Or happily tying him to the railroad tracks—that's one of my favorites."

Jolie stood and brushed Essie's bangs off her forehead. "So much for maturity. Where's Mama?"

"Tendin' the animals. She said she would milk Margaret."

Jolie gazed out the open east side of the barn, her hand on a rough wooden post. "Milking is my chore."

"I think she wanted you to cook." Essie made circles with her fingers and peeked through them. "Lawson cleaned out your stove this mornin'. He said you can cook in the house if you want."

"Yes, that will be good. I'll be right out as soon as I clean up."

"I'm goin' to go help Gibs," Essie declared. "How do you think I would look with spectacles?"

"You would look fine. Why do you ask? What's Gibs doing?"

"Gibs is tryin' to get Max to drink some of Margaret's milk. I was just wonderin' if I'd look more mature with spectacles."

"Where is the fawn? Do you want to look more mature?"

"In the pen with Mudball. I'd like to look more everything," Essie sighed.

"How does a pig like sharing a stall with a fawn? No one wears spectacles for looks."

"Mudball has been sleeping ever since he came home. I think he was a very naughty pig and is resting up. Mary Vockney tried on her mama's spectacles, and she said she looked more mature."

Jolie laughed.

"What's so funny?"

"I just can't imagine Mary Vockney ever looking mature."

"Can you imagine me lookin' mature?" Essie asked.

"Yes, I can."

Essie skipped out of the barn.

Jolie washed her face, brushed down her green dress with lace cuffs and collar, buttoned up the dress, fastened on tiny gold earrings, and dabbed her neck with lilac perfume.

Lord, I know the only ones who will notice the perfume are Maxwell Dix and Shakey Torrington, but I like to smell nice. I think it's important to always look my best.

Jolie checked the hand mirror to make sure every auburn hair was in place and then hiked out into the yard. The sun was not up yet, but the homestead was bright with reflected light from the passing clouds.

Sometimes, Lord, this looks like such a barren, lonely place. No neighbors. No trees. No flowers. No yard.

Her oldest brother sat on the front uncovered step of the house, a knife in one hand, a stick in the other. He looked up as she approached. "Mornin', Jolie."

"Good morning, dear Lawson. Thank you for cleaning out my stove."

"Wasn't much in it except ashes. The mud was on top. Mama said I should wait and see if you want me to build a fire in it."

"Yes, thank you. I'll get going on potato cakes. I would imagine Mr. Dix and Mr. Torrington are hungry."

Lawson studied the stick as if it were a treasure. "They're gone, Jolie."

"Gone? When will they be back? Did they go hunting?"

"They went to Scottsbluff. Said they wanted to check out the sides in this railroad war."

"War? It's not really a war." She stared north. In the distance sunlight broke across the white cliffs of Scott's Bluff, making it look like an ancient Roman ruin. "I'm sure they'll be back."

"Why do you say that?"

Jolie raised her chin. "Because they haven't said good-bye to me."

Lawson stared at her. "I guess not ever'body's life centers around you, like ours does. I'll go get some dry firewood."

Jolie folded her arms and studied the roof of the sod house.

You told him to say that, didn't You, Lord? And You are right, of course. I want to know everything first and be at the center of everything. I think I'm afraid to lose control. I suppose that's what scares me most about marriage. Will Tanner make decisions for both of us, and I'll have no say? I know he will. I just don't know how I'll accept it. Maybe this is practice.

Lawson hiked back with an armload of pine and cedar. "Jolie, I didn't mean to blurt that out."

She put her hand on her brother's shoulder. "Lawson Pritchett Bowers, I hope you always feel free to tell me what's on your heart and mind. You're the oldest son. I'm the oldest daughter. I think that means we have to look out for each other as well as for the others."

"Thanks, Jolie. Do you think we can get the roof shingled in one day?"

"I don't know. It looks like Maxwell and Shakey finished the rafters and purling. Have you ever shingled anything?"

"I helped at that chicken coop behind 'Dog' Manley's house in Helena. I know how to lay the shingles, but I don't know what to do up at the peak of the roof."

"I guess we'd better learn. These clouds could turn threatening," Jolie said.

"That's what Mama thinks. I don't reckon we'd have the heart to shovel out the house one more time."

"I'll cook a quick breakfast, and we'll get started. Why don't you and Gibs see if you can roll the wagon over here next to the house. I think the shingles will be easier to hand up from the wagon bed."

None of the mattresses or leather webbing survived the collapse of the sod roof, but the bed frames and the table did. They sat around a scrubbed table perched in the barren front yard as Jolie served potato cakes and pickled eggs.

"We need to go to town and buy groceries today. And we need to shingle the roof," Mrs. Bowers said between bites. "I don't know how we can do both."

"Mama, you could go to town. We'll shingle," Jolie offered.

Mrs. Bowers studied her children. "That would not surprise me. But it's too difficult a job to leave to you. I could never do that. We can go to church in Scottsbluff tomorrow, but the stores will all be closed, so we couldn't shop then."

"Maybe we can hurry, Mama," Lawson said, "and get finished in time to go to town today."

"Darlin', we can't do an inferior job. A good roof will be much more important than a big meal."

"If we get real hungry, we can roast Max," Gibs suggested.

"No," Essie called. "No, no, no, no!"

"Mama, let's all go fishin' after the roof is done. Maybe we can have fish for supper," Gibs proposed.

"You think they'll bite in that muddy water after such a storm?"

"If they're hungry, they will."

"We only have two hammers, Mama," Lawson reminded her.

Jolie scooped more potatoes onto Gibs's plate. "This is the way I have it organized. Mama and Lawson will have to hammer because they are best at that. Gibs will keep Lawson supplied with shingles and nails. I will assist Mama and work from the back of the wagon because Gibs is better on the ladder than I am."

"What about me?" Essie interjected.

"You need to be on the ground running for supplies and doing errands."

"Can Francis help me? He promised that he would never, ever run away again."

Jolie stood on the wagon, holding shingles, the pockets of her white apron filled with slightly rusty nails from the keg given to them by

Mr. Culburtt. She handed another shingle to her mother. Lissa Bowers propped herself on the purling boards with half a dozen nails between her lips.

"Mama, it will be more difficult once these bottom rows are done. I won't be able to hand you up one shingle at a time."

She handed her mother a shingle and turned to pick up another from the pile in the wagon. She could hear Lawson hammer on the other side of the roof. The air was still. The clouds were thick but white. A cedar splinter pricked Jolie's finger, and she pulled it out.

She waited for her mother's pounding to stop and then handed up more nails. "I believe these are too long for shingles. There's no reason to have them stick through that far. If this new roof ever collapses, it will hurt a lot more than the mud and rain."

Mrs. Bowers nodded and reached for the nails.

"I think you're ahead of Lawson," Essie called out. Francis stood beside her, wearing a dirty blue bandanna.

"Poor Gibs has to climb up and down the ladder. It must be tiring," Jolie said.

"He said he was pretending to be storming a castle," Essie informed her.

"Yes, he would make a game out of it," Jolie said.

"Do you want a drink, Mama?" Essie asked.

"Hmmpht, naysatmer."

"What did she say?"

"She said, 'No, thank you,'" Jolie interpreted.

"Hey, someone is comin'," Gibs hollered.

"I'll go see," Essie shouted.

"I guess that means the roads are drying out. I suppose I should stay here and wait for them to come to me," Jolie said.

Lissa Bowers nodded her head and kept hammering.

"You see, Mama, I am learning. Wait for the men to come to you. Maybe Maxwell and Shakey came back. They left rather abruptly, you know."

Mrs. Bowers rolled her eyes and reached for the last nail in her mouth.

"It's a wagon," Gibs shouted from the other side of the roof.

Essie ran back across the yard, Francis following close behind. "We're hiding in the privy and won't be out until he's gone," she hollered.

"Bullet Wells?" Jolie queried.

"And his daddy and brothers," Essie called out as she scampered toward the barn.

Gibs hiked around front as the wagon rolled into the yard.

"Smooth your skirt down. I think your ankle is almost showing," Jolie whispered.

Mrs. Bowers laid the hammer down on the shingles and tugged her skirt over her lace-up shoes. "Yes, Mama."

"Hi, Mr. Wells," Jolie greeted him.

The tall, thin man handed the lines to Greg and stepped off the wagon. "And greetings to the Bowerses. We came to help with the roofing. It's too wet to do any work in the fields over at our place."

"Hi, Jolie," the taller of the teenage boys called out.

"Hi, Theo. . . . Hi, Greg," Jolie replied. "Hello, Bullet."

"Where is she?" Bullet hollered.

"Who are you looking for?" Jolie asked.

"Estelle."

"She's, eh, ill-disposed at the moment," Jolie replied.

"That's a fine shinley," Bullet grumbled.

Mr. Wells hiked over to the house. "Mrs. Wells sent some squash and a mess of snap beans."

"Thank you, Mr. Wells. That's very generous of you," Jolie replied.

"You've got a lot of work done already. Look at this lumber. I didn't know there were that many cut boards in the whole county," Mr. Wells remarked.

"Jolie procured those for us," Lissa Bowers explained.

"And nails! Ready-made nails," Mr. Wells added. "Where would you like me and the boys to begin? We only have one hammer. The boys aren't too good at hammerin', but they can work hard."

"Hey, can I go look at your pig?" Bullet blustered.

"Yes," Jolie replied, "but don't ride him, please. He's tired."

"What do you think, Jolie Lorita?" Lissa Bowers asked. "Do you have this new crew organized?"

"Yes, Mama. If Mr. Wells, Greg, and Theo would like to pull their wagon around back, they can work on the other side with Lawson. Gibs can come around here and help on this side."

The man shaded his eyes with his hand and stared up at the roofline. "Your mother shouldn't be up there hammerin'. This is no work for a lady."

"Thank you, Mr. Wells. I will accept that as the compliment you intended. But until someone comes along who can out-hammer me, I will stay. We could get rain today, and we must get this finished," Lissa Bowers insisted.

Mr. Wells shook his head. "Don't reckon I've ever known any-one like you, Mrs. Bowers."

Lissa Bowers lined up another shingle. "Very few have, Mr. Wells."

"Did you grow up on a farm?" he quizzed.

"I grew up on a Michigan estate as an only child. I was a spoiled, little rich girl. By the time I was twelve, I hated it."

He shook his head and drove the wagon to the other side.

"Gibs, come up on the wagon and help me," Mrs. Bowers instructed. "We'll let Jolie do other chores."

Jolie hiked over to the barn and stared at the stack of buffalo robes caked with dried mud.

"Is he gone yet?" The voice filtered across from the canvas-draped stall.

Jolie tugged back the canvas. Essie lounged behind the empty copper tub. A brown and white calf stood inside it. "I thought you were at the privy," Jolie stated.

"Francis doesn't like hidin' in the privy."

"I can't blame him for that. Bullet is still here. Mr. Wells and the boys are going to help us roof. So I guess you're stuck with him for a while."

"Why am I the one who is stuck with him?"

"Because he's your age."

"That's not fair. Just because you like his big brother doesn't mean I should get stuck with Chester," Essie complained.

"You're right. Would you like to help me with a difficult chore?"

"Anything is easier than bein' with Chester."

"We need to beat, brush, and comb the buffalo robes."

"Will I get dirty?" Essie queried.

"Filthy."

"I'll do it."

"Let's drag them out to the clothesline," Jolie suggested. "We'll beat them and then start combing and brushing."

"Do you really think we can get them clean?"

"Yes, I do."

"Will they still stink when we're done?"

"No, they'll smell like lilacs," Jolie teased.

Essie lifted Francis out of the tub, and the calf followed her across the barn. The girls dragged the first seven-by-four-foot buffalo hide out to the clothesline rope.

"What're we going to beat it with, Jolie? I think our rug beater is too light."

"Let's try the broom," Jolie suggested.

"I think it's too light too."

"How about this axe handle?" Jolie offered.

"Yes, but we would have to stand so close we would really be caked with dirt after a few swings," Essie warned.

"Hey, there you are!" A muddy Bullet Wells jogged toward them. "Hello, Estelle!"

Essie sighed and slumped her shoulders. "Hello, Chester."

"Hey, what're you doin' with that axe handle? Are you playin' a game? It's my turn next," Bullet demanded.

"We do like making a game out of it," Jolie said. "It's called—eh, Spank the Buffalo."

Bullet Wells's eyes brightened. "Wow, I like it. How does it go?"

"We hit the back side of this buffalo hide with the axe handle just as hard as we can, and then we check our score."

"What do you mean?"

"If we do a good job and really spank it, dust will fog all over us," Jolie explained.

"If you can write your name in the dust on your sleeve, you get ten points," Essie responded.

Jolie nodded agreement. "If it's moderately dusty, you get five points."

"And if it's a smidgeon, only one point," Essie concluded.

Bullet's brown eyes grew wider. "How do I win?"

"Get the highest score on one buffalo hide," Jolie replied.

"What's the record?" he demanded.

"It's 487 points," Essie reported. "Mama did that a long time ago."

Jolie sighed. "No one has come close to that in years."

Bullet stared at the buffalo robe. "I bet I can beat it."

"This is Essie's hide," Jolie said. "I'm afraid she gets first crack at it. Sorry."

"But—I'm company. I'm supposed to go first," Bullet demanded.

"I know she had her heart set on that one." Jolie put her arm around Essie's waist. "What do you think, sis?"

"I don't know." Essie faked a pout. "You promised me that I could have that one."

"Please," Bullet pleaded.

Essie rocked back on her heels. "I suppose it is my Christian duty to think of others first."

"Oh, thank you, thank you, thank you." Bullet danced around and around. "Give me that axe handle."

Jolie handed it to him. "Wait for us to stand back."

"Don't you want to get dirty?" he pressed.

"That wouldn't be fair. That's your dirt. No one else should stock up on it as if it were their own," Jolie explained.

"Oh . . . yeah. You're right. Get way back over there by the barn." Jolie and Essie giggled as they scooted back to the barn.

"Is this all right, Chester?" Essie called out.

"Yeah," he hollered. "Now watch this."

With two hands on the axe handle, Bullet Wells wound up and smacked the buffalo hide so hard that his feet left the ground. Dust fogged high. When it cleared, two round white eyes peered out from a thick mask of dirt.

"How was that? Was that good? That was good, wasn't it?"

"Oh, Chester," Essie swooned, "you're so good at that. I couldn't do that in a hundred tries."

"Was it a ten?"

"That was a perfect ten points," Jolie hollered.

"If you thought that one was good, watch this!"

With even more enthusiasm he slammed the hickory handle into the back side of the buffalo hide. This time the dirt rained down like locusts in a plague. He coughed, spat, and rubbed his eyes on his shirttail. "Wow, that was even better. Can I get a fifteen?"

"Ten is the highest, Bullet," Jolie said. "And that's definitely a ten."

"That ol' record doesn't have a chance."

"Okay, Chester, you have twenty points. Keep going and see how you do."

"Aren't you goin' to stay and watch?" he asked.

"No, you have to keep your own score," Essie told him.

"I do?"

"Yes, but we'll be watching from time to time," Essie assured him.

"Oh, man, this is goin' to be easy. I'll be the champ in no time."

Essie and Jolie hiked around the barn where Bullet Wells was no longer in view. There was a loud "twaap" and then a shout of victory.

"I can't believe he thinks it's a game," Essie giggled.

"It *is* a game."

"It is?"

"Sure. We just made it up. That's how all successful games get started," Jolie explained.

"I don't think it will be too successful. Not many would fall for it besides Chester."

"Then he'll truly be the champ!" Jolie exclaimed.

"Do you want to come see Max? He took Margaret's milk in a pan."

Jolie glanced at the railroad-tie pen. "Okay, just for a minute. I need to start thinking of what I can scrape up for lunch. If yesterday was meager, today is a near dearth. We have a bigger crew now. And when Bullet figures it out, we have to beat the rest of the buffalo robes."

They tramped out to the corrals.

"I don't think Max likes bein' in there with Mudball," Essie commented.

"Why did you put him in the pigpen?"

"Because it's solid enough that he can't get out and tall enough that he can't jump over it yet."

"That's quite a pair," Jolie said. "A 300-pound hog and a 30-pound fawn."

Essie took Jolie's hand. "I told Max that Mudball was his older brother."

"You think he believes that?"

"He's young and impressionable. Maybe he'll go along with it for a while," Essie laughed.

"At least, until he sees himself in a mirror."

Essie climbed up on the wall of the pigpen. "He's gone!" she shouted.

"Mudball?" Jolie peered over the rails.

"No, Max!" Essie jumped down and surveyed the yard. "He's gone. How did he get out?"

"Maybe he can jump better than you think," Jolie commented.

Essie's eyes got wide. "Do you think Mudball ate him?"

"No," Jolie shot back. "Of course not. Perhaps we should ask Bullet if he saw Max."

"That's right. He was in there! I can't believe it. If he did something to Max, I'll kill him," Essie fumed.

Jolie put her hand on her sister's shoulder. "You'll what?"

"Eh, I'll give him what he deserves."

Jolie and Essie trotted back around the barn toward the dust cloud.

"Would you look at that one?" Bullet shouted. "That's another ten. I have 143 points in only fifteen hits. I'm really good at this."

"Chester Wells," Essie shouted, "what did you do with Max?"

He shook his head, and dust fogged everywhere. "Max who?"

"Don't lie to me. You went to the hog pen and—"

"Hey, you'll never guess what I found in your hog pen. A baby deer. Must have gotten stuck there in the night, but don't worry—I set him free."

"You did what?" Essie cried.

"I threw him out of the pigpen. Watch this." Bullet wound up and slammed the axe handle into the buffalo robe. A light fog of dirt and dust hung in the air.

"Chester, Max was my fawn. You had no right to turn him loose," Essie sobbed.

"Where did you put him, Bullet?" Jolie asked.

"I put him on the ground between the pen and the horse corral."

"Where did he run off to?" Jolie pressed.

"I don't know. Watch this." Bullet slammed the axe handle into the buffalo hide. "Wow, that was another ten. I haven't had this much fun since I found the six cats in the gunny sack."

Jolie glanced at Essie. "Don't ask him."

Essie sprinted back to the corral, Jolie trailing behind.

"He'll die on his own, Jolie. You know he will," Essie wailed.

When Jolie caught up, she tugged on her sister's shoulder. "Essie, wild animals are supposed to live on their own all their lives. Some live long lives, some short lives. I believe we can trust the animal population into the Lord's hands. They belong to Him."

"And He gave me Max. I'm supposed to look after him, Jolie. Don't you see?" Essie sobbed.

"Then let's look for him. If the Lord wants us to find him, we will. But we can't go traipsin' all over. So if he's not on our homestead, perhaps the Lord has something else in mind."

"I'll check with Francis and see if he's seen Max," Essie called out.

Jolie searched the barn, stalls, and feed bin. *Lord, I know that little deer isn't in here, but I'll look for Essie's sake. She has such a sweet, tender heart. Her empathy for animals is incredible. They sense it too. From Stranger and Pilgrim down to that little fawn, they know Estelle Cinnia is on their side. But it means she can be hurt easily too. Toughen her up a little, Lord. In this world there are pains and failures. I don't want life and people to crush her.*

When Jolie finished searching the barn, she paused and glanced over at the roof. Shingle by shingle, nail by nail, hammer blow by hammer blow, the roof grew. The clouds to the east had thickened and looked darker than the ones straight above.

Jolie rested her hand on her narrow hips. *Lord, if we actually get that roof on before it rains again, we'll be better off than before the storms hit. Does it always take a tragedy to get us to do what we should have done in the first place?*

She studied the woman on the roof.

Lord, I can never be like Mama. Where does she get the strength and energy? My back hurts every night, and I never plow the field, shoe the horses, or climb on the roof and nail shingles. I don't think I've ever met anyone like her. She's a remarkable lady. Help me always to be as energetic in my life as my mother is in hers.

"Did you find him?" Essie ran up with Francis following. He now wore a red bandanna around his neck.

Jolie brushed Essie's long light brown bangs out of her eyes. "No, dear, sweet Estelle. Perhaps it's time to release him to his destiny."

"Yeah, and I'm goin' to release Chester to his destiny too. If I can get that axe handle away from him, I'll see how much dust I can raise out of him."

"Now, Essie, you don't mean that."

"I do too!" Essie broke toward Bullet Wells.

Jolie threw her arms around her and held her back. *Lord, I might have been a little overboard on the sweetness trait.*

"Let me go. I'll kill him," Essie muttered.

"We haven't finished looking."

"We haven't?"

"No, did you check the—the shed?"

"No."

"You and Francis check the shed. I'll check the . . . well."

"The well?"

"Perhaps he went for a drink. Animals are attracted to water."

"Oh, yeah."

Mud circled the well, and Jolie held up her skirt as she approached. She opened the wooden trapdoor behind the red pump handle and peered into the blackness. *I'm not sure why I'm looking down here. There's no way the fawn could open the door and fall in. Of course, a boy could open the door and throw a fawn in.*

Jolie cleared her throat. "Are you in there, Max?" Her voice came back in a shallow echo. When she turned around, Essie and Francis stood beside her. "Eh, I was just making sure . . ."

"Did you hear him?" Essie asked.

"No."

"He's not in the shed either. What're we goin' to do, Jolie?"

"We will just wait. Remember how Mudball came home when he was hungry?"

"But Francis didn't," Essie reminded her.

"He might have, but we found him before he had an opportunity."

"I don't want Chester to ever come to our house again," Essie fumed.

"I suppose we should keep a better eye on him."

"You mean . . . play with him?"

"If you had gone with him to look at Mudball, maybe you could have prevented this."

"That's not fair."

"I believe you're right." Jolie glanced back over her shoulder. "What's Francis doing?"

"I think he wants to go back into the privy," Essie said.

"I thought you said he didn't like it in there."

"He doesn't, but that was before he met Chester," Essie replied.

"It seems strange to have a calf waiting at the privy door. If a traveling photographer came by, I'd have him take a picture of that." Jolie smiled.

"Yeah, you could label it, 'Hurry it up, buddy. I don't have all day,'" Essie giggled.

"Maybe Francis thinks someone is in there."

"Maybe someone is," Essie shouted. "Max! Maybe he found Max." She ran over and threw open the privy door.

Jolie strained to see. "Is he . . ."

Essie spun around, and her shoulders slumped. "It's empty."

"We looked all over, Estelle. There's nothing else we can do," Jolie said as the calf wandered into the privy.

"I can beat the tar out of Chester," Essie grumbled.

"No, you can't. Chester didn't know Max was a pet."

"He could have come and asked first."

"Yes, I agree with that."

The calf bawled, and both girls turned back.

"What does he want?" Jolie asked.

"I think he wants me to close the door." Essie shoved the wooden door closed and scurried back to Jolie.

They circled around the clothesline where a panting, dirty, sweating Bullet Wells leaned on the axe handle. "I don't think I'm goin' to break the record."

"Would you like to have a second chance and beat another robe?" Essie offered.

"You'd let me do another?"

"Of course she would," Jolie assured him.

"Wow, Estelle, you're a pal. Which one do I get?"

"Shall we let him have the muddiest one?" Jolie asked.

Essie's eyes lit up. "But—but—I thought Mama wanted that one."

Jolie shrugged. "Sorry, Bullet. You'll have to—"

"I guess we could let him have the worst one," Essie said.

"Really? Oh, man, this might be the best day of my life," Bullet exulted.

Jolie studied the twelve-year-old covered with fine yellowish brown dirt. *Lord, I guess I have no idea what Bullet's life looks like from the inside. But I trust that he has had better days than this.*

"Come on, Essie, let's go see if the roofing crew needs water. Then you can help me cook lunch."

They hiked to the house.

"Are you goin' to use the stove?" Essie asked.

"Not with them roofing over it. I'll have to cook outside. Looks like I'll be cooking in the skillet again." They paused by the wagon where Gibs handed shingles to his mother.

"Mama, would you like a drink now?" Jolie called.

Lissa Bowers pulled the nails out of her mouth. "That would be nice, dear."

"Did you hear what Chester did?" Essie cried out.

"Looks like he's beating the buffalo rugs for us. That's very kind of him."

"No, what I mean is—"

"Baby, while Jolie Lorita gets us all a drink, I need you to move your fawn out of the backroom before he messes things up."

"Max?" Essie hollered. "He's in the house?"

"Yes. I don't know how he sleeps through all of this racket," Lissa Bowers added.

Jolie had just finished drying the last of the dishes in the yard when Lawson stood up on the half-finished north side of the roof and hollered, "There's a rider comin' in."

"Can I go see, Jolie?" Essie asked.

"Help me put the rest of the lunch dishes back in the barn first. I think it's goin' to rain by nightfall."

When the dishes were crated, Essie sprinted across the yard. Jolie followed as far as the wagon. "Mama, your braid is coming loose."

Lissa Bowers pulled the nails from her mouth. "Darlin', whoever it is isn't coming here to see me."

"Have you ever noticed how everyone stops and stares anytime we get someone on the lane. I suppose it's a sign of living in an isolated place," Jolie said. "I wonder if I should build up the fire?"

"Just relax, Jolie Lorita. Could just be someone ridin' down the wrong lane."

"He's wearin' a wide-brim hat and brown leather vest," Essie reported.

"Is he sitting straight in the saddle?" Lissa Bowers asked.

"Yes. Straight back like he was tied to a board, and he has a gun across his lap," Essie answered.

"A carbine or a rifle?" Gibs asked.

"How would I know? He's way down there."

Lissa Bowers stood and stretched her legs. When she did, she glanced over her shoulder. Then she sat back down on the purling strips. "It's Captain Richardson."

Essie ran around to the side of the house and stared, then sprinted back. "How can you tell, Mama? He's still way down there."

"By the way he sits that horse, baby. Some men are born to ride horses. The captain is one of them."

Jolie waited at the wagon as Essie ran back out to the lane. She glanced up and noticed that her mother was reweaving her long auburn braid.

"I don't want to embarrass my daughter," Lissa explained.

By the time the man with silver-gray hair rode into the yard,

Lissa Bowers was once again driving nails. The rancher rode over on the long-legged blue roan gelding. "Afternoon, Mrs. Bowers, Miss Jolie, li'l sis, and young Mr. Bowers."

"Captain Richardson, we're happy to see you," Lissa greeted him. "I'm sorry we're not more accommodating, but we're racing the clouds. We lost our sod roof night before last."

He pushed back his head and studied Lissa Bowers. "Yes, ma'am. That's what Jocko told me. He and the boys wanted to come help, but I need them at the ranch. That storm scattered cattle everywhere. We have a lot of sortin' out to do."

"Captain, may I fix you some dinner? We just finished, but I would be happy to cook you something," Jolie offered.

"Thank you, Miss Jolie, but I'll pass. I ate a big breakfast, and the spicy gravy didn't seem to agree with me. I'd be better off not eatin' for a while."

"What brings you here?" Lissa Bowers asked.

"Mr. Bowers isn't home from Lincoln yet, is he?"

"No, we don't expect him until tomorrow. May I do anything for you?"

"No, but I believe Miss Jolie can."

"What can I do for you, Captain Richardson?"

"Miss Jolie, can a group of us hold a meeting at the schoolhouse tomorrow night? I asked Ernie Vockney, and he said the school board don't mind, but you were in charge of the building, and it would be your decision."

"A community meeting? Of course," Jolie replied.

"It won't be the whole community. Just some ranchers and farmers who are disgusted with the railroad rate increase. We didn't want to meet in town. There are plenty of railroad sympathizers there."

"I do trust there's some way to resolve this problem," Jolie said.

"Besides with fists or bullets," Lissa added.

Captain Richardson combed his gray hair back with his fingers. "I reckon that was aimed at my behavior. And you're right, Mrs. Bowers. I didn't handle that situation correctly. Havin' a dime-store attorney from Omaha tell me that if I couldn't make it, perhaps I should retire from the cattle business just didn't set well with me."

"Did you beat him to a pulp?" Gibs asked.

"I flattened him with one punch, son. Broke his nose, I reckon. He had me arrested and is threatenin' to sue me. But, as I told the judge, I was clearly in the wrong. When Jocko brought in the funds, I paid my fine and left." He glanced up at Lissa Bowers. "Now, ma'am, I'd like to trade places with you and do a little roofin' myself."

"That's generous of you, Captain, but I'm doing very well, what with Mr. Wells and the boys on the other side."

Richardson stared up at the clouds. "Mrs. Bowers, I have no doubt that you can roof the house or build a house, for that matter. But it's goin' to rain again by dark. And I couldn't live with myself, knowin' I left a purdy lady on the roof nailin' shingles. So if you'll practice kindness to an old cattleman, I'd appreciate havin' the opportunity to release a little of my temper on those nail heads."

Lissa Bowers flashed a wide smile. "Captain Richardson, you are indeed a persuasive cattleman. Under those conditions, I surrender my hammer. Gibs, go around to the other side and borrow the ladder so I can get down."

Captain Richardson pulled off his spurs. "I'll stick my pony in the corral and be right back."

Jolie walked back to the barn with him. "Captain, are you sure you wouldn't like some coffee?"

"I think my gut would feel better with nothing in it. Is that one of your brothers beatin' that buffalo robe?"

"No, that's a neighbor boy."

"Don't reckon I've ever seen a lad attack a chore with such vigor."

"He's very good at it."

"Say," the captain's eyes searched the yard, "eh, which way is your . . . My stomach is hurtin' somethin' fierce."

She took the reins from him. "It's around the corner behind that shed. I'll put your horse up."

Jolie had just pulled the bridle off the captain's horse when she heard a commotion. She rushed out of the corral and around to the front of the barn. Bullet Wells stopped beating on the buffalo robe.

"Did you know there was a calf wearing a bandanna in your privy?" the captain shouted.

Jolie made the rounds with water as Captain Richardson replaced Lissa Bowers on the roof. Gibs handed the shingles up to the cattleman.

Lissa strode to the barn with Jolie beside her. "Where's Essie?"

"Still with the fawn, I suppose."

"Tell her to clean up. We're goin' to town."

"You, me, and Essie?" Jolie asked.

"Yes. Lawson and Gibs can help the others with the roofing. Gibs needs the ladder on this side now, and so they won't miss the wagon. There are no more hammers; there is nothing we can do to make it go any faster."

"I'll tell Gibs to move the buffalo robes back inside if it starts to rain," Jolie said.

A dirt-covered Bullet Wells ran over. "Miss Jolie, can I spank another buffalo robe? I think I figured out how to beat the record, but I need one more chance at it."

Lissa Bowers raised her eyebrows.

"He's playing Spank the Buffalo, Mama," Jolie explained.

"Oh? I suppose you're very good at it."

"Miss Jolie said it was a natural talent I have," Bullet reported.

"Since you're having such fun, I suppose you could spank one more," Jolie offered.

"Thanks, Miss Jolie. Tanner is right. You are a fine shinley, indeed." Bullet ran back to the clothesline.

"I believe that's a compliment," Lissa Bowers replied.

"I'm never quite sure. There doesn't seem to be any definition for 'a fine shinley,'" Jolie added.

"You wash while I rig up Stranger and Pilgrim," Lissa Bowers instructed.

Jolie stared out at the corrals. "And they thought they were going to get the day off. But at least they won't be chasing any trains today." She stopped and looked at her mother. "I suppose there could always be some surprises on the trip to town."

Lissa Bowers grinned. "That's exactly what I was thinking."

Traffic on Telegraph Road had returned to normal as they rattled to town in the big farm wagon. Essie sat in the middle between Jolie and Mrs. Bowers. "If Chester does somethin' else to little Max, I don't think I can control my anger," Essie declared.

"Emotions have a way of controlling us, don't they?" Lissa Bowers pointed out.

"Sometimes when I cry, I want to stop, and I can't no matter how hard I try. One time in class I was reading about a little boy who was lost on the prairie during the covered-wagon days, and I started crying. I was so embarrassed, but Jolie called on Mary Vockney to read, and I don't think anyone else noticed it."

Lissa Bowers hugged her youngest daughter. "Baby, our emotions aren't always wrong and sinful."

"But it's scary not being able to control yourself, isn't it?" Jolie said.

"Yes. It's like running downhill and not being able to stop," Essie replied.

"When I think of little Landen losing his mother and being with her all alone when she died," Jolie sighed, "I can hardly keep from crying."

Lissa Bowers reached across and patted her daughter's knee. "You still thinking about him?"

"About little Landen?" Jolie asked.

"Yes. Who did you think I meant?"

"I suppose I think about him a little. Tragedies like that happen all the time—only they seem distant. Landen was up close."

"Mama, are we goin' to buy new mattresses?" Essie asked.

"No, baby, we don't have the ones that were ruined paid for. But we'll get some more leather straps and go back to using the buffalo robes. I'm quite proud of Bullet Wells."

"Mama, I wonder if we could buy Bullet a few sticks of candy and drop it by his house on the way home?" Jolie queried.

"To thank him?"

"We could call it the prize for being the best at Spank the Buffalo," Essie suggested.

Lissa Bowers nodded. "I think we could afford that."

At the edge of town, Lissa yanked back on the reins and slowed the horses down to a mild trot.

"Scottsbluff looks crowded," Essie observed.

"Can we go by and see how Trip Cleveland and Case Ragsdale are doing?" Essie asked.

"The railroad men?" Lissa Bowers said. "Yes, I think that would be nice."

"What if he asks about buying me a new dress?"

"What do you want to do?"

"I'd like to have a new dress. What would you do, Jolie?"

"I'd wait until Daddy comes home and have him talk to Mr. Cleveland first."

"Big sis may be right," Lissa added. "That keeps girls from having things bought for them that shouldn't be bought."

Lissa Bowers jerked the horses to a stop in front of Snyder's Livery. "Andrew, water the boys and park them in the shade if you can. Leave them hitched."

"Yes, ma'am," the fifteen-year-old replied. "Howdy, Miss Jolie."

"Hi, Andrew. Are you growing a beard?"

"Me? Oh . . . no, Miss Jolie. I was shovelin' this mornin' and kind of got my face smudged, I reckon."

"Oh, good. You look quite handsome clean-shaven, and I was hoping you'd keep it that way."

"Yes, Miss Jolie, I was thinkin' the same thing," the boy replied.

All three females climbed down off the wagon.

"Hello, Andrew," Essie drawled.

"Eh . . . hi, Miss . . . little Miss Bowers."

"Essie. My name is Essie."

"I knew that."

"You forgot."

"No, I didn't. I reckon I just misplaced it for a minute, that's all. I didn't forget."

The three Bowers ladies strolled down the uncovered boardwalk along Main Street. Men lounged on the steps and benches. Most watched their every step.

"They surely are lookin' Jolie over," Essie whispered.

Jolie shook her head. "They're looking at all of us."

"No, I think little sis is right," Lissa Bowers murmured.

"Nonsense," Jolie insisted.

"Little sis, let's you and me stop at this next store and have Jolie Lorita walk on ahead of us. We can prove who they're watching."

Jolie adjusted her straw hat and continued to stroll west. Three cowboys on the corner turned to follow her.

Oh, my . . . Lord, when men watch me, I always feel like I've done something wrong. My dress is at ground length. My collar is buttoned high on my neck. My hat is on straight. I will not be intimidated.

Jolie spun around and marched back. The cowboys glanced away.

A man in a suit and tie stepped out of the store and stood next to Mrs. Bowers as Jolie returned.

"Ephraim Mendez," Lissa Bowers greeted him, "how nice to see you." She held out her hand.

Mendez gawked at a gray mule tied to the rail in front of the Colorado Furniture Emporium as he shook her hand. "Lissa Bowers, it has been several weeks since I've seen you in town." He nodded at the mule. "Nice to see Miss Jolie and Miss Esther."

"Essie."

Jolie studied the middle-aged man with a small mustache. *Lord,*

I never know where Mr. Mendez is looking. His vision is quite alarming. I suppose it must have been difficult for him all these years.

Lissa brushed her bangs off her eyes and flipped her waist-length braid behind her back. "We've been very busy trying to catch up with the crops. How is your family?"

"Much better now that the additions to the house are complete and we have that new cedar roof. Did you ever get those shingles on your place?"

Lissa glanced up at the cloudy sky. "I hope they'll finish putting them on this afternoon."

"And how are the new mattresses? I told you they are superior to all others."

Lissa took a deep breath and glanced over at Jolie.

"They got ruined when our sod roof caved in on them. We had to throw them out with the mud and sticks," Essie blurted out.

Mendez's face turned white. "Ruined? But—but—but . . ."

"Now, Ephraim," Lissa soothed, "I'm sure you realize that we always pay our debts and that you will indeed receive your money."

It was as if he were talking to the mule. "But—but—ruined? Completely ruined?"

"Mr. Mendez, I'm teaching school now, and so I could start paying you two dollars a month," Jolie offered. She opened her handbag.

"They're ruined?" he repeated.

Jolie placed the coins in his hand. "Would you please put this on our account?"

"But—but . . ." He stood straight up. "Yes, of course. What happens to the furniture is certainly your business."

"Thank you, Ephraim," Lissa said. "Tell Gerta hello for me. We had such a pleasant visit the day I delivered those shingles."

"Yes, of course. Thank you." He shuffled back into the store.

"I think Mr. Mendez is taking this rather personal," Lissa Bowers said.

Jolie nodded. "For him, it's like losing a family member."

"Darlin', you didn't have to pay him with your money."

"Mama, we've been through that. The only reason I took the teaching job was to help out with expenses until the homestead begins to pay. You and Daddy promised I could help."

They strolled west past a dress shop and a bakery where a short man slept on a bench.

"Jolie, that man was using a loaf of bread for a pillow," Essie whispered. "Why's he doin' that?"

"I suppose he's not hungry yet."

The sound of boot heels slamming into the boardwalk caused all three to spin around.

"Sheriff," Jolie called out, "how are you?"

He tipped his hat. "Things are going crazy, Miss Jolie." He turned to Lissa. "Mrs. Bowers, is your husband at home?"

"He's in Lincoln. He should be home tomorrow," she reported.

"I need to talk to him as soon as he gets here."

"What's wrong?" Jolie asked.

"The town's goin' crazy—that's what. I've had half a dozen fistfights in the past three days. Can't be long until they reach for knives and guns."

"Oh, dear. What is it about?" Lissa Bowers asked.

"They claim it's over the railroad fee hikes, but most of them fightin' don't even live around here. I'm scared different ones are joinin' in for their own reasons."

Lissa Bowers studied several men who loitered across the street in front of the drugstore. "What can my husband do about it?" she quizzed.

"He's a reasonable man, Mrs. Bowers. Perhaps there's a solution to this that no one has considered. I ain't takin' sides. I just don't want anyone gettin' shot dead over it."

"I'll have him contact you before he leaves town tomorrow," Lissa said.

"Thank you, ma'am." He tipped his hat. "And tell that young deputy I'm needin' him more and more."

"Gibs will be delighted to hear that."

They waited for a stagecoach from Chadron to pass and then crossed the street.

"Jolie, do you have anywhere you want to go before we buy groceries? I need to make a quick trip over to Fleister's Hardware."

"I suppose we could check out the Platte River Armory," Jolie purred.

"Yes," Lissa grinned. "I thought you might want to do that."

The Armory was marked by a ten-foot wooden Winchester rifle pointing out at the street. Jolie and Essie ambled west toward the sign.

"Jolie, I like coming to town with you."

"I certainly like having you along." She reached over and laced her fingers into Essie's. "I always get in trouble when I'm by myself."

"You get into trouble when I'm along too. That's why I like coming with you. It's an adventure."

"Not today, sweet Essie. Just groceries and home. No adventure. No trouble."

"No boys fightin' over you?" Essie swung their hands back and forth.

"Absolutely no fights."

Essie dropped Jolie's hand, skipped ahead to the gun shop, and peeked through the window. "He's got a customer."

"That's good. A business should have customers."

"A blonde lady," Essie reported.

Jolie straightened her straw hat. "Yes, well, she's probably picking something up for her husband."

"It's Bailey," Essie squealed.

Jolie flinched as her hand flew to her chest. *Why did I do that, Lord? Bailey is a friend of Tanner's. She's a friend of mine. I don't know why I feel possessive and jealous. Tanner is a good man. I surely don't have to worry about him.*

Essie waited by the door as Jolie pulled it open. When Jolie walked in, Tanner had just reached over and given Bailey Wagner a hug.

"Ehhh hmmm." Jolie cleared her throat.

"Hi, darlin'," Tanner called out. "I was just congratulatin' Bailey."

"Hi, Jolie. Hi, Essie," Bailey greeted them.

"How come you were huggin' on Jolie's sweetie?" Essie blurted out.

"I got really good news." Bailey's eyes danced.

Jolie studied the bright blue eyes of the blonde girl. *Good news? Are you moving? Lord, forgive me. Relax, Jolie Lorita. You are so unsure of yourself it's pathetic. And no one has a clue.* "What's the news?" Jolie waltzed over and took Tanner's callused hand in her own.

"The judge decided that Jeremiah and me don't have to go to trial since Mr. Saddler got all his money back at the store."

"That *is* good news." Jolie hugged Bailey. *Sweet Bailey, we may be friends now, but that is NOT the same hug you gave Tanner.*

"It gets better," Bailey said.

Jolie's hat raised with her eyebrows. "It does?"

"Yes. Jeremiah and me have been run out of town."

Essie tugged at her earlobe. "What?"

"Sheriff Riley said it would be best if we leave town. Folks have heard we stole some money from Mr. Saddler and that I shot Jeremiah, and they might not give us a fair shake. He advised that we leave town."

"He did? That sounds horrible," Jolie replied. "I'll go talk to him about it right now. He has no justifiable cause to do that." *What am I saying? Lord, forgive me for being so hypocritical.*

"I knew you'd say that. Didn't I tell you, Tanner, that Jolie would pitch a fit?"

"Yes, you did."

Bailey threw her arm around Jolie and hugged her again. This time it was very enthusiastic. "Jolie, you're the best friend I ever had."

Jolie bit her lip and tried to hold back her tears. *Lord, I'm a lousy friend. So jealous and possessive. Relax, Jolie Lorita. You're tighter strung than Grandma Pritchett's corset. I worry too much . . . way too much.*

Bailey stood back. Several strands of her long blonde hair draped down over her eye. "Jeremiah and me are movin' to Deadwood. Jeremiah is already there."

"I didn't know he felt like traveling," Jolie said.

"There's a train into Deadwood now. And the important thing is, I have a job," Bailey announced.

"That's wonderful. Are you working in a cafe?"

"No, I got a job with the telephone exchange."

"They have telephones in Deadwood?" Essie asked.

"Sam Fortune hired me personally," Bailey replied.

"The gunslinger from down in the Indian Nation?" Essie gasped. "My Leppy told me all about him."

"He's not a gunslinger anymore. He's very nice. He even helped us find a house to rent. It's owned by one of his brothers. There are a lot of Fortunes in Deadwood."

"That's a curious statement." Jolie grinned. "But I know what you mean."

"Are you and Jeremiah goin' to live in sin?" Essie blurted out, then grabbed her head and closed her eyes. "Sorry."

Bailey laughed. "I love it, Essie. That's the kind of thing a good friend should say."

Essie peeked out between her fingers. "Really?"

"Sure. And you'll be happy to know that Jeremiah and me will be gettin' married in two weeks."

"That's wonderful," Jolie said. *Thank You, Lord. It was a very selfish prayer, I know . . . but You answered it anyway.*

"We're goin' to get married in Deadwood, and you're all invited, of course. I didn't want Jeremiah to have to come to Scottsbluff and then travel back again. He's staying in our little house. I'll be in a room above Mr. Fortune's wife's dress shop until we get married."

"Does Sam Fortune know about your trouble down here?" Essie asked.

"Yes, he does. Said he kind of likes givin' folks a second chance, since he had a few of 'em himself."

"That really is wonderful news," Jolie said.

"Yes, it is. Now will you forgive me for huggin' your Tanner?"

"Oh, well, certainly," Jolie stammered. "That didn't bother—"

"Of course it did. I read it in your eyes."

Jolie began to laugh. "I don't hide anything well, do I?"

"Never play poker, Jolie Bowers. You would lose every hand. Now if you all will excuse me, I have a few more things I need to do. The wedding is October 24 at 2:00 P.M. at the church right there at the head of Sherman Avenue."

"Bailey, I really am happy for you," Jolie said.

"I know." Bailey winked. "All the purdy ones will be married off soon except for our Essie."

"I'm goin' to marry Leppy Verdue," Essie stated.

"If you like the driftin' cowboy type, the town's full of them right now," Bailey said.

"This is crazy, isn't it? I don't understand why they're all coming here. I'm sure Daddy and the others can work out something with Mr. Culburtt and the railroad." Jolie's voice turned serious. "So I don't know why they're hanging around like buzzards waiting for the cow to die."

"I can say one thing." Tanner spoke up. "It's been good business for me."

"That's a horrible thing to say," Jolie gasped.

Tanner scratched his head. "It is?"

"If you make money selling bullets and guns to men who are going to shoot each other, it doesn't seem good at all."

"Jolie, I'm in the gun business, and business is good this week. That's all I'm sayin'."

"All this talk about a railroad war scares me," Jolie admitted. "Daddy will be standing with the homesteaders. What if one of these gunmen like—like—"

"Galen Faxon?" Essie offered.

"Yes. What if one of these gunmen like Galen Faxon shoots Daddy with a bullet bought at your store?"

"Darlin', your daddy isn't goin' to get involved in a gunfight."

"Who did you say?" Bailey blurted out. Her forehead wrinkled. Her lips were taut.

"We met a man named Galen Faxon. He and some others were headed to Scottsbluff. I suppose they're here already," Jolie explained.

Bailey spun around to the glass gun case. "Tanner, I want to buy that Whitneyville pocket pistol and half a dozen bullets."

"What're you talking about?" he sputtered.

"I'm talkin' about Galen Faxon," she snarled.

five

Jolie watched Bailey Wagner stomp out of the Platte Valley Armory. "Tanner, I don't think you should have sold her that gun."

He shoved a small green cardboard box of bullets back onto the shelf behind the counter. "She would have bought one someplace else."

Jolie paced the wooden floor, her heels marking time with her heartbeat. "That's not the point. You should never sell a gun to an agitated woman."

Tanner folded his arms across his chest. "How about an agitated man?"

Jolie stopped in front of him. "You shouldn't sell him one either."

Tanner shoved his hands in his pockets and walked away from her. "And just how do I tell if a woman is agitated?"

Jolie followed right behind him. "Bailey was angry. She said so."

Essie spun a .44-caliber bullet around on top of the glass gun case. "She might pull the trigger. She shot Jeremiah in the back."

When Tanner whirled, Jolie almost stumbled into him. "Should I sell a fearful woman a gun?"

"What do you mean?" she mumbled.

He rubbed his square chin. "Suppose a woman is livin' out in Carter Canyon in a little shack, and she's scared of sounds in the night. So she comes in here all scared to death and wants to buy a gun. Should I sell her one?"

"Of course, but I don't see—"

"Jolie, how do I tell the difference between an angry woman and a scared woman when she walks through my door?"

Jolie felt her teeth grind. "That's a different question, Tanner Wells, and you know it. Bailey Wagner was angry. That was obvious."

Tanner stood by the front window and stared out at the street. "And angry people do not have the right to have a gun? What if they are justifiably angry? Should I give them a test first?"

Jolie tried to keep her voice from rising. "Tanner, you know what I'm talking about." It came out someplace between a whine and a shout.

"Are you two goin' to fight? 'Cause if you are, I'm goin' to go shop with Mama," Essie declared.

"We aren't fighting," Jolie snapped.

"I'll meet you at the grocery store." Essie marched to the front door.

Jolie followed her sister. "I'll go with you."

"We aren't through talkin'," Tanner insisted. "This is important to me."

Jolie straightened the lace cuffs on her beige dress. "I can't see what it will accomplish to stay here and argue. Maybe I can go talk some sense into Bailey."

Tanner stepped up behind her and put his hand on her shoulder. "It will take care of itself, darlin'," he insisted. "Bailey will come to her senses."

"I'm leavin'." Essie pushed her way out the door.

Jolie spun around. Tanner's hand dropped to his side. "What do you mean, it will take care of itself?" Her voice grew louder with each word. "Good-bye."

His reply was soft. "Jolie, we need to talk."

She shoved open the door. "I need to get some fresh air. There's too much I don't understand."

"About you and me?" he asked.

"About you." She stomped out to the boardwalk where Essie waited.

Jolie buried her face in her hands as she heard the door close behind her. *I'm out of control, Lord. I have to think. What's going on here?*

"I don't think that was the scene you were dreamin' of this mornin'," Essie said.

"I don't understand, Essie. Bailey needs help with her anger, and Tanner puts a gun in her hand. Why would he do that?"

Essie shuffled along the boardwalk. She rolled her lower lip down with her finger until it touched her chin. "Remember that lady in Helena who bashed in her husband's skull with an iron skillet? Maybe they ought to be careful who they sell skillets to."

"The fatality rate with iron skillets is quite puny compared to guns," Jolie huffed. "There's no comparison."

"I guess." Essie placed one foot in front of the other on the boardwalk as if she were walking a tightrope. "But I don't know why you didn't want to stay in there and talk it out with your sweetie."

"I noticed you didn't want to stick around."

"He isn't my sweetie."

Jolie retied her hat string. "I need to find Bailey."

Essie peered one way and then the other down the dirt street. "Where do you think she is?"

"Looking for Galen Faxon."

"And where would Mr. Faxon be?" Essie asked.

"At a saloon, I would guess."

"Are *we* going to saloons?" Essie gasped.

"Just take a quick peek in front of them." Jolie stomped along the boardwalk. "I can't believe he sold her that gun."

Essie jogged to catch up. "Are you going to sit in the shop after you're married and tell him who to sell to and not sell to?"

"Of course not." Jolie spun around and glared. "I'll be at home with the children. At least I won't have to know."

Essie waited for a noisy stagecoach to rattle by. "So it would have been okay for Tanner to sell the gun to Bailey as long as you didn't know about it?"

"No, it was wrong, it was stubborn . . . prideful . . . greedy for profit. He knew I didn't want her to have a gun," Jolie fumed.

They walked two blocks in silence. Every open doorway spilled out conversation and laugher that failed to drown out the drumbeat of Jolie's heels. Essie spoke first. "There's a saloon over there, the Imperial House. Mary Vockney says it's the biggest and busiest one in town."

"How does Mary know that?"

"She knows all that kind of stuff."

"Are any of those men out front the ones who were with Galen Faxon?"

Essie tugged at the big yellow bow that kept her waist-length hair draped down her back. "I forget what they looked like."

"So do I. But I remember Faxon. They don't look familiar to me. Have you noticed how many men in town look the same?"

"The dirt, the guns, and the hats look alike. After that, they're all different. There's one way to find out if they were with Faxon," Essie declared.

Jolie paused at the edge of the boardwalk. "Oh?"

Essie grabbed her sister's arm and stepped out into the street. "We can troll you along as bait."

"What?"

"If you go struttin' by, and one of them has seen you before, he'll call you 'Miss Jolie.'"

They paused in the street as a four-bench surrey went by with only one passenger.

"I doubt it very much."

Essie tugged her on across the street. "Let's try it."

"I've never seen any of those men."

"Then there's nothin' to worry about." Essie took her arm. "Come on, bait."

"Estelle Cinnia!"

"Come on, just strut along."

"I do not strut."

"You strut when you're around Tanner."

"He's not here."

"Well, then, stroll or sashay or amble or meander, but do something," Essie hissed.

"This is absurd."

Essie pushed her ahead. "Go on."

"You're coming with me."

"Sure. It doesn't matter. No one ever recognizes me."

"I'm not goin' to look at them," Jolie whispered.

"You won't need to. Keep walkin'."

They passed several men sitting on the bench in front of the Imperial House. A man cleared his voice. "Afternoon, Miss Jolie."

As she turned, all three men pulled off their hats and grinned.

"See." Essie beamed.

"Did you come to town to spend the money your mama earned racin' that horse?" a tall, thin man asked. "It was my horse she won on."

Jolie brushed her auburn bangs off her forehead. "Good to see you men again. I'm sure we'll spend the money. We came to town for supplies. Say, I need to talk to Mr. Faxon. Is he around?"

The big man wearing a brown leather vest and smelling like spice tonic pointed his hat to the open doorway. "He's inside the Imperial, Miss Jolie. Last table at the back near the rear door."

Jolie peeked through the open doorway but hesitated.

"Do you want me to tell him you're out here?" the thin man asked.

Jolie laced her fingers in front of her waist. "If you don't mind."

The man with black stove-top boots outside his duckings drifted through the open twelve-foot-tall double doors of the Imperial House Saloon.

Jolie and Essie stepped out to the edge of the boardwalk. "I feel funny standin' here," Essie said.

"It's a public sidewalk. Why shouldn't we be here?"

"Yes, but it looks like we're hangin' around a saloon door waiting for a man."

"We aren't," Jolie insisted.

"What do you call it then?"

"In one way, we're waiting for a man. But it's to warn him of impending danger. That's quite different indeed."

Essie pointed across the street where several women in bonnets huddled in conversation, each with a child in tow. "If a person was walkin' on the other side of the street over there at the dress shop . . . say, where that carriage is parked, could they tell the difference between some girls hanging around outside a saloon waiting for a man and some girls waiting to warn someone of impending danger?"

"Of course not." Jolie stared into her sister's eyes. "What kind of question is that?"

"It's a make-believe question."

"You aren't talking about me and Tanner again, are you?"

"I don't think you gave him a say in the matter. Maybe he had an explanation," Essie murmured. "Everybody has an explanation for what they do even if they're wrong. Ever'one except maybe Chester."

"What was there to say? He sold a pocket pistol to a girl who is liable to use it to murder a man."

"I don't think she'll use it that way," Essie countered.

Jolie studied the women across the street who seemed to be looking at her and Essie. "How can you say that?"

"Bailey stayed with us for almost a month." Essie shaded her eyes and peered down the street at a barking black-and-white dog. "Sometimes when you and Tanner went someplace, me and her would talk and talk and talk. She thinks Mama and Daddy are the most wonderful people on earth. I don't think she would do anything she knew they would disapprove of."

The tall cowboy ambled out the door. His thick, drooping mustache made a permanent scowl. "Galen said he can't leave the poker hand right now, Miss Jolie. It's the best hand he's had all day. Are you sure you won't go in and see him?"

Jolie's chin stiffened. "I'm a schoolteacher, and I'm not entering a saloon."

"You're a schoolmarm?" the big man in a brown vest said. "My mama was a schoolteacher in Indiana. I don't reckon there has ever been a finer woman—rest her soul." Then he jammed his hands in his pockets. "Miss Jolie, Galen said unless it's a life-or-death matter, you would just have to wait."

The big man in the vest stood up. "You and little sis can sit over here and wait if you want, Miss Jolie."

"She needs to warn Mr. Faxon of impending danger," Essie confided.

Jolie nodded. "It could be that Mr. Faxon's life is at stake."

The man glanced at the others on the bench and then back inside the Imperial. "Okay, I'll tell him, but he'll not be happy."

"Better unhappy than dead," Essie replied.

The tall man disappeared into the shadows of the smoky room. Layers of boisterous conversation tumbled out the door behind him.

Essie ambled out to the street edge of the boardwalk. "I still say Bailey wouldn't shoot Mr. Faxon," she whispered.

Jolie stood close to her. "She said she would."

"But what a person says and what a person does is different. Chester is always saying he's goin' to run away and join the circus, and he never does," Essie sighed.

"Does he want to be a clown?"

"He wants to be an elephant trainer."

Jolie covered her chuckle with her hand. "Oh, my, that does sound dangerous."

"Chester won't get hurt because he only talks about it but never does it."

"He's only twelve."

"Yes, well, he's not gettin' any younger," Essie declared.

Jolie laughed out loud. Then she glanced back at the men on the bench. "So you and Bailey talked a lot when I wasn't there?"

"The weekend you went to Sydney to that teachers' rally, me and Bailey laid in bed and talked until almost midnight."

"She never talked that much to me."

"I think she's shy with you. You scare her."

"What do you mean? Bailey and I are good friends."

"Yeah, but you don't ever get in any real trouble, Jolie. And you always look beautiful. And you're a schoolteacher at seventeen."

"I'm almost eighteen."

"Bailey said she's never been around anyone like you. Anyway, little sisters aren't scary. She never had a little sister to talk to. So she talked to me."

"Does Bailey have any sisters or brothers?"

"She had a brother that was older," Essie said, "but he was left out on the prairie, and the Comanches killed him."

Jolie felt her heart jump. "Left out on the prairie? That's horrible. Who would do that?"

"Some bad man from Texas. She was cryin' too much to tell me how it happened. I was cryin' too, and I didn't even know why."

Jolie put her arm around her sister's shoulder as they walked back to the saloon door. "That is a sad story."

The tall cowboy scooted back outside, his hat in his hand. "Sorry, Miss Jolie, Faxon ain't comin' out. It's that good a hand."

Jolie could feel her neck muscles tighten. "But I'm tryin' to save his life."

The cowboy glanced down at his boots. "I'm sure he'll appreciate it later on."

Jolie turned to Essie. "Wait here."

"Are you goin' in there alone?"

"Yes, you shouldn't have to see a place like this."

"The Imperial House is a nice saloon, Miss Jolie. It ain't like the Gemstone or one of them," the cowboy reassured her.

Essie grabbed onto her arm. "Jolie, if you go in by yourself, it's like a girl goin' into a saloon for who knows what. But if you go in with your little sister, well, obviously you ain't lookin' for you know what."

The tall cowboy shrugged. "Little sis is right, Miss Jolie. They'll think you are coming in to find your daddy and take him home. I seen that a time or two."

"Our father doesn't drink," Jolie snapped.

"You know what I mean," he mumbled.

"Okay, come on, Estelle."

"I'm really called Essie," she told the cowboy. "She only calls me Estelle when she's angry."

"I am not angry," Jolie insisted as she tromped into the saloon, towing Essie.

Laughter and loud voices rolled out from the smoky corners. Jolie coughed and wiped the corners of her eyes.

"I don't think anyone even saw us come in," Essie said. "Everyone is talking loud and smoking so much."

Jolie pulled her handkerchief from her sleeve and wiped her neck. "So much for shocking the clientele."

"Where's Mr. Faxon?"

"Somewhere at the back. I can't tell in all this smoke." Like a schoolteacher in a noisy classroom, Jolie stomped the heels of her lace-up boots until the crowd quieted. "Gentlemen, I need to speak to Mr. Galen Faxon immediately."

Out of the hushed silence a man at the bar called out in a high-pitched voice, "Yes, ma'am. He's right by the backdoor."

"Mr. Faxon, this is urgent and private," she called out.

Grumbles and curses echoed from the back of the room.

"What did he say?" Essie whispered.

"You don't want to know."

"Not even when I'm sixteen?" Essie asked.

"Not even when you're sixty."

Galen Faxon stomped toward Jolie and Essie as if leading troops into battle. "Young lady, do you know—"

"Her name is Jolie Bowers. I'm her sister."

"The grass widow's kids? I remember you." He pushed his black hat back. Thick eyebrows tinted with gray accented his dark eyes. "Is your mama in trouble?"

"My mother is not a grass widow. Daddy is in Lincoln with the Young Farmers' Alliance," Jolie reported.

Faxon raised his eyebrows. "I thought you all said . . ."

Jolie pulled off her straw hat and fanned herself. "You assumed some things."

Faxon rubbed the bridge of his nose. "Yep, and I shouldn't do that. I know better. I guess that long auburn braid and ridin' skill of your mama blurred my judgment. But it didn't blur my poker. This better be important. I just tossed in five spades on the biggest pot of the day."

"We have no idea what that means, Mr. Faxon, but I can assure you this is important," Jolie replied.

"You had a flush?" Essie gasped.

"In spades."

"Five-card draw?"

"Yep."

"What was your high card?"

"The ace."

Essie rolled her eyes. "I can't believe you tossed in."

"Neither can I," Faxon moaned.

"Estelle Cinnia, where did you learn such things?"

"Eh . . . remember all those times in Helena when I went over to Rebekah Browne's house to play with her dolls?"

"You played poker instead of playing with the dolls?" Jolie asked.

"We set the dolls up and played poker with them," Essie grinned.

Faxon pulled a gold watch from his pocket and glanced at it. "Miss Bowers, tell me, what is this life-and-death news?"

Jolie lowered her voice and stepped closer. "Do you know a girl, a young woman—she's a little older than I am—by the name of Bailey Wagner?"

"Nope, never heard of her."

"She has pretty blonde hair," Essie added.

"Look, I don't know anyone named Bailey Wagner. I never met any gal named Bailey. So I hope you have more to tell me than this," he bristled.

"She knows you. She was in the Platte River Armory a few minutes ago and bought a pistol, claiming she was going to kill you." Jolie felt her heart race with frustration.

Faxon's eyes narrowed, and his hand rested on his gun handle. "That's it?"

"It's not a laughing matter."

"Miss Bowers, if I had a cow for ever' time someone threatened to kill me, I'd own Montana by now. Thank you for the warnin'. I'll watch out for blondes."

"Why does she want to kill you, Mr. Faxon?" Essie asked.

"Probably because I interrupted her poker game one time when she had a spade flush. That'll drive a person to contemplate murder."

A roar and a groan rumbled out of the cigar smoke at the back of the room.

"Hey, Faxon, you lucky skunk," someone shouted. "The pot went up two hundred more, and Doc Stillwell was holdin' a full house. You got out at the right time."

"Wow, you would have had to stay in with that ace-high flush. We just saved you two hundred dollars!" Essie grinned.

Faxon shook his head. The leathery creases around his eyes relaxed. "That you did, girls. But stay out of saloons and gamblin' halls."

Jolie turned toward the front door. "Are you sure you don't know any Wagners?"

Faxon's hand slipped down to his revolver. "Sly . . . Sly Wagner."

"Who is that?" Jolie asked.

"Is she related to Sly?" he queried.

"Her brother's name was Rood Wagner," Essie supplied.

"That's him," Faxon said. "He went by the name Sly."

"He was abandoned on foot in the desert and killed by Comanches."

Faxon let out a long, deep sigh. "Is that what she said?"

"Sort of," Essie replied. "She said she heard it from the Naylord brothers."

Faxon lowered his voice. "Girls, I'll tell you what really happened, but it won't matter to his sis. She's goin' to believe whatever she wants. When it comes to death in the family, I learned a long time ago, family always see it different."

Jolie scooted to the side as several men swaggered into the Imperial.

Faxon followed them to the corner by an empty faro table. "It was at least ten years ago. No, eleven. The last big herd I brought north . . . Anyway, I was pushin' contract beef from Texas to the Wind River Reservation in Wyomin'. Sly Wagner was one of the fourteen cowhands I hired. He was night herdin' when the Naylord brothers came along and rustled thirty-two head of my beef. Sly said it was dark, and they jumped him before he could do anything. We chased 'em down, and the Naylords escaped."

"Did you recover all thirty-two?" Essie asked.

"Thirty-one of 'em. We lost old Five Spot."

"Your cows have names?" Essie asked.

"Some do. Anyway, we were out on the plains above the Cimarron. It was open country and a moonlit night. There ain't no way someone could jump you unless you were asleep in the saddle or you were in cahoots with the rustlers. One of the boys said Sly had been pals of the Naylords over in Bolivar, Missouri. I fired him right there on the spot."

"Guilt by association?" Jolie asked.

"Miss Bowers, when the boys hire on, I tell them I'm hirin' them to stand and fight if anyone tries to take a cow. That means rustlers or Indians or anyone. I used to tell 'em, if they didn't want to draw their gun and defend my herd, not to sign on."

"So you fired him out on the plains?" Jolie pressed.

"Yes, I did. I couldn't count on him anymore; nor could the other drovers. That don't work movin' cattle. You got to know who to trust. He had his own saddle and guns. I gave him the pay that was comin' to him, minus ten dollars for my horse. I wouldn't ever put a man on the ground. Not in those days anyway."

"And he rode off?" Essie asked.

Faxon drummed his fingers on the green felt that covered the table. "Yep. We were goin' north. I told him Valverde was about thirty-five miles east of the herd, and the Naylord brothers had high-tailed it west toward New Mexico. I didn't care which way he headed as long as it wasn't north. But I told him not to go back toward Texas because I had spotted some Comanche sign. They won't attack a dozen guns, but they surely would one lone rider. I gave him some biscuits, jerky, and sent him off."

"That seems fair enough," Jolie said.

"When we finally got to Wyomin', I heard that Sly was killed by Comanches when he rode south. He had run his horse down and was hoofin' it, draggin' his saddle when they caught him. Now I'm sorry he died, but if I had it to do over again, I'd do the same thing. The cattle-drive business was rough, and you made it by the guts and deter-mination of your crew. Don't let them kid you—there was nothin' glamorous about those old cattle drives except the excitement you felt when you delivered the herd and actually lived through it all."

"Bailey thinks you abandoned him in the desert."

"She believes the Naylord brothers, and they aren't around to clear it up."

"What happened to them?" Essie asked.

"They were hung in Ft. Smith for rustlin' cattle down in Oklahoma. But like I said, it doesn't matter much to family. Sly is dead. And his sister wants revenge. It's an old pattern. Now, gals, thanks for the warnin', but I'm goin' to get back to my game. I can't stand to save much more money."

"Mr. Faxon, thanks for the explanation. Bailey is a friend of ours, and she was just getting things settled down in her life."

"She accepted Jesus as her Lord and Savior. I heard her pray with Daddy," Essie blabbed.

"But she still wants to kill me?"

"She doesn't read real good. Maybe she hasn't come to that part of the Bible yet," Essie said.

"Mr. Faxon, may we tell her your side of the story?" Jolie ventured.

"Help yourself. But I told you, it won't make any difference."

"It made a difference to me," Jolie stated.

He paused for a minute and tipped his hat. "Thanks for believin' me, Miss Jolie. A man's reputation is based on the quality of people who believe his word. And your sayin' that just enhanced mine greatly."

"That's a nice thing to say, Mr. Faxon."

He started to the back of the room, then turned around. "By the way, thanks for saving me two hundred dollars."

Essie led them out to the sunlight of the boardwalk. As they exited, Jolie heard a young voice ring out, "It's them, Strath. I was right. They were in the saloon!"

Jolie set her hat back on her head and tied the ribbon under her chin. She squinted into the diffused sunlight of the cloudy day. "Landen?"

"I told Strath I saw you and her go into a saloon, Miss Jolie, but he said I was mistaken."

"I'm Essie."

"How come you were in a saloon?"

Strath Yarrow strolled up. His felt hat was tipped to the side, his shirt collar unbuttoned, his black tie one-tug loose. "Landen, that's the ladies' business, not ours."

"We went in there to see a notorious gunman and warn him that a lady was trying to kill him," Essie chattered.

Strath Yarrow's eyes lighted on Jolie. "I love it. Sounds like your sis has as good an imagination as Landen."

"It was basically the truth," Jolie explained.

Yarrow peered into the smoky room. "There's a famous gunman in there? Is it Earp? Masterson? Brannon?"

"Faxon," Essie replied.

Strath Yarrow's back stiffened. "Galen Faxon?"

"So you've heard of him?"

Yarrow led Landen and the women away from the door. "I've read the news accounts. What's a Texas gunman doing in a Nebraska farm town?"

"Everyone seems to think there'll be trouble with the railroads and the farmers and cattlemen," Jolie explained.

He rubbed the stubble of a one-day beard. "I thought that when we bought in the Nebraska panhandle, we would be a long way from all of that."

"There isn't any trouble yet. Perhaps it will resolve itself," Jolie tried to assure him and herself.

Essie licked her hand and brushed down a cowlick in Landen's blond hair.

He pulled away. "How come you rubbed your spit on my head?"

"Your hair was sticking up. I just mashed it down."

"I think he slept on it wrong," Strath said.

"We got to sleep on the benches in the train station last night," Landen announced.

"Oh, dear," Jolie replied.

"It's my fault. We rented a buggy and drove out west of town to find our place. Got all the way out to Ft. Mitchell and realized that the map was drawn wrong. I guess it was flipped over. Someone pointed out that Scott's Bluff was across the river and southwest of Gering. By the time we got back to town, there wasn't a hotel or boardinghouse room to be found."

"I think all of these cowboys are fillin' up the town," Essie remarked.

"We'll find our place today. And we'll have a sod house to sleep in, even if no furniture. Would you recommend a furniture store?"

"The Colorado Furniture Emporium," Jolie said. "Ask for Mr. Ephraim Mendez."

"I figured you'd know. When I spotted you across the street, I wanted to talk to you," Strath announced.

"She's already got a beau," Landen reminded him.

"What I wanted to say was . . ."

Landen tugged at his father's coattail. "Strath said you were—"

"Landen Yarrow, don't go embarrassing me," Strath Yarrow interrupted.

"He thinks you—"

"Landen, don't tell Jolie that. Please."

The blond boy stepped over to Essie and said with a loud voice, "He thinks your sister is the purdiest girl he's seen since my mama. My mama was purdier, of course."

"Landen!" Strath Yarrow's eyes squeezed shut.

"I didn't tell Miss Jolie. I told Bessie."

"Essie."

"Yeah, her."

"Miss Jolie, I'm sorry. I shouldn't have ever told him that." Yarrow pleaded with his eyes.

Jolie brushed away a soft tear. "That's quite all right. That was a very wonderful compliment."

Strath tugged his tie a little looser. "That's not the reason we wanted to see you. I asked around about how to get to our place, and a couple of men at the grocery said they spotted you and your mother in town."

"That's Luke and Raymond. They're always at the store," Essie said as they all walked west on the boardwalk.

"Maybe you can read our map and tell us how to get to our place." Strath handed the paper to Jolie. "If it helps you to locate it, it used to be called the 'Avery place.'"

"Another one!" Essie groaned.

"Another what?" he asked.

Jolie took his arm. "Oh, dear Strath, we own the Avery place, but that rascal Mr. Avery seems to be making a career out of traveling around and selling the same homestead."

"You're kidding me! No, you aren't. You wouldn't. This can't . . . ," he stammered.

Jolie bit her lip and held onto his arm. A wide, dimpled grin broke across Strath Yarrow's face, and he started to laugh.

"I didn't think it was that funny," she said.

"Oh, Miss Jolie, don't you see? I'm an attorney, and I just got swindled into buying a piece of property that wasn't even his to sell. There's nothing I can do but laugh. Oh, Landen, we're either crying or we're laughing. There doesn't seem to be any in-between. It's famines or feasts for us."

"I appreciate your good nature. Usually they cry or get mad at us," Jolie said.

"How many others have there been?" he asked.

Jolie turned to Essie. "Six, I believe."

Essie shrugged. "The Riggers were the sixth."

"That's right. You're the seventh."

"Strath, what're we goin' to do?" Landen pressed.

"Miss Jolie, do you know of any other places for sale?"

"Some say every place is for sale if you have cash," Essie announced. "But ours isn't."

"Essie's probably right. If you had the cash money, there's one homestead just north of ours that's for sale. It's at the railroad tracks where I tried to flag down the train."

"Daddy says they want way too much for it," Essie remarked. "That's why no one has bought it."

"Is it a nice place?" Strath asked.

Jolie glanced up at Yarrow's soft blue eyes. "Mama says it's the best farmland around. It's entirely level, cleared, and right next to Telegraph Road."

He rubbed his chin. "How much do they want for it?"

"I'm almost ashamed to say," Jolie answered. "I heard they were asking ten dollars an acre."

Landen laced his fingers together and plopped them on top of his head. "How much is that, Strath?"

"Sixteen hundred dollars."

"Is that a lot?" the young boy asked.

Jolie watched Strath's eyes. *He didn't even flinch. I don't think that's a lot to Mr. Strath Yarrow.*

"Good property is never cheap," he replied. "What's the house like?"

Essie plucked a piece of straw from the back of Landen's shirt. "It doesn't have a house."

"No house? How could they prove up a homestead and not have a house?" he asked.

"Mama said they either had a house on wheels, or they bought the patent deed to start with. It may never have been homesteaded," Essie explained.

"It sounds promising. I'd like to look at it. Are you headed that way now? Landen and I can follow you out there in our buggy."

Jolie stepped to the street side of the boardwalk to allow two women to pass behind them. "We have to buy groceries first."

"Can I meet you somewhere? I would rather not get lost like yesterday," Strath said.

"How about down at Snyder's Livery in an hour or so?" Jolie glanced at his eyes again, then looked down. "It really is a nice place. I think it would make a wonderful homestead."

"I look forward to seeing it. I think it's wise this time to inspect the place before we buy it."

"You'll have to come out and stay the night with us," Jolie offered. *Lord, I trust I know what I'm doing. And I don't know why I feel guilty saying that.*

"We're putting a cedar roof on our house. We slept in the barn last night," Essie told him.

"Yes, but there's plenty of room in the barn."

"I wouldn't want to put you out," Strath Yarrow insisted.

"Jolie invites people to spend the night with us all the time," Essie said.

"She does? Don't your parents mind?"

"They mind her most of the time." Essie giggled. "Jolie Lorita runs the house. It's her chore."

"We just might take you up on the offer if we can't find a room here in town. A haystack would be better than a depot bench. I'll look around for a room, and then we'll meet you at the livery in an hour." Strath's shoulders were back and his posture perfect.

"I still can't believe how you took the news. Most were so devastated," Jolie said.

"It's a question of place, not money, Miss Jolie. This is where I want to be. This is where Landen wants to be. And I believe this is where the Lord wants us to be. So we'll just find our farm and settle in. How are the winters? I understand the temperatures drop low, but the snow doesn't pile up too high."

"We've just been here a few months," Essie said.

"That surprises me. Everyone in town I've talked to seems to know you like you were well established."

Jolie watched his expression. *He's been asking all over town about me?*

"Me?" Essie asked.

"Eh, Miss Jolie anyway," he added.

"Oh, everybody knows Jolie. But most can't remember my name."

"Is that right, Evangelina?" He winked.

"It's not . . ." Essie held her breath. "You're funnin' me, aren't you?"

"Yep, Estelle Cinnia. May I call you Essie?"

"Yes! I can't believe you remembered my whole name."

"I never forget the name of a pretty lady."

Essie rolled her eyes. "Another one of those sweet-talkin' men, Jolie."

"So I noticed," Jolie laughed. "We Bowers girls have run across sweet-talking men before."

Strath grinned. "Jolie, I've known you for ten minutes, and I've smiled and laughed more than in the past two years combined."

"I hope that's okay. I don't mean to trivialize your pain and grief," Jolie said.

"It's wonderful. That's exactly why we sold the real estate in Illinois and moved here."

"We used to own Chicago," Landen announced.

"You owned Chicago?" Essie laughed.

Strath shook his head and grinned. "No. We only owned one city block of it."

"You aren't kidding, are you?" Jolie quizzed.

"Nope. But we sold it and moved here. We are Nebraskans now," Strath announced.

"If we buy the place by the railroad tracks, will we be neighbors?" Landen asked.

"Yes, won't that be fun?" Jolie replied.

"Are there any other neighbors?"

Jolie studied the young boy's face. "To the east is the lane back to our place and some open land sloping down to the river. It looks too rough to farm." *His eyes are just like his daddy's.* "To the north is the railroad. We are to the south, and the Wells family lives just west of there."

"That's Jolie's sweetie's parents' place. Tanner doesn't live at home anymore though," Essie declared.

"Oh?"

"He lives in a very messy room behind his gun shop."

"It's not messy; I cleaned it." Jolie paused. "Eh, recently."

Landen turned to Essie. "Are there any kids for me to play with, or are they all old like you?"

Essie's mouth dropped open. "Chester! You can play with Chester!"

Jolie seemed to bounce on her toes as she and Essie strolled east.

"The grocery store is over that way." Essie pointed.

"Yes, but I need to stop and see Tanner again."

"Are you goin' to pitch another fit?"

"I didn't pitch—well, perhaps it was a small one. No, I need to apologize for my behavior. He's a gunsmith by trade, and I'm not going to be negative about it."

"I haven't heard you apologize very often," Essie remarked.

"That's because I'm usually right."

Essie rolled her eyes.

"I'm teasin', sis."

"I have to admit that you're right more times than anyone I know," Essie said. "You're surely bouncin' along. Why is that?"

"I'm happy."

"Why are you happy? The town is full of men wanting to shoot each other; Bailey is loose on the streets with a pistol; it looks like it's about to rain, and the roof isn't finished on our house . . ."

"My, aren't you a pessimist!"

"Are you happy because Strath Yarrow is movin' into the place next to ours?"

"He won't be moving soon. He doesn't have a house."

"Yes, but you invited him to stay with us."

"That's only temporary, and they might find a room here instead."

"Where would you put them?"

"It depends upon whether the roof is finished."

"Suppose it is?"

"Then until Daddy comes home, maybe Mama will sleep with us, and they can have the front room. Or you and I can sleep in the barn and—"

"Us sleep in the barn?"

"If the roof isn't fixed, we'll all sleep in the barn."

"Is that why you're dancin' along like a calf full of milk?"

"Oh, Strath Yarrow has something to do with it, I'm sure," Jolie replied. "I'm happy because for the past twenty-four hours my mind's been cloudy, and now things are clear again."

"Sometimes I get sick like that too," Essie said. "I think I felt a drop of rain. Did you feel one?"

"No, I didn't. But rain wouldn't surprise me at all."

The bell on top of the door rang when she pushed the door open. "May I come in?"

Tanner glanced up from a workbench in the back of the gun shop. "Hi, darlin'. I was hopin' you'd stop back."

Essie skipped across the room. "What're you doin'?"

He glanced at the bench. "I'm installing new toggles in this Winchester '73, replacing the mainspring, straightening the rear barrel sight, and adjusting the set trigger."

"I didn't want to know that much." Essie shrugged.

"I'm fixing this rifle," he amended.

"Thank you."

Tanner wiped his hands on his white shop apron. "Jolie, I'm sorry. I—"

Jolie stared down at the floor. "No, I'm the one who needs to apologize. I had no—"

Tanner yanked the apron off and scooted next to Jolie. "If I thought for a minute you didn't want me to do this kind of work, I'd quit and take another job, Jolie."

She looked at his eyes, took a deep breath, and held her chest. *He means it. Oh, he would quit his work for me.* "No, Tanner, I would never ask that. I know I worry a lot. I probably will always worry a lot."

"She even worries about worryin'," Essie added.

Tanner took Jolie's hand. His rough, callused fingers slipped into hers.

The bell above the door tinkled. Tanner's hand plunged to his side. Bailey Wagner marched across the room, waving the pocket pistol in front of her.

"Tanner Wells, I want to talk to you," she demanded.

Jolie stepped in front of Tanner and faced Bailey. Tanner's strong arms moved her to the side.

"I trust you didn't use that pistol," he said.

Bailey pointed the barrel at Tanner.

Essie gasped.

Jolie held her breath.

Tanner reached over and took the gun by the barrel. "Your money is still lyin' on the counter up there."

"You knew I'd change my mind, didn't you?" Bailey said.

"You didn't try to shoot Galen Faxon?" Essie quizzed.

"No. After years of hating a man I never met, I realized things are different now. I have my life up ahead of me. Jeremiah and me and that cute, little house in Deadwood and a good job workin' for Sam Fortune. The past is the past." Bailey folded her arms and sighed. "May the Lord deal justly with the likes of Galen Faxon."

Jolie felt her body relax. "Bailey, I think the Lord is really working in your life."

"Yes, He is. Between the help of the Lord Jesus and the deceit of Tanner Wells, I might amount to somethin' yet."

"What did Tanner do?" Essie asked.

"Hold out your hands," Bailey instructed.

Essie cupped her hands together and held them out in front of her. Bailey opened her left hand, and half a dozen shiny bullets tumbled into Essie's hands. "He gave me these."

"How did that help you?" Essie asked.

"They're the wrong bullets."

"They don't fit the gun?" Jolie glanced at Tanner.

"Nope. At first I was disgusted because I thought he had just made a mistake. Then I realized it was no mistake and got mad. But finally it dawned on me—he didn't want me to get in trouble. I like havin' good people like you Bowerses and Tanner worried about me."

Jolie spun around and looked at Tanner. "You gave her the wrong bullets on purpose?"

He forced a grin. "Those are .38s. This gun is a .32. I thought it was the best way to handle it."

"All the time we were arguing, you knew she could never use the gun?" Jolie pressed.

"Yep."

Jolie paused with hands on her hips.

"Are you mad at me, darlin'?" he asked.

Jolie threw her arms around his neck. "I love you, Tanner Wells." Then she kissed his lips hard.

Essie turned to Bailey and shrugged. "She ain't mad at him."

"No," Bailey grinned. "I believe you're right."

With his arms still around her, Tanner pulled back a little. "I love you too, darlin', but you're embarrassin' Estelle."

"Me?" Essie giggled.

"Tanner Wells," Bailey accused, "you're the only one in the room who is blushing."

"I knew it was one of us," he mumbled.

Jolie released him. "This has been a good day. I thought it might be a tragic day, but it's been a good day."

"What makes a good day for you, Jolie Bowers?" Bailey asked.

"When she comes to town, and the boys don't fight over her," Essie said.

"That's what makes Jolie different than any other gal," Bailey observed. "For the rest of us, that would be a bad day. But no more of that for me. I found my man. I had to shoot him to figure it out. I'm goin' back to Deadwood first thing in the mornin'. That's where my future is."

Jolie hugged Bailey. "Tell Jeremiah we're really happy for both of you."

"You come up to see us. We won't be comin' back this way for a long while, I reckon."

"We'll come, you know . . . when we . . ." Jolie paused and bit her lip.

"When we have enough money," Essie finished.

"You can stay with us. It's a small place, but it's surely bigger than—than . . ."

"Than our sod house?" Jolie asked.

"Yes, and you're always so generous about inviting people over."

Essie rocked back on her heels. "She just invited . . ."

Jolie's strong grip on her sister's shoulder silenced Essie.

Bailey strolled to the front door, then turned back. "Tanner, thanks. Thank you for lookin' out for me. Never in my life have I had friends like that. It does feel good."

When the door closed, Tanner turned back to Jolie. "Are you two hurrying back home?"

"Yes, Mother is probably waiting at the store for me already."

"Are you coming in for church tomorrow?" he asked.

"We plan on it. Daddy is supposed to come home tomorrow, and Mama is pinin' for him somethin' terrible."

"She talks about him, does she?" Tanner pressed.

"Not too much, but she doesn't sleep hardly at all," Essie reported. "She says she can't sleep unless his arms are around her all night."

"Estelle Cinnia," Jolie scolded.

"Well, she does."

"It's not proper to say things like that."

"Even to Tanner? He's goin' to be family on June 14."

"It's not June 14 yet," Jolie insisted.

"Boy, Tanner, on June 15 do I have a lot to tell you."

"You might want to make it a little later in the month," he said.

"Oh . . . oh . . . oh!" Essie slapped her hand over her mouth. "Bye." She scampered out the front door.

"We do need to find Mama and get the groceries," Jolie said.

Tanner took her hand and walked her to the front of the store.

Jolie paused in the open doorway. "I'm sorry I embarrassed you with that hug and kiss."

"Darlin', I was a little startled, but I wasn't embarrassed. You can kiss me anytime you want."

"Thank you very much," she grinned.

"You're welcome."

Jolie threw her arms around his neck and kissed him on the lips again.

Hard.

"I, eh, didn't mean right now," he mumbled.

"Of course you did," Jolie giggled.

Essie led the way toward the grocery store. "Jolie Lorita, what has gotten into you? I ain't never seen you kiss Tanner like that, and you did it twice. In fact, I've never seen anyone kiss a boy like that—except Mama kissin' Daddy. But don't worry, I won't tell her."

"Essie, Mama would understand."

"Jolie, do you think Rev. Leyland ever kisses Mrs. Leyland like that?"

"What?" Jolie felt her cheeks and neck redden. "Where did that question come from?"

"Some Sundays while he's preaching, I watch Mrs. Leyland . . . and I was wondering if a minister is allowed to kiss."

"Of course they are."

"I mean, they have five children. So I reckon they kissed at least five times, haven't they?" Essie stated. "But I wonder if they ever kissed like you and Tanner?"

"I think you should find other things to think about during church," Jolie snapped.

"Look, there's Mama." Essie ran up the boardwalk. "Hi, Mama!"

"Where have you been?" Lissa Bowers asked.

"Jolie's been savin' lives and kissin' on Tanner."

"At the same time?" Mrs. Bowers asked.

"Essie!" Jolie reprimanded.

"You said Mama will understand."

"You'll have to tell me on our way home. We'd better get some groceries. I felt a sprinkle or two, and I want to hurry back and make sure the roof gets finished."

"What did you buy?" Essie asked.

"Plow tips and a sack of whole oats. They're down at the wagon. I ran into Sherry DeMarco at the livery."

"How is she, Mama?" Jolie quizzed.

"Sad, of course. She sold the place to Mr. and Mrs. Wells. In fact, she was on her way out of town. She hired Mr. Snyder to drive her down to Sydney. She's going to live with a sister in Turkey Run, Colorado. She just got a letter today and decided to leave immediately. She was hoping Mrs. Fuentes could find another boarder."

"The town is full of men lookin' for a place."

"You know Mrs. Fuentes. She won't rent to single men who aren't employed."

"Strath!" Essie called out. "She can rent it to Strath Yarrow."

"Did you see him?" Lissa asked.

"Yes. Mama, you won't believe what they did. Come to think of it, you probably will believe it," Jolie corrected.

Jolie plopped down on a bench in front of the grocery store next to two big crates of supplies. Two men meandered out of the store and stood on the boardwalk beside her.

"Raymond and Luke, you both look very nice today."

"Thank you, Miss Jolie. Are you waitin' for a fight to break out?" Luke queried.

"We thought we might just stand out here and watch," Raymond added.

"No fights, boys. I'm just waiting for Mama and Essie to fetch the wagon. Contrary to popular rumor, I really don't attract fights."

"I reckon you'll have one tomorrow night," Luke said.

"What're you talking about?"

"It's all over town that some kind of confrontation is goin' to take place at Miss Jolie's schoolhouse," Raymond explained.

"No, it's not a confrontation at all. It's just an informational meeting. Some want to discuss how to survive with the increased railroad rates."

"We heard that the farmers and ranchers were meetin' to plan battle strategy, and some of the gunmen the railroad has hired aim to break up the meeting," Luke revealed.

"Where did you hear that?"

"At the barber shop, the meat market—places like that," he said. "It must be true."

"There will be no fighting at my schoolhouse," Jolie insisted. "I will not tolerate it."

A black buggy pulled by a single large gray horse swung around in the dirt street and pulled up in front of the store. Two men in dark suits tipped their hats.

"Miss Bowers!"

Jolie remained seated. "Mr. Culburtt, how are your ankles?"

"They hurt like they were caught in a bear trap, but the doc says they aren't broke, only sprained bad. You met Mr. Davenport, our chief railroad detective."

"Yes, I did. But I didn't remember his name. He almost arrested me, my mother, and my sister."

"Miss Bowers, I trust you won't hold that grudge long," Davenport said.

"It's already dismissed."

Culburtt cleared his throat. "Two days ago I owed you a deep debt of personal gratitude for assisting myself and two employees."

"How are they doing?"

"Trip is resting in the hotel. Doc said he'll be weak for a month but should recover fine."

"And Mr. Ragsdale?"

"He woke up with a splitting headache and can't keep any food down, but the doc thinks if she keeps him there for a week, he could pull through. Nothin' is paralyzed, and he has most of his memory; so we're grateful."

"That's wonderful news," she said.

Culburtt gazed at the two men standing next to her.

"Mr. Culburtt, these are my friends Raymond and Luke."

"Yep," Luke drawled. "We've known Miss Jolie since she first came to Scottsbluff."

Culburtt glanced back at her. "The reason I stopped is to say that you and your mother's heroics yesterday are worth more than a bundle of boards and a keg of nails. I telegraphed my superiors, and one of the vice presidents is coming out here to meet you two personally."

"What did Miss Jolie and her mama do?" Raymond asked.

"They outraced the train, parked across the tracks, and forced us to stop, instead of letting us plunge off into Bobcat Gulch," Davenport reported.

"I'll swan—I didn't hear that one." Luke shook his head. "You was drivin' Stranger and Pilgrim, I surmise."

"Them is the only two horses that can outrun a train on muddy roads," Raymond said.

"And," Luke added, "Miss Jolie and her mama are the only two people in Nebraska that can drive that team."

"In the meantime, Miss Bowers, if I can be of any help to you in any way, please don't hesitate to let me know. If that train had barreled into the canyon, not only would lives have been lost, but the company itself would have been devastated, perhaps to the point of bankruptcy. We owe you a big debt," Culburtt announced.

"I believe it was the Lord's timing for us to be there, Mr. Culburtt."

He nodded. "I believe you're right, Miss Bowers. He has the right people in the right place. But sometimes they don't listen to what He says."

She watched as the buggy lurched on down the street.

"I can't believe you palled around with ol' Culburtt," Luke remarked.

"He's a nice man."

"It's that nice man who is raising the railroad rates and will put you homesteaders out of business."

"You're wrong, Luke. He's a reasonable man. When Daddy gets home, we'll figure out a workable solution."

"I hope you're right, Miss Jolie, but I ain't felt this much tension in a town since Tombstone ten years ago. It don't take a reasonable spark to start a fire," Luke warned.

"And the man over there on the black horse has a reputation for not bein' reasonable," Raymond added.

Jolie glanced across the street. A tall, strong man with gray at the temples rode toward her.

"You better get inside, Miss Jolie," Raymond cautioned.

"Nonsense. Mr. Faxon is a friend."

"Me and Luke is gettin' inside."

Both men slipped back into the grocery store.

The man on the horse tipped his hat. "Miss Jolie, you look like you're waiting for a ride."

"Mother went to get the rig. I'm not sure what's keeping her."

Faxon glanced back down the street and shook his head. "Your mama is quite a gal. I reckon you know that."

Jolie sat up straight. "Yes, I do. And my daddy thinks so too."

He smiled and nodded, then pushed back his hat. "I'm sure. She's married and happy. I'm glad. But when you get old, Miss Bowers, you look back on some of the forks in the road and ponder what life could have been if you had made a different decision. At the time some of them didn't seem momentous. But now you ponder it and wonder about the 'what ifs.'"

"What was her name, Mr. Faxon?"

He sat straight up, his hands on the saddle horn. "Whose name?"

"The woman my mama reminds you of. I see it in your eyes when you look at her."

His shoulders slumped. "Elizabeth Pryor."

"Did you ride off and leave her?" Jolie pressed.

He stared southwest at the cliffs on Scott's Bluff. "One more cattle drive, I said. It was goin' to be the last."

"But it wasn't?"

"I got stuck in Montana snow all winter. I didn't write to her 'cause I had no good reason for not tryin' to make it back. When I went home to Texas about a year later, she had married a judge and was carryin' a baby."

"Did she look like Mama?"

"She wore a long braid when I met her. She was wearin' a green dress with black lace at the collar and cuffs and danglin' earrings that looked like they dropped off a rainbow. Her lips were a fine dark red, but they didn't have any paint on them. Her left eyebrow had a little curl in it that made her look like she was questionin' ever'thin' you said. But when she smiled, it warmed me from boot to hat."

"How long ago was that?"

"When I first met her?"

"Yes."

"Eighteen years ago last July 3rd."

"You have a good memory."

"It haunts me, Miss Jolie."

"And you are ponderin' what if you had stayed in Texas and married Elizabeth Pryor?"

"And settled down and run some cows or a store and raised children. I wonder, would I have a daughter like you? And a woman like your mama waitin' for me when I come in ever' evenin'? Like I said, Miss Jolie, the forks in the road plague a man."

"Daddy says we must do those things in life we would regret not doing."

"Your daddy sounds like a smart man though I've never met him." Faxon patted the neck of his horse. "Enough of the melancholy. Thanks for the warnin'. Have you seen the Wagner woman?"

"She's had a change of heart. She turned in her pistol and is moving to Deadwood tomorrow."

"That's good. I don't take much guff from an angry man, but I don't know what to do with an angry woman. What would be your advice to me?"

"On how to deal with an angry woman?"

"Yep."

Jolie tucked a finger under her chin. "Stand still and really listen to her. Take every word without arguing back until she's completely spent. She'll feel better getting the words out."

"How old are you?"

"I'll be eighteen soon."

"Now I know for sure your daddy is the luckiest man on earth."
He tipped his black hat. "Good day, Miss Jolie."

"Good day, Mr. Faxon."

As soon as he rode west, Luke and Raymond shuffled out to the
bench.

"I cain't believe you and Faxon is chums," Luke began.

"You two are just looking at reputations. There are real people
behind reputations."

"I reckon so, but reputations come from somewhere," Raymond
replied.

At the roar of a wagon, Jolie jumped up from the bench. Stranger
and Pilgrim thundered down the middle of the street. A gray tarp was
lashed down over a load in the wagon.

Jolie stepped out to the edge of the boardwalk. "Mama, what do
you have in the wagon?"

"We got mattresses," Essie called out.

"Mr. Mendez sold you some more mattresses?"

"No, it was Mrs. Mendez. She gave them to us," Lissa Bowers
reported. "They aren't new. When she found out what had happened
to our roof, she said it was time to replace her own mattresses. So she
got new ones from the store and wanted us to have her old ones."

"That's wonderful!" Jolie exclaimed.

"Yes. I'm hoping the roof is on when we get home," Lissa Bowers
added. "We might be racing the rain. Sorry I kept you waiting so
long."

"Oh, I've had some nice visits."

"Is your daughter pals with ever'one in Nebraska?" Luke
chortled.

"Nebraska, Montana, Wyoming, and parts of New Mexico,"
Lissa Bowers said. "But mostly just the men."

Jolie studied the street to the east.

"Mother, did you see . . ."

"Yes."

"Is he . . ."

"Yes, but he won't be . . ."

"But where's he going to . . ."

"Sherry DeMarco's room at . . ."

"That's good. I didn't want . . ."

"Landen said . . ."

"It's nice when some things work out," Jolie concluded.

Luke gaped at the women. "I don't reckon you two even need words, do ya?"

"Not really," Lissa replied. "Luke, will you and Raymond shove those grocery crates into the back of the wagon? I don't want to turn these boys loose. They are prancin' like someone at the livery slipped them sweet feed."

They had just secured the groceries in the back of the wagon when Sheriff Riley galloped up and yanked his buckskin horse to a halt. "I'm glad I caught you before you left town."

"What's wrong, Sheriff?" Lissa asked.

"You have to get over to the telegraph office."

"Why?"

"We got word from Lincoln. There's been trouble."

Jolie watched her mother's face turn white. "What're you saying?"

Sheriff Riley pulled off his hat. "There's been some gunfire. It's about Mr. Bowers, ma'am."

Six

"Sheriff," Lissa Bowers's voice quivered like her hands, "exactly what are you saying? If you're telling me I'm a widow, then come right out and say it. I will surely lie down on this street and die right now. Don't be vague with me. My heart won't take it."

Essie started to cry.

Jolie bit her lip and held her breath.

"No, ma'am—that is, I don't think so," the sheriff stammered. "Two telegrams came in, one to me and one to you. Mine said there was a violent riot in Lincoln by the Young Farmers' Alliance led by Matthew Bowers of Scottsbluff. That's all it said."

Lissa Bowers's hands were clenched, her knuckles white. "That's preposterous. My Matthew isn't a violent man at all."

"Sheriff, how violent was the riot?" Jolie asked. *Lord, we would be devastated to lose Daddy, but Mama's right. Her life centers in that man. She wouldn't eat. She wouldn't sleep. She couldn't live two weeks without him. Please, Lord . . .*

Sheriff Riley fanned his face with his hat. "I don't know any more than that. Violent means fightin' enough that shots were fired, I reckon."

Lissa's voice was a measured monotone. "What does my telegram say?"

The sheriff glanced at the envelope in his hand. "I didn't read it, ma'am. I reckon you can read it here. I figure you might need to write one back. That's why I mentioned readin' it at the telegraph office."

She took a deep breath. "I can't wait that long. Hand it to me."

The sheriff rode his buckskin horse closer to the wagon and leaned over.

"No!" Lissa Bowers blurted out and drew back. "Give it to Jolie Lorita. Read it to me, darlin'. Read it real slow."

Jolie slipped open the tan envelope and tugged out the note. She opened it one fold at a time. Lissa Bowers clutched her oldest daughter's arm.

Jolie swallowed hard. "'To: Mrs. Matthew Bowers. Melissa, darlin', I'm fine . . .'"

Lissa Bowers began to sob. Her shoulders rocked back and forth, and she gasped for breath.

"It's okay, Mama," Essie soothed. "Daddy's fine. Daddy's okay, Mama. Don't cry."

"I know, baby, I know," Mrs. Bowers sobbed. "That's why I'm cryin'. I'm so happy and relieved."

"'I'm in jail,'" Jolie read.

"Jail!" Lissa Bowers sat up and wiped her cheeks. "Why is my husband in jail?"

Sheriff Riley shrugged. "I reckon because of the riots."

Jolie continued, "'Be home as soon as I clear this up. I love you. M.B.'"

"Daddy's in jail?" Essie echoed.

"It must be a misunderstanding," Jolie said.

"I have to go to Lincoln and get him," Lissa announced. "Sheriff, is the evening train at the station yet?"

The lawman pulled out his gold watch and glanced at it. "Yes, ma'am. It should be leavin' any minute now."

"Jolie Lorita, do you have any money left?" Mrs. Bowers asked.

"Mama, I spent it all on groceries. The rest is at home." Jolie glanced up at the lawman. "Sheriff, please hurry and find Mr.

Culburtt. Tell him Jolie Bowers needs two train passes. He'll give them, I'm sure."

"Two?" the sheriff questioned.

"So Mama can bring Daddy home."

Sheriff Riley galloped off toward the train yard.

A buggy rolled up beside them. Strath and Landen Yarrow peered over at them. "Look, Strath, their mama is with them," Landen called out.

Strath Yarrow surveyed the three tear-streaked faces. "Jolie, what's wrong?"

"Oh, Strath, I'm so glad to see you," she replied.

"You are?"

"Would you lend me five dollars? I will pay you back when we get to the homestead. I don't have the money with me."

Yarrow took several coins from his vest pocket. "Certainly."

"Jolie Lorita, we do not take money from someone we hardly know." Lissa Bowers wiped her eyes with a lavender-embroidered handkerchief.

"Mama, please take it. Strath isn't a stranger. He's going to be a neighbor. I'm just sure he'll want the place north of us. And we have to get you on that train now, not tomorrow."

"If I have a pass, why do I need money?" Lissa Bowers asked.

Jolie pointed to the telegram in her mother's hand. "For bail."

"Bail?" Strath called out. "What happened?"

"Daddy seems to have gotten arrested for leading the farmers' protest," Jolie informed him. "It's a mistake, but until it can be cleared up, we'll need bail, I'm sure."

"Here." He held out his hand. "Take twenty-five."

"Oh, my," Lissa Bowers gasped. "I don't need that much."

"His bail will be twenty dollars if it has anything to do with a riot. Trust me. I've handled such cases."

"But I don't have that much at home to repay you," Jolie protested.

"Just repay me the five. The bail will be refunded after this matter is cleared up. Take it. I insist."

Lissa Bowers tugged on her braid and shook her head. "Jolie, I can't do this. I just can't take that much money."

"You have to, Mama. Now pull yourself together. You have to go be with Daddy, and you know it. He needs you, Mama."

Lissa Bowers heaved a sigh and took the money. "Mr. Yarrow, I don't know what to say."

"Mrs. Bowers, you and your daughters either saved our lives or saved us from serious injury yesterday at great risk to yourself. A temporary loan is the least I can do. The funds will not be missed. Trust me."

"It's not a gift?" she asserted.

"No, ma'am," he replied. "Just a loan to future neighbors because their funds are miles away."

"All right." Lissa Bowers let out a long, deep sigh. "May the Lord bless you for your generosity."

Jolie raced the team to the train station. When she climbed down, a crutch-wielding Edward Culburtt handed her the passes.

"We got here in time," Jolie exulted.

"Just a tad late. I held the train. The sheriff explained everything."

Lissa Bowers gave the gray-headed man a hug. "Thank you, Mr. Culburtt. You're a generous man."

He nodded and wiped his gray mustache. "And perhaps foolish. Your husband, as I understand it, was arrested for leading a riot against our railroad. I just gave him and his wife a free pass. I'll need to think up a way to explain this. 'Bless those who curse thee,' I suppose."

"Daddy doesn't curse," Essie corrected him.

Within minutes the eastbound train pulled out with Lissa Bowers aboard. Jolie glanced over at the man and the little boy in the buggy now parked beside them. "Mr. Yarrow, are you ready to go look at that homestead?"

"I believe we are. I trust all will be well with your mother and father."

"If they're together, all will be fine. They're quite dependent on each other," Jolie said. "I see you've already checked out the room at Mrs. Fuentes's."

"How can you tell that?" he asked.

"You washed Landen's face, combed his hair, fastened the top button on your shirt, and tightened your tie. You both look very nice."

"Thank you, Miss Jolie. You're very observant."

"I can't do anything without her catchin' me," Essie called out.

"You didn't see that I changed my stockings," Landen said.

She glanced over at the young boy's wool trousers that hung down over black high-top shoes. "No, I must have missed that. We'll go east on Telegraph Road. I'll go by the property about five miles out. We'll wait for you there."

"I hardly think a loaded farm wagon will get too far ahead of a buggy," Strath called back.

Essie grabbed the iron rail of the wagon seat. "Oh, you shouldn't have said that."

With a slap of the lead lines, Stranger and Pilgrim plunged into the middle of Telegraph Road. They were at a gallop by the time they reached the edge of town.

Essie glanced over her shoulder. "I think you're leaving them behind."

"They'll catch up."

"I like Strath Yarrow," Essie announced.

Jolie kept her eyes on the road ahead of her. "I thought Leppy was your fella."

"I didn't mean for a boyfriend," Essie giggled. "Jolie, do you like Strath?"

"Yes, I do."

"For a boyfriend?"

"Of course not. Tanner is my sweetie. You know that."

"What if Tanner hadn't moved to Scottsbluff? What if you weren't goin' to be married on June 14? Would you be interested in Strath Yarrow?" Essie pressed.

"I don't think it's advantageous to meditate on hypothetical scenarios," Jolie objected.

"Does that mean you don't want to talk about it?"

"Yes."

"That's what I thought," Essie replied.

There was a steady rhythm to the bouncing, squeaking wagon. Jolie stared down the road between Stranger's ears. *Lord, it seems to me that ever since we moved to Nebraska, our lives have been out of control. I started this day in the barn, hurryin' to cook breakfast for Maxwell and Shakey. I was going to spend the day helping to roof the house and clean up dishes and clothes. Now I'm driving back home with groceries, mattresses, and a handsome man following me.*

Jolie glanced back over her shoulder.

He's back there somewhere. I marched into a saloon. Confronted an angry woman with a gun. And kissed my Tanner in public. Twice. I put my mother on the train with borrowed money to go fetch Daddy out of jail. None of that was in my plans.

Jolie sat up and stretched her neck.

Okay, the second kiss was planned. But the rest seems to be a reaction to situations You bring our way. Sooner or later things have to settle down. Even at school I don't test the students all the time. That's it, isn't it? This is a test. Each unplanned event is a test. You want to see what I've learned. I think I'm glad I don't know what my grades are. But I do need some recess time, Lord. And some study time.

Essie poked her in the ribs. "What're you thinkin' about, Jolie?"

"Supper. I wonder what I should cook for supper."

"We have fresh groceries; so there are lots of choices."

"It's more difficult to decide when you have new supplies. Too many choices. Feasts are harder to plan than famines. Besides, I don't know how many I'll be cooking for. I trust Captain Richardson will stay for supper."

"I hope Chester isn't there," Essie said as she bounced on the seat.

"I'm sure the Wells family will be going home before dark."

"Did you feel a sprinkle?" Essie asked.

"Yes, I did."

"I hope the roof is finished. Won't it be nice, Jolie?"

"It'll be wonderful. No more muddy roof dripping into our stew."

"Or our bed." Essie turned and stared back down the road. "I can't see them at all."

Jolie wrapped the lead lines around her wrists and threw herself back. The team slowed.

"Were you just racin' to get ahead of him?" Essie asked.

"Yes, I guess I was."

"Jolie, do you think Daddy is okay? I mean, what's it like bein' in jail?"

"I'm sure he's just sitting there visiting with the other men, waiting for the situation to be resolved."

"Kind of like being at the barbershop?"

Jolie brushed her auburn bangs back and adjusted her straw hat. "Except behind bars, of course."

By the time they reached the turnoff to their place, a light rain drizzled. Jolie parked the rig at the side of the road.

"It's goin' to be slick for Strath to get back to town," Essie declared.

"Yes, I believe you're right. I'll have him take a quick look and turn back immediately."

"I think I have an answer to your question," Essie announced, wiping rain off her cheek.

"What's the answer?"

"Ham and cabbage soup."

"Oh, that question," Jolie said. "Yes, that does sound good."

"What other question was there?"

"Eh, none. I had just forgotten."

"Here they come," Essie shouted.

The buggy wheels flagged a narrow stream of fresh mud as they approached.

"Those horses are really fast," Landen called out as they pulled up alongside.

"Yes, aren't they?" Jolie hugged herself and felt the dampness of her dress sleeves.

"Is this the property?" Strath called out.

"Yes, it stretches over to the wheat field, I believe. That place belongs to the Wells family now."

"That's Jolie's sweetie's parents," Essie piped up.

"Yes, I believe you've mentioned that on several occasions," Strath remarked.

"And it borders this lane," Jolie said.

"Which goes back to our place," Essie added.

Strath pointed south. "Are there any other homesteads down there?"

"No, just the river."

"So the far border is against your place?" he quizzed.

"Not more than a hundred feet from our house," Jolie replied.

Strath Yarrow pulled off his dark hat and shook water off it. "I like it."

"It's been scraped and tilled, as you can see." Jolie waved her arm at the open field. "But not for a couple of years."

"I wonder how deep the water level is for a well?" Strath asked.

"Ours is less than twenty feet, but we're much lower and closer to the river."

"We'll put the house out here near the road, I suppose," he said.

"Strath and me are goin' to buy a ready-cut house," Landen announced.

"There's a company in Chicago that makes ready-to-build houses," Strath explained. "It's a precut and packaged complete house that they ship out on the train. We'll assemble it."

"You mean, a clapboard house?" Jolie said.

"Yes."

"That'll be nice."

"Daddy is goin' to build us a wooden house too," Essie said. "After he gets out of jail and all."

"I would like to drive the boundaries of the place. Do you think I can do that in this light buggy?" Strath asked.

"Perhaps—if it doesn't rain too much more. You need to know that until the county grades these roads different, they're slick and almost impassible after a rain."

Yarrow pointed to Stranger and Pilgrim. "Your team seems to do all right."

"These two big boys love the mud," Jolie said.

"I'll follow you down and then swing by the boundaries and back to town," Strath called out.

"There's a gulch that cuts across the southwest corner. You should avoid that with a buggy."

The drive back to the homestead grew muddier as they approached the house. Jolie pulled up just short of their property and waited for the buggy.

"If you go straight to the sage, you'll find the gulch and the edge of this place. But you might be better off going right back up the lane. It's getting slick," she admonished.

"We seem to be doing all right, but I certainly won't dawdle. Thank you, Miss Jolie. We really like this place."

"I thought you would. Bye, Landen."

"Bye, Miss Jolie. Bye, Esther."

"Essie."

Jolie watched as they bounced east across the fallow ground.

"We're goin' to have neighbors," Essie said.

"*You* will have neighbors. Remember, after June 14 I'll live in town."

"It's a long time between now and June 14," Essie replied.

Jolie trotted the team toward the sod house. *I was thinking the very same thing.*

Behind the storm clouds the sun sank into the Laramie Mountains of Wyoming. The air hung dark gray and damp. Lantern light filtered out from the open front door. Gibs ran out to meet them.

"Mama, we got the roof all done. Where's Mama?" he asked.

"She went on the train to Lincoln to get Daddy out of jail," Essie informed him.

Gibs stared at her for a moment and then turned to his older sister. "Jolie, where's Mama?"

"Leppy!" Essie shouted at a thin man with a black hat who strolled out of the barn. She leaped from the wagon and sprinted across the yard.

Jolie glanced at Gibs. "Leppy's here?"

"Yep. Leppy, Chug, Maxwell, and Shakey," Gibs reported. "They asked to use the barn. No rooms in town, they said, and they didn't want to spend the night in the rain. Lawson said it was all right since the roof got finished."

"I'll have to make lots of soup. Have Lawson put up the team. Get Leppy and the others to help unload these mattresses."

"You bought new mattresses?" Gibs asked.

"No. They aren't new."

"You bought used mattresses?"

"We didn't buy them."

"Where is Mama, really?" Gibs pressed.

"She took the train to Lincoln to get Daddy out of jail."

"You got a lot of explainin' to do," Gibs said.

"Yes, I do."

Jolie was slicing ham into one-inch chunks by the time Leppy Verdue and the others finished unloading the wagon.

Lawson tromped back into the house. "Sis, there's a man and a boy hikin' across the field toward us."

"Oh, my, it's Strath and Landen. They must have gotten stuck. Essie, set two more places at the table."

Ten people crowded into the small front room of the sod house by the time supper was prepared. Jolie stood by the stove. She felt sweat trickle down the back of her neck and soak into the collar of her dress. Her shoulders hurt. Her feet felt swollen. "Men, we have ham and cabbage soup, bread, and an apple cobbler."

"A very large apple cobbler," Essie added.

"If I had had more time," Jolie said, "I might have been able to fix more."

Within minutes after Lawson had said a blessing, everyone in the room was busy with a bowl of soup. Landen scooted in between Gibs and Lawson. Essie huddled next to Leppy. Maxwell, Chug, and Shakey lounged on the floor with their backs against the wall. Strath sat down next to Jolie. "I should have taken your advice and driven right back to town."

"Yes, you should have." Jolie passed him the blackberry jam.

Leppy waved his soup spoon across the table. "Strath, if Miss Jolie or her mama tell you to do something, you'd better do it. You can take their word to the bank."

"I suppose that's a lesson we all have to learn," Yarrow said.

"Ol' Leppy learned it when she pointed his revolver at his temple and told him to back off," Chug hooted from the other side of the room.

"Whoa, I didn't hear that story," Maxwell said. "I thought it was the law that ran you out of Scottsbluff."

"No," Chug said. "You ought to see her do a one-handed Dakota spin on that cylinder and drop those bullets in the dirt. It was almost poetic."

"You're a girl with many talents," Strath commented.

She skimmed her spoon across the steaming soup. "I was stopping a silly fight, that's all."

"This cobbler is delicious, Miss Jolie."

"Thank you, Shakey. You know, most folks eat their soup and bread first and then the dessert."

"I never could figure that out. What if I got full on soup and didn't have much room for dessert?" Shakey reasoned.

"I can see that would be a tragedy."

"My sentiments exactly, Miss Jolie. Shoot, I may skip the soup completely and just have seconds on pie."

At the sound of a crash in the yard, Lawson peered out into the darkness. "Looks like the wind is pickin' up. That was just some boards tumblin' off that stack of lumber. It's a good thing there isn't a campfire. It would have blown to Chimney Rock by now."

"Is it rainin' still?" Maxwell asked.

"Nope. I think it blew over. There are some stars up there," Lawson reported.

"It will dry the roads," Jolie remarked.

"And perhaps the field," Strath added. "I appreciate your putting us up after all."

"Miss Jolie runs the smallest hotel in Nebraska," Leppy said. "All sorts of folks have stayed in this one room."

"We'll stay in the barn," Maxwell offered.

"No, I insist you all stay in here," Jolie said. "It sounds too windy out there. The barn only has three walls. Besides, you moved all the furniture back in here and repaired what was broken. I would feel much better if you were all in here."

"I think I'd better go settle down the horses," Lawson called from the doorway. "The wind is rattlin' ever'thing around in the corral."

"I'm goin' to help him," Shakey announced. "Sounds like demons cryin' out there."

"I think we'd better tie our ponies to a picket line so they don't bolt off in the night," Chug suggested.

"I'll make some more coffee, boys." Jolie scurried back to the stove. "Bring your bedrolls in. Strath and Landen can use Mama and Daddy's bed."

It took two hours to secure things outside and calm the horses. They huddled inside the front room of the sod house, most with cups of steaming coffee. Landen slept on the living room bed. Lawson was asleep in the backroom. Jolie and Essie washed and dried the dishes as they listened to the men talk.

"The railroad is payin' six dollars a day for guards," Maxwell announced.

Chug sipped from a tin cup. "That's more than the miners up in Deadwood are makin'."

"Shoot, that's more than anyone is makin'—legal," Leppy added.

Shakey squatted by the woodstove. "I heard the ranchers would offer five dollars, but you don't get paid until later in the fall."

"Don't cotton much to promises in a deal like this," Maxwell murmured.

"You think the farmers will toss in some more? I mean, you get a couple dollars now and five promised. That might make it worth-while," Chug said.

Leppy pulled off his hat and ran his fingers through his thick black hair. "If this gets solved in two days, who's goin' to stick around to pick up their money come fall?"

"You got to take the daily cash," Chug maintained. "It's the only way."

"Chug's right. You take a bullet some night, and them promises don't do a thing for you," Maxwell added. "Go with the ones that pay you ever'day."

"Do you really believe there'll be shooting?" Strath asked.

All four turned to look at the man in the suit and tie.

"Yeah, I do," Leppy said. "Not 'cause the situation warrants it but 'cause you got all sorts of quick tempers comin' to town. Someone will get drunk and take a shot, and then it will all cut loose. That's what happened down in Lincoln. It's the newspapers that make it political."

"I don't understand why you're willing to chance your lives on a mercenary cause," Strath puzzled.

"What's a mercenary cause?" Shakey asked.

"When you hire out to the highest bidder, and you really don't care how it's settled," Jolie said.

"That's not true. I do care." Maxwell grinned. "I want the side I'm on to win."

"There's a lot of personal feuds loungin' in Scottsbluff right now," Chug mumbled. "Some of them boys will see this as an excuse to set-tle up old scores."

"The longer they hang around, the more chance of somethin' bustin' loose." Shakey nodded.

"You boys do what you want," Leppy Verdue said, "but if the farmers come in with the ranchers on this deal, I'm takin' that side. I won't go up against my Essie darlin' and her kin."

Essie grinned and poked Jolie. "Did you hear that?" she whispered. "He called me his darlin'."

Jolie nodded.

"You might have to look down the gun barrels of Galen Faxon and that bunch," Maxwell warned. "I hear he's leadin' the railway bunch."

"Ol' Davenport don't back down either," Chug said. "The railroad is linin' up tough cases, for sure."

"I'd rather meet Saint Peter and explain why I went up against Faxon than meet him and try to explain why I opposed the Bowerses of Nebraska."

"Leppy's got a point there," Chug conceded.

"I say, take the daily cash 'cause the odds are nothing will happen, and it will all be solved. Shoot, how do we know it ain't solved already?" Maxwell declared.

"Ol' Dix might be right," Shakey said. "I'll check the horses one more time and then get some sleep. Reckon I'll let tomorrow's trouble take care of itself. That's in the Bible someplace, isn't it, Miss Jolie?"

"Yes, you're right, Shakey."

Torrington rubbed his beard. "Mama used to read the Bible to us kids purtneer ever' night."

"Shakey, does your mother live around here?" Jolie asked.

Torrington rubbed his chin, jammed his hat down tight, and pushed his way out into the stiff wind.

"Shakey's mama was Osage. She died last winter in the cold," Maxwell reported. "They ran out of firewood when me and him was in Colorado."

Essie was snuggled under the covers when Jolie finally came to bed, but she wasn't asleep.

"How's the mattress, little sis?"

"Comfy like our other ones. Only these smell."

"What do they smell like?"

"Like lilac perfume."

Jolie sank down next to her sister.

"How come we have so much company at this house? It's the smallest, most remote place we've lived in, and we have people here all the time."

"I was wondering that myself. I suppose it's the Lord's doing."

"Why do you think He's doin' it?" Essie asked.

"What do you mean?"

"They're not starving to death. I think they can all afford to eat in town. So it's not like the Lord is wanting us to feed the hungry," Essie pointed out.

Jolie pulled the sheet up to her neck. "That's very true."

"And did you notice there are a lot of unmarried men that come over?"

Jolie giggled into the pillow. "Yes, I did notice all five were unmarried."

"Six." Essie laughed. "Landen isn't married either."

"You're right. What do you think the Lord is telling all these unmarried men?"

"I think He's tellin' them it's too late for them," Essie whispered.

"Too late? It's never too late. If they give their hearts to the Lord, then they can—"

"No, I meant, He's telling them it's too late for them to get Jolie Bowers." Essie giggled.

"Essie!"

"Why do you think they hang around?"

"Because they miss their own families, and they like being with ours."

"I still say the Lord has a purpose in bringing them all here. Daddy would know."

"I believe you're right about that."

"I wish he and Mama would get home," Essie said.

"She just left this evening. She isn't even in Lincoln yet."

"I know, but I can wish. Did you notice that you and me are in a house with eight boys?"

"Does that trouble you?" Jolie asked.

"No . . . I reckon it's about even. Don't you?"

Jolie giggled and hugged Essie. "I believe you're right, little sis."

When the strong hand grabbed Jolie's shoulder in the dark, she slapped at it and connected with a square jaw and thick mustache.

"Don't you—"

"Jolie Lorita!" the man whispered.

She sat straight up in bed. "Daddy?"

"Hi, darlin'. Looks like you got a houseful," he whispered.

She rubbed her eyes. "It was too windy and stormy to have them stay in the barn."

"I visited with Leppy a little. Who's in Mama's and my bed?" he asked.

"That's Strath Yarrow and his son Landen. He's a widower, an attorney from Chicago who thought he bought the Avery place. But now he's—"

"You can explain it in the mornin', darlin'. I'm tired."

Jolie clung to her father's strong arm. "I didn't expect you to be home so quickly."

He patted her hand. "You read the telegram?"

"Yes," Jolie whispered. "What happened?"

"Some organizers from Saunders County pulled out guns when we rallied in front of the statehouse. When I disarmed one of them, the gun went off."

"Did it hit anyone?"

"No, but it hit the tree above the sheriff, and he had me arrested as the leader. He had seen me speaking to the crowd earlier and assumed I was leading a rebellion."

Jolie's eyes started to adjust. She could see her father's outline. "What did you tell the crowd, Daddy?"

"That we should go home and farm."

She hugged him. "I'm glad you're home. But I didn't think there was a train west until morning."

"Some railroad big shot has his own train. One of the workers slipped me into the caboose. I think the sheriff wanted me out of town. Anyway, I'm home. Remind me *not* to go to Lincoln for a long time."

She rubbed her hand up and down his arm and waited.

"Is Mama putting away the horses?" Jolie finally asked.

"No," he replied. "She sleeping in the barn?"

"She is?" Jolie mumbled. "You can have our bed. Essie and I can go to the barn. Is it still windy?"

"No, it's not windy." He grabbed her by both shoulders. His voice was very soft, yet firm. "Jolie, is Mama sleepin' in the barn?"

"Why do you keep asking me that? She was with you, Daddy, not me," Jolie insisted.

"What?"

"Mama brought you home, didn't she?"

"Mama's here, Jolie. Are you still asleep, darlin'?"

"After we got the telegram, she went to Lincoln to get you, Daddy."

"She did what?"

"The telegram said you were in jail. She caught the evening east-bound and went to bail you out. You didn't see her?"

"Mama is in Lincoln?" he gasped. "Why did she do that?"

"She went after her man, Daddy. She'd march into Hades and fight the demons to pull you out. You know that."

"But—but—I didn't ask her to come."

"Daddy, you know Mama. She doesn't wait for anything."

"She's in Lincoln?" he repeated.

"Do you want our bed?" Jolie offered.

"I'm goin' out to the barn," he mumbled. "Melissa's in Lincoln!"

Jolie swung her legs out of the bed. "I'll warm up some coffee and be out in a few minutes."

It took until daybreak for Jolie to report everything to her father and for him to give his account of the farmers' meetings.

Maxwell Dix was the first of the men out the door. He wore his bullet belt and holster around his bare chest and carried a tin cup of coffee as he walked toward them. His blond hair curled from under his faded gray hat out over his ears.

Shakey Torrington scooted out barefoot and shuffled to the privy. Leppy came out of the house completely dressed and wearing a black silk bandanna around his neck. Chug's shirt was untucked, and he was hatless as he emerged. Strath Yarrow's tie was loose and his vest unbuttoned as he ambled toward the barn.

"How many more are in there?" Matthew Bowers laughed.

"Only Landen and your other children. I think. Of course, some have been known to stop by after I go to sleep. I think I'll go start breakfast." She hugged her father. "I'm glad you're home."

"Darlin', that was my last trip to Lincoln . . . I surely wish."

"Mama will be fine, Daddy. She's got a train pass and will be home today."

"I miss her, Jolie."

She studied her father's eyes. "I know you do. And you know how she misses her Matthew." *Someday, Lord, I want to look into Tanner's eyes and see that same kind of longing. They both are like orphan pups when the other is not nearby.*

Jolie was cracking eggs into a bowl when the sound of a gunshot caused her to spin around. Essie laid down a handful of forks and scampered to the door.

"What're they doing out there?" Jolie asked.

"Can I go see?"

"Put on some shoes. I don't want you to have dirty feet at church today."

"Are we just goin' to drive off and leave them all here when we go to church?" Essie pulled on her black high-top shoes.

"I suppose. Tell them breakfast will be ready in about ten minutes. I don't intend to call them twice."

"Yes, Mama." Essie giggled as she tied her shoes.

Several more shots rang out. Gibs ran into the house and grabbed his Winchester 1890 pump .22.

"Gibson Hunter Bowers, what're they doing out there?" Jolie asked.

"They're havin' a target shoot. You ought to see it. Leppy and Maxwell Dix are matchin' shot for shot."

"Are they the two best shots?"

"Oh no. Strath can outshoot them both."

Jolie flipped her auburn bangs back off her forehead. "He can?"

"He used to do trick shooting. He's goin' to show me how to shoot my .22 backwards over my shoulder, using a knife blade as a mirror."

"That sounds dangerous."

Gibs grinned. "Yeah, don't it?" Then he ran out the door.

By the time they huddled in the small kitchen/living room/dining room of the sod house, Strath Yarrow's rented black carriage had been pulled out of the mud and stood hitched in front of the house. Four saddled horses stood tied at the barn.

"Miss Jolie," Chug offered, "if you ever want to open a cafe, I'd surely eat there every day when I'm in town."

"Why, Chug, you're welcome at our table anytime you're in town now. If I had a cafe, you'd have to pay for meals, and that means you could complain. I like doin' it this way. Everyone is happy."

"Yes, ma'am, but you go marry that gunsmith, and he might not want us boys stopping by for supper."

Jolie laughed. "I think you're right about that. You should just find yourself a nice farm gal that can cook well and marry her, Chug."

"Me—get married?"

"You have something against steady meals and a warm home at night?" Jolie challenged.

"No, ma'am. It's just that I ain't the marryin' type."

Jolie marched over to him. "What does that mean?"

"Ma'am?"

"I've heard that time and again. Didn't you tell me that same thing, Mr. Dix?"

Maxwell swallowed his eggs and swigged some coffee. "That's right. I'm a drifter. Don't think that sits well with a wife."

"I still don't understand the term, 'not the marryin' kind.' Shakey, does that mean you don't like to be around women?"

"What?" Shakey Torrington sprayed his coffee across his plate.

"Do you remember ol' Mr. Kenton west of Helena, Lawson?"

Lawson smeared a spoonful of butter across his biscuit. "Yeah, he was a hermit . . . lived in a cave, but he always had nice pelts to sell. But he wouldn't sell them to Jolie or Mama. Me and Daddy had to go buy them 'cause he swore he would have nothin' to do with women."

"Is that what you mean when you say you aren't the marryin' type?" Jolie prodded.

"No, ma'am," Shakey replied. "I do like women."

"You ought to see him out on the floor with them girls at the dance hall," Maxwell hooted. "Where do you think he got the name Shakey?"

"That's my type of girl, Miss Jolie," Shakey added.

"So you don't like bein' around non-dance-hall girls?"

"I jist ain't at ease around them."

"So you're probably anxious to leave this morning," Jolie remarked.

Shakey Torrington scratched his neck. "What?"

"Bein' around Essie and me makes you feel uncomfortable, I suppose."

"No, Miss Jolie, you two is different."

"I surmise you know that we're the marrying type," she countered.

"We all knew that," Shakey replied.

"So you can be at ease around non-dance-hall, marrying type women after all?"

"Careful, Shakey," Leppy warned. "The schoolteacher's going to trap you."

Jolie spun around. "How about you, Mr. Verdue? Are you the marryin' type?"

"Are you proposin' to me?" Leppy's deep dimple flashed when he grinned.

"Hardly. But you didn't answer my question."

"With a reputation like mine, it ain't fair to take a wife."

"Tell that to Sam Fortune," Jolie challenged.

Maxwell Dix banged down his coffee cup. "The Oklahoma gunman?"

"He lives in Deadwood now. He's married, settled down, and runs the telephone exchange there. Bailey Wagner just got a job working for him. Would you say your reputation is greater than Sam Fortune's?"

"Leppy ain't in Galen Faxon's league—let alone Sam Fortune's," Chug said.

"So a man's reputation doesn't make him a non-marrying type, Mr. Verdue. What could it be?" she pressed.

"Maybe we're scared to death," Shakey admitted. "What decent gal is goin' to cotton up to the likes of us?"

Jolie passed the strawberry jam to Chug. "There's only one way to find out."

"There is?"

"You men will just have to spend some time around gals who are the marrying kind and see what happens," Jolie suggested.

"You plan on invitin' them over for a party?" Maxwell teased.

"I just might. In the meantime, you can all go to church with us today."

"Ah, hah! There you have it. She's tryin' to sucker us into goin' to church," Maxwell proclaimed.

"I wasn't deceptive. Was there anything I said that wasn't true?"

"No, Miss Jolie. I reckon not," Chug said.

"Shakey, your mama went to church, didn't she?"

"Yes, ma'am, she surely did."

"What if someday you meet a young lady who has a lot of the same qualities as your mama? Would you be interested in gettin' to know her better?"

"Yes, Miss Jolie. I reckon I would."

"Do you think a young lady like that would go to church?"

"If she's like Mama, she would."

"Did your mama ever go into a dance hall?"

Shakey Torrington looked offended. "Never in her life."

"Then why in the world do you think you'll find a gal like Mama in a dance hall instead of church?" Jolie pressed.

Leppy laid down his fork. "Are you sayin' we should go to church to find women to marry? That don't sound very spiritual."

Jolie cracked a tight-lipped smile. "No, I'm sayin' you should go in order to become the kind of men that good women will be attracted to."

"I'll go to church with you, Miss Jolie," Shakey offered.

"I don't reckon I need to," Leppy replied. "I already have a good woman who likes me." He grinned at Essie.

"Leppy, would you go to church with me today?" Essie asked. "Please."

"What?"

"You heard me. I'd like you to go to church with me today."

Leppy Verdue sighed. "They trapped us, boys."

"I'll go with you, Miss Jolie," Chug offered. "But I ain't much to look at. I ain't got a clean shirt."

"Daddy has one you can borrow. Jolie scrubbed up every piece of clothing in the house two days ago," Essie said.

"I'm not goin'," Maxwell Dix declared. "I don't like being railroaded into anything."

"Good," Jolie responded. "I was hoping you'd say that."

"You were?"

"I wanted one of you to stay back here at the house."

"I'll volunteer," Maxwell Dix offered.

"And wash the dishes and sweep the house. We won't have time this morning if we're to get to town for church. There's an apron over there." She pointed to a yellow one on a peg near the door.

"It'll look good with your golden hair," Shakey teased.

Dix shook his head. "I can just saddle up and ride away."

"Yes, you can," she said. "And someday when Leppy, Chug, and Shakey are snug in their homes with Mama and the kids around the fireplace, and you are out in that shack of a cabin sellin' pelts, you'll say to yourself, 'I wonder if it would have been different if I had gone to church with Miss Jolie?'"

Maxwell Dix shook his head. "Mr. Bowers, what's a man to do?"

"The most painless thing is to give in," Matthew Bowers laughed. "She won't turn loose, boys. She's like her mama that way."

"I'd like to see the church folks' faces when we all saunter in and sit down." Maxwell Dix smiled.

Jolie clapped her hands. "Yes, we're all going."

Strath Yarrow scratched the back of his neck. "Was there ever any doubt?"

The Bowers sisters rode in the big wagon behind Pilgrim and Stranger. Jolie wore her yellow satin dress with a large black ribbon on the back but no bustle. The trim was black lace, as was the ribbon that held down her white straw hat.

"How come you dressed up so fancy?"

"I don't think my rose dress is sufficiently clean after all that mud collapsed on it. I need to wash it again."

Essie leaned closer. "Really, how come you wore that dress?"

"Because it looks rather stunning, don't you think?" Jolie admitted.

"Ever'thin' looks stunning on you. I don't think I ever stunned a boy. Not with my looks anyway," Essie said. "I stunned Chester with my fist one time."

"I remember that."

Essie glanced over her shoulder. "How come Daddy brought the other team and wagon?"

"He's goin' to stay in town and wait for Mama to come home. I need to come back in time to straighten the schoolhouse for tonight's meeting."

"Can I stay with Daddy and the boys and wait for Mama?" Essie asked.

"Certainly."

Essie glanced back again. "This is almost like a parade. Our wagon, Strath and Landen in their buggy, Daddy and the boys with Mrs. DeMarco's team, and the four cowboys."

"Either a parade or a funeral."

"Ever'one is talkin' and laughin'. It can't be a funeral. I can't believe you talked them all into goin' to church," Essie said.

"We aren't in the door yet. But it's all your fault, Estelle Cinnia."

"Mine?"

"You challenged me yesterday with your question about why the Lord would bring so many men to our door. I decided that if the Lord is doing it, there must be some spiritual reason."

"So you decided to take them to church?"

"It *is* spiritual."

"What do you think Rev. Leyland will say?"

"I think he'll be delighted. You know how he prays for the lost around here," Jolie said.

"What about Mrs. Leyland?" Essie pressed.

"She'll ask them if they can sing, and would they like to be in the choir."

Essie started to giggle. "I was thinking about those four standin' up front with the McMasters sisters in the choir."

"Some things are difficult to imagine," Jolie concurred.

"What do you think Mrs. Fleister will say?"

"She'll pull me aside and say, 'Jolie, dear, those are not our kind of people.'"

Essie held her dress down as the wind caught it. "What would you do?"

"I would say, 'Mildred, honey, they're the Lord's kind of people. He came to seek and to save the lost.'"

Essie's eyes grew wide. "Really?"

"Probably not. But that's what I'd like to say."

"I think Mrs. Fleister will like Strath."

"Yes, once she finds out he's a widower, she'll adopt him for dinner every Sunday after church."

"Sometimes Mrs. Fleister is okay."

"Essie, sweetie, that's about all any of us can say, isn't it?"

The rigs were parked.

Horses were tied at the rails.

Well-dressed people filed into the church. On the concrete sidewalk out front, ten of them huddled as the one in a yellow dress gave a final inspection.

Jolie straightened her father's tie. "You look handsome, Daddy."

"I'd feel more handsome if Mama was on my arm."

"I know, Daddy . . . but Essie makes a beautiful substitute."

"Yes, she does."

Jolie retied the blue bow in the back of Essie's hair.

"You have a little smudge on your neck just below your right ear," Jolie whispered.

Essie rubbed her neck and licked her fingers. "I think it's raspberry jam."

"But we haven't had any raspberry jam since . . ."

"Don't think about it," Essie whispered.

"Are you goin' to spit on my hair?" Landen asked.

"Eh, no, your hair looks fine. Let me fasten the top button on your shirt," Jolie requested. "There. You look quite handsome."

"What about his daddy?" Strath Yarrow grinned.

"Well, Mr. Attorney, my prediction is that Mrs. Fleister will have you introduced to every eligible young woman within fifty miles by evening."

"Which one is Mrs. Fleister? I'll try to avoid her."

"Strath Yarrow, no one . . . *ever* . . . avoids Mrs. Fleister."

Jolie moved down the line. "Gibson Hunter Bowers, you said you'd brush your boots."

"I forgot." Gibs rubbed the toes of his boots on the back of his wool trouser legs. "Is that better?"

Jolie shook her head.

"Have you seen Miss April?" Lawson asked.

Jolie looked at the crowd filing into the church. "I haven't seen the Vockneys. Perhaps they're running late. Is that top button too tight?"

"It's sort of tight," Lawson replied.

"You need larger shirts. Why don't you unbutton the top button?"

"Do you think it would be all right?" Lawson asked.

"Yes, it would."

Lawson unfastened the button and let out a deep sigh.

She moved to the biggest of the cowboys who stood with hat in hand. "Charles Quintin LaPage, you look very nice. I don't believe I've seen you after a shave."

"Thanks, Miss Jolie," Chug replied. "I can scrub up kinda good, can't I?"

She squeezed his big, rough hand. "Yes, you can." Then she moved on. "Leppy, that black silk bandanna really looks nice with your black hair. But let me straighten it." She fussed at his bandanna. "Now, Mr. Verdue, don't be flashing those irresistible dimples at the ladies during the service. I don't want you distracting them from spiritual matters."

Maxwell Dix's blond hair draped down to his shoulders. "Are you goin' to fuss over me too?"

She pulled out her linen handkerchief, licked a corner of it, and then wiped his cheek beside the blond sideburn. "No," she laughed.

"Listen, there's a cute yellowed-haired girl in the choir. Her name is Celia Delaney. She faints real easy. So I don't want you winkin' at her, or she'll faint right there in the choir loft. You promise?"

"I can't believe I'm doin' this," Maxwell mumbled.

"Going to church?"

"Leavin' my gun on my saddle," he replied.

"No one ever had a gun stolen while in church," she insisted. *Lord, I have no idea if that's true. I hope it is.*

"How about me, Miss Jolie?"

She moved to the last man in line. "Shakey, you look fine."

"I'm nervous, Miss Jolie."

"Why don't you sit next to me."

"You don't mind?"

"Tanner sits on my right. You can sit on my left."

"Thank you, Miss Jolie."

"Shakey, I think you should take your knife off your belt for church."

"Yes, ma'am. I didn't know . . . eh, can I slip it in my boot?"

"That would be fine."

She strolled back up to the head of the line as Tanner Wells ambled over to them.

"Hi, darlin'," he called out. "You have lots of friends today."

"Jolie shamed them all into comin' to church with us," Essie told him.

"I think most of you know my Tanner," she said to the men. "Tanner Wells, this is Mr. Strath Yarrow, formerly of Chicago. He's going to buy the place between your folks' homestead and ours."

Strath Yarrow reached out his hand.

"And this fine-looking boy is his son Landen."

"Oh . . ." Tanner grabbed Strath's hand and shook it.

"Strath is a widower," Essie announced.

Tanner paused.

Jolie took his arm. "And contrary to popular opinion, I did not shame them into coming to church. Did I, boys?"

There was a chorus of "No, ma'ams."

Tanner held her arm as he led the procession up the front steps.

Most of the eyes at the Scottsbluff Baptist Church were focused on the front two pews on the west side of the building. Matthew Bowers, Essie, Tanner, Jolie, Shakey, Lawson, and April Vockney occupied the front row. Behind them sat Strath Yarrow, Landen, Leppy, Chug, Maxwell, and Gibs.

When they stood to sing, "Oh, God, Our Hope in Ages Past," it was Maxwell Dix who had the best voice. But it was Shakey Torrington who had all the words memorized.

Jolie sensed that each of the cowboys watched her to see when to sit and when to stand. Shakey jammed his hat back on after the opening prayer but quickly yanked it off when Jolie gently jabbed his ribs with her elbow.

Matthew Bowers sang a solo in the choir number, and Jolie watched as Celia Delaney stared at Maxwell Dix. Her mouth barely moved. Jolie was surprised to see Maxwell and Shakey volunteer when Rev. Leyland asked for help to replace shingles that had blown off the parsonage roof in the windstorm.

The church was silent as the offering plate was passed to the row behind them, and Chug LaPage leaned back and grumbled, "Mister, I reckon you can do better than that. I'm just a driftin' cowboy, but I put in more money than you did." The chagrined man dug for his wallet again.

Shakey sat straight up when Rev. Leyland read the text about the Good Samaritan. "I remember this one, Miss Jolie," he said.

Jolie patted his arm and nodded.

The reverend launched into the sermon, and she reached over and held Tanner's hand. *Mama holds Daddy's hand in church. Of course, Mama holds Daddy's hand everywhere they go. Sometimes she reminds me of April Vockney. Lord, please bring Mama home safe today. And, Lord, do Your spiritual work in my friends. I don't know what they're struggling with, but I know You can help.*

When they stood for the closing hymn, Leppy had to poke Chug to wake him. "I was dreamin' of heaven," he mumbled loud enough for Rev. Leyland to smile.

They filed out of the church, and Mrs. Fleister grabbed Jolie's arm and led her aside. "Jolie, dear . . ."

"Mrs. Fleister, I wanted to see you."

"You did?" the large woman seemed taken aback.

"Yes. Do you see the nice-lookin' man and his son?"

"His son?"

"That's Mr. Yarrow from Chicago, an attorney and a widower."

Mrs. Fleister's eyebrows raised like mountain peaks. "A widower. Poor dear."

"Yes, and I wondered . . ."

"Say no more, my Jolie." Mrs. Fleister sailed through the crowd toward the Yarrows.

"Where's Shakey?" Maxwell asked.

"He wanted to stay and talk to the reverend," Jolie said.

"I've been with him three years and have never heard him mention religion."

"Some keep a lot inside, I suppose," Jolie said.

A blonde girl tugged at her shoulder.

Jolie spun around. "Oh, Mr. Maxwell Dix, this is Celia Delaney."

"Jolie and I have been friends for a long time. Well, at least a month," Celia giggled. "You have a wonderful tenor voice, Mr. Dix. I could hear it in the choir."

He yanked off his hat and strolled to the street with the blonde.

Chug sauntered over to Jolie. "Do you see that man over there?" He pointed to a bald man in a neat, dark suit.

"That's Mr. Meynarde from the bank," Jolie informed him.

"Is he the church treasurer?" Chug asked.

"Yes, he is."

"He came over and thanked me for tellin' that stingy man to give more. He said that was the best offerin' they had in six months. Said if I was to come regular, he'd have me pass the plate ever' week. I think he was joshin' me."

Jolie leaned close to Chug's ear and whispered, "I think he might have been serious."

Leppy strolled over with Essie. "Miss Jolie, the boys and me want to take the Bowers family out to Sunday lunch at the hotel."

"Leppy, that's not necessary, but thank you anyway."

"Miss Jolie, we've been givin' you the opportunity to practice Christian charity by feedin' us. Are you goin' to deny us that same opportunity?"

Jolie shook her head and grinned. "You're a persuasive fellow, Mr. Verdue."

"And quite handsome as well," he added.

"Does that invitation include Tanner?" she asked.

"If you insist." Leppy smiled, revealing two deep dimples.

"I do."

"Yeah," Leppy laughed, "I figured you would."

It was three o'clock when Jolie drove the big wagon by herself out of Scottsbluff. Several men on horseback rode single file toward her. They pulled off the road and waited, tipping their hats as she rumbled along.

Men are still coming to town. I don't understand this, Lord. It's a matter that can be solved when reasonable people sit down and discuss it. It's as if a greater force is at work. What's bringing all these men here?

Perhaps at the meeting tonight they will find a solution. Daddy and Strath were together during dinner talking about legal matters. They can figure it out. I like Strath, Lord. Daddy likes him too—I can tell.

But he isn't Tanner.

Strath Yarrow needs a wife and a mother for Landen.

Tanner Wells needs Jolie Bowers.

There's a difference.

A big difference.

Stranger and Pilgrim settled into a rhythm. Jolie relaxed the lead lines and let them run. The constant bouncing of the wagon seat, the warm sunlight, and the wind in her face caused her eyelids to sag.

After I get home and change, I think I'll take a very short nap before I go clean the schoolhouse. It's been a good day. Now it would be nice to have a good evening.

I'm proud of Shakey Torrington, Lord. Whatever he needed to square with You, I know he did it. I could see it in his eyes. And that might be the most important thing I've been a part of since we moved to Nebraska. That and finding my Tanner.

Jolie slowed the team and turned off Telegraph Road down the lane to their homestead. *I don't think I've driven this rig completely alone before. I don't think I've done anything by myself since we moved here. It does seem rather strange. Our place doesn't seem remote when it's filled with people.*

She rolled past the sod house and parked the rig in front of the water trough. Jolie tied off the lines, plucked up her handbag, and climbed off the big wagon. She hiked across the yard. *Right now it feels empty, like we're on the edge of the earth.*

With her dress changed and her face washed, Jolie lay back on the living room bed and closed her eyes. The room was warm, a little stuffy, and still smelled of fried ham.

Her eyes felt heavy.

The mattress was soft.

She let out a slow, deep sigh.

And the pain in her back melted.

Until a voice shouted in from the yard, "Matthew Bowers, if you come out that door carrying a gun, you'll be shot on sight!"

Seven

Her bare feet hit the wooden floor when Jolie stood, and she could feel sweat around the collar of her dress. The air in the sod house hung heavy and stale.

What time is it? I overslept. I was dreaming something. . . . Someone shouted at me. . . . Did they tell me to wake up? I should never lie down. I'm much too tired to nap. Now I'll have to hurry to get down to the schoolhouse.

"We said, come out unarmed!" a deep voice bellowed.

"And don't carry any guns!" a higher voice added.

Jolie brushed her auburn hair back from her forehead. *I wasn't dreaming. What do they want? Unarmed? No guns? They're rather redundant.*

She stepped to the two-foot-square lone window to the left of the front door and peeked out.

"Someone's in there, Bob. I done seen the curtains move."

The man wearing coveralls waved a shotgun at the door. "Come on out without a weapon, Bowers. We know you're in there. You only got one door!"

"He could go through a window," the other man muttered.

Why do they want Daddy? Jolie stepped to the door and then scooted back to the other side of the room and picked up a mirror. *There's no excuse for not looking one's best.* She studied her hair.

"If you ain't out of the house by the time we count to ten, we start shootin' your horses, Bowers," the man yelled. "Bill, start countin'."

Jolie resat her hair in her combs. *That's a little better. I'm certainly going to pull on my shoes. I don't know these men. They're not going to see my bare feet.*

"Bill, I said to start countin'."

"Countin' down or countin' up?"

"It don't matter. Start countin'."

"I ain't goin' to count, Bob."

There was a pause. The deep voice softened. "You always been the counter, Bill—ever since you was small."

"I ain't countin' this time, Bob. It's an empty threat."

Jolie pulled on her stocking and then her shoe.

"How do you figure that?"

"'Cause you cain't kill them horses with your shotgun from way over here."

She pulled on her other stocking and shoe and began to lace the shoe.

"I could maim 'em."

"The way you shoot, you'd be lucky to annoy 'em, Bob."

"Then you ain't countin', Bill?"

"Nope, Bob. This time you're on your own."

Jolie checked her mirror one more time, opened the door, and stepped out on the porch. "Would you boys like me to count?"

Bill whipped off his hat. "It's a purdy lady, Bob."

"I can see that." Bob trained his shotgun toward the front door. "Lady, send your husband out. We want to talk to him, and we want to talk to him right now."

Bill waved what appeared to be a severely rusted cap-and-ball pistol at the other man. "Take your hat off, Bob."

The man in the coveralls lowered the shotgun to his lap. "What?"

"You're supposed to remove your hat when talkin' to a lady. Mama taught us that much," Bill insisted.

The big man pulled off a tattered brown slouch hat. "Ma'am, send your husband out. We're the Condor boys. Maybe you've heard of us."

"Ain't nobody in Nebraska ever heard of us, Bob."

"Maybe she ain't from Nebraska, Bill."

"I don't reckon anyone outside of Ash Flat, Arkansas, has ever heard of us."

"They will after today. Yes, sir, Bill. This time they'll remember the Condor boys."

Jolie shaded her eyes with her hand. "Who're you looking for?"

"Ol' man Bowers," Bob replied. Tobacco dribbled down his chin, and he wiped it off with the back of his hand, then smeared it on the neck of the chocolate brown horse. "The one that led the riot in Lincoln."

"Not Abe Lincoln," Bill added. "He's dead. But Lincoln, Nebraska. It's mostly dead, after dark anyway."

"My father is Matthew Bowers," Jolie reported. "But he's not at home."

"He's her father, Bob."

"I heard her, Bill."

"My father is not here, boys."

"Did you hear that?" Bill murmured.

Bob scratched his unshaven face. "How do we know we can believe her?"

"She ain't never lied to us before," Bill declared.

"That's because we ain't never seen her before."

"That's true, Bob. I ain't never seen her. I don't forget the purdy ones. She's just as purdy as she can be."

"What do you want?" *Lord, maybe I am still dreaming. This conversation is ludicrous.*

"We got ourselves a plan," Bill grinned.

"Don't tell her the plan," Bob cautioned.

"She ain't goin' to use it herself."

"I know she ain't, but it's bad luck to tell a plan before you carry it out."

"It is? How come you told me this plan, Bob?"

"Never mind, Bill." The big man turned back to Jolie. "Do you expect your daddy to come home today?"

"Yes, I do."

"Is your mama in there?"

"No, I'm alone."

"I'll swan . . . She's alone, Bob. What're we goin' to do now?"

"I guess we wait."

"Yeah, he'll come home after the schoolhouse meeting."

"It'll be too late then."

"It will?" Bill asked.

"The railroad ain't goin' to give us money for kidnapping him after the meeting. Especially if he stirs them all up again."

"They might give us somethin'," Bill mused.

"It won't be a hundred cash dollars—you can bet on that."

"Kidnapping my father? What're you two talking about? Do you work for Mr. Culburtt?"

Bob scratched his chin. "Who's he?"

"Boys, I have to go to a meeting soon. Would you like to come back and talk to my father some other day?"

"You ain't goin' nowhere," the big man growled.

"Bob, don't wave that shotgun at the lady. It could go off accidental. You remember Aunt Beulah."

"If I don't wave it, how will she know I'm serious, Bill?"

"That's what you said to Aunt Beulah—rest her soul."

"Lady, you ain't goin' nowhere." Bob slid off the brown horse, and Jolie noticed that his saddle didn't have a left stirrup. "Water the horses, Bill."

Bill jumped off a tattered McClellan saddle. "How come I always have to water the horses?"

Bob scratched the back of his neck with the barrel of his shotgun. "'Cause you're the youngest."

"That ain't my fault."

"Water the horses, Bill!"

"Someday you ain't goin' to have me around to water and feed your horse."

"You keep promisin' that." Bob hiked over to Jolie.

Bill hesitated. "Where are you goin', Bob?"

"To see if she's got some grub."

"You got to promise to save me some, or I ain't goin' to water your horse. And he'll fall over dead in the middle of the desert and leave you stranded, and the buzzards will eat ya."

"I promise to save you some grub."

"Do you promise on a stack of fine shinleys?"

"Yeah."

Bill led the horses toward the barn.

Jolie folded her arms across her chest. *Lord, is this still a dream? These two aren't real, are they?*

"Where's your food, lady?" Bob stepped up on the porch.

She pursed her lips at the stench. "In the kitchen. Where did you expect?"

Bob shoved open the front door and stomped in. "Whoa . . . you got yourself a nice house here, ma'am. This is very roomy."

Jolie followed him in but left the door open wide. *This is a tiny two-room sod house stuffed with belongings. No one has ever called it roomy. Where do these two live? In a hole in the ground?*

He meandered over to the shelf near the woodstove and tore off a hunk of bread. "You got any meat?" he mumbled. "I like meat."

"I believe I have some ham." *Lord, I need to get rid of these two. I can't believe Mr. Culburtt or anyone would hire them. I must get to the schoolhouse.*

"You got any potatoes?" he asked.

Jolie motioned at a green pottery crock. "Just those in the bowl."

Bob picked up a raw potato and took a bite.

"Did you want me to cook it first?" Jolie blurted out.

He put the potato, minus the bite, back into the bowl. "Oh, say," he mumbled, "that would be fine, wouldn't it?"

Jolie grabbed the big black iron skillet and shoved it on the cookstove. She plucked a knife from the chop block.

"What do you intend to do with that knife?"

"Peel the potatoes."

"Peeled and cooked." Bob grinned. "This is just like a cafe! What's your name?" he asked her.

"I'm usually called Miss Jolie." She stabbed a potato with her knife.

"Jolene? That's a purdy name. You surely are purdy."

"My name is Jolie. J-O-L-I-E."

"We had a cousin by the name of Jolene." Bob peered out the front window at the bare yard. "At least, I think her name was Jolene."

Jolie studied the iron frying pan. "Bob, would you like the ham cooked in with the potatoes?"

He spun around with a wide grin on his face. "Yes, ma'am. Do you have any of them little red hot peppers?"

"No."

"That's okay. Come to think about it, maybe Jolene wasn't a cousin of ours," he mumbled. "She must have weighed three hundred pounds—that much I can remember. Some things a man don't forget."

I really don't have time to feed them. There must be some other way to handle this. As Jolie bent over and shoved two small sticks of wood into the firebox, she felt a hand grab her hip. She stood up suddenly and jerked her head straight back. It cracked into Bob's face. He let out a yelp, and when she spun around, he was holding a bloody nose.

"You shouldn't have done that," he growled.

"Bob, it's not the worst thing that's goin' to happen to you."

"And just what do you mean by that?"

"Have you ever heard of Mrs. Iron Skillet Wainwright from Helena, Montana?"

"Nope."

"Good."

The iron skillet slammed into Bob's head just above the right ear, and he dropped to the floor unconscious, still holding his nose. Jolie stared at the motionless body. *Lord, I don't want him dead. I just want him gone.*

She had just put the heavy skillet back on the stove when Bill wandered in, hat in hand.

"Bob, what're you doin' on the floor?"

Jolie spun around, grabbing the skillet. "Bill, do you want your ham cooked in with the potatoes?"

A wide grin broke across his face. "Yes, ma'am. Cooked potatoes! You're treatin' us good."

"Would you like some of those little red peppers stirred in too?"

"That would be mighty fine, ma'am." He stepped over closer to his brother. "Say, what happened to Bob?"

"I believe he's resting." Carrying the skillet, Jolie stepped closer to him. "Have you two been sleeping well at night?"

"Mama always had us sleep on the floor. She said she didn't want us gettin' the furniture dirty," Bill mused.

Jolie scooted between the men so that Bill could no longer see Bob. "Well, he doesn't look too comfortable to me." She forced a smile.

Bill scratched under his arm. "Say, what's your name? You surely are a purdy girl."

"My name is Jolie—I mean, Jolene," she replied.

"How about that. We used to have a neighbor girl named Jolene. At least, I think that was her name."

Jolie stepped back away from the man on the floor. "It will take me a while to cook this food. Would you like to take a nap with Bob?"

"Come to think about it, maybe that Jolene wasn't a neighbor. But she was all skin and bones—that much I can remember. Some things a man don't forget." Bill pointed across the room. "Can I have some of that bread?"

"Help yourself." She watched as he meandered over, tore off a hunk of bread, and then wandered back. The iron skillet felt heavy in her hand. "You could take a nap while I'm cooking these potatoes."

"I ain't sleepy. Course, Bob always could sleep better than me.

He slept through a tornado once. Shoot, it lifted him up and carried him clean out to the barn. Funniest thing I ever saw. He claims he don't remember a thing."

The iron skillet began to sag in her hands in front of her. "Are you sure you don't want to take a nap too? You could lie down there next to your brother."

Bill bent low and stared at his brother. "I think he's bleedin', Miss Jolene."

"Oh, my . . . wake him up."

Bill dropped down to his knees and shook Bob's shoulders. "He surely is a sound sleeper."

The iron skillet whammed the back of Bill's head. He dropped on top of his brother.

All right, Jolie Bowers, now what're you going to do? You've got to get to the schoolhouse. You're not going to leave these two at your house.

Lord, I don't know why You brought them to my door. For the life of me, I can't figure out any spiritual good that will come from it. But they're not going to make me late. I'm not about to have a community meeting in my schoolhouse until after I straighten it up.

Jolie found that tying up the men's hands and feet with lead ropes was the easy part. Dragging them out to the front porch was more difficult.

She drove the big wagon up next to the porch and pulled out the tailgate. She used it as a ramp from the step to the wagon. With concerted effort at pulling, pushing, and lifting, she managed to get both men into the back of the wagon. Bob was shaking his head and starting to mumble when she tied his filthy bandanna into his mouth. She did the same to an unconscious Bill and then climbed out of the wagon and tied their horses to the back.

"Bob, if you two lie real still, I promise I won't shoot you. And you know I've never lied to you before."

Jolie went inside and washed her hands and face.

I will not wear this now dirty, smelly dress to the meeting. I'm afraid they'll get the yellow satin after all. I know, I'll be overdressed. But other than opening the door and closing it when the meeting's over, I won't have much of a role. Perhaps I'll get some things ready for class tomorrow.

Jolie hurried to pull on her good dress in the back room and tied on her hat. She grabbed her handbag and opened the door just as a black leather buggy pulled into the yard. Both men in it wore suits and ties.

"Mr. Culburtt, what're you doing out here? You should be at home with those ankles raised up."

"Thanks for your concern, Miss Bowers. We have some urgent company business. This is Mr. Hubert R. Monroe, vice president of the railroad."

She walked over to the carriage to greet the man with silk top hat and dark gray wool suit. "Are you looking for my father?"

"No, we understand he is, eh, incarcerated in Lincoln. We wanted to see you," Mr. Culburtt declared.

"Actually," Monroe said, clearing his throat, "I came to see you and your mother. But I understand your mother is also in Lincoln."

"What did you need?" Jolie asked.

Mr. Culburtt pointed across the yard. "Excuse me, Miss Bowers, are there two men bound and gagged in that wagon?"

She glanced back. Bob and Bill wiggled and grumbled. "Yes, there are."

Culburtt glanced around the yard. "What exactly is going on out here?"

She folded her arms and stared at the railroad men. "I was hoping you could tell me."

"Tell you what?"

"Bob and Bill Condor seemed to think the railroad would pay them big money for kidnapping Daddy and keeping him away from tonight's meeting."

"Bob and Bill Condor?" the vice president mumbled. "What's this all about, Culburtt? I specifically said that all railroad personnel were to avoid that meeting."

"I have no idea. I didn't hire them. I won't pay them. I don't care if your daddy makes it home for the meeting," Culburtt declared. "If they claimed to be hired by me, they're liars."

Jolie glanced over at the big farm wagon. "No, I don't think anyone hired them. Bob and Bill have it in their heads that it would be advantageous to the railroad if Matthew Bowers did not attend the meeting at the schoolhouse. But how did they get such an idea? I don't think they're capable of an original idea between the two of them."

Monroe held his top hat in his lap. "But your father is in jail in Lincoln."

"Daddy came home last night," Jolie declared.

"Good heavens," Monroe gasped, "the authorities turned him loose?"

"Yes, but mother went to Lincoln."

"But I assumed he wouldn't be here," Monroe muttered.

"So you wanted to visit a man's wife and daughter when he's gone?" she questioned.

"I just wanted to avoid any violence, I assure you. How did he get home so quickly? There was no train last night . . . except . . . mine," Monroe mumbled.

Bill thrashed about, and Culburtt waved his hand toward the big wagon. "What happened to them?"

"I think my cooking didn't agree with them. Now I'm late. I need to clean the school and open it up for the meeting. I'm sorry Mama isn't here. What did you need to see me about?"

Culburtt pointed at the vice president's brown leather satchel. "Mr. Monroe has a presentation to make."

Jolie surveyed the case. "A what?"

"Oh behalf of a grateful railroad, I have a conferral to make," Monroe explained.

"Now?" Jolie protested. "I really must be going."

"Mr. Monroe needs to journey on later tonight. I'm afraid his time is limited," Culburtt insisted.

"Especially since Matthew Bowers is not in a Lincoln jail?" Jolie pressed.

"Perhaps you should go ahead and make the presentation," Culburtt told the railroad executive.

"It would be inappropriate to give a citation when Mama isn't here," Jolie protested. "She's the one who drove the wagon."

"I understand that," Monroe mumbled. "Culburtt is right. I should avoid confrontation and yet demonstrate the railroad's gratitude."

"That would look good in the newspapers, wouldn't it?" Jolie remarked.

"Quite. However, since she is in Lincoln, I feel I need to proceed. Are there other credible witnesses?"

"No one is here," Jolie replied, "except Bill and Bob over there. It would be a stretch to call them credible. Perhaps you could come back later. Mama will be coming home in time for her and Daddy to make the schoolhouse meeting. In fact, they might be there already."

"Where is the schoolhouse?" Monroe asked.

"Just a few miles down the road," Culburtt replied.

"No, we're not going that way," Monroe insisted. "I do not want to be within five miles of that meeting."

"What about your presentation and speech?" Culburtt asked him.

"Speech?" Jolie asked.

"A short one, of course. I have copies for the press."

"Perhaps you should just give it to me and Miss Bowers," Culburtt said.

Monroe pulled some papers from his vest pocket. "Well, I did have a few notes. We have to have witnesses. This just isn't what I had planned."

Jolie glanced at the carriage. "Mr. Culburtt, does this all seem a little strange to you?"

"I couldn't agree with you more."

"Perhaps we could come to town tomorrow. You could inform the newspaper, even stack the crowd with railroad men," Jolie pressed. "I have to go to the school now."

"But I need to assure the board of trustees of the railroad and the public that I personally expressed our deepest gratitude."

"What time is it, Mr. Culburtt?" Jolie interrupted.

He pulled out his watch. "Almost five o'clock."

"I'm sorry, gentlemen. Some will be showing up early for this meeting, and I'm not about to let them in my schoolhouse before I straighten it. Now if you'll excuse me."

"What about my presentation?" Monroe huffed.

"I'll let Mr. Culburtt know when Mama gets home, and perhaps we could plan something then."

"But heroism and sacrifice can never go unheralded, no matter what the source."

"That's a very nice line, Mr. Monroe. Did you write it yourself?"

"I did have some help, but I assure you it was heartfelt."

"Thank you very much. What Mother, Essie, and I did was no more than any Good Samaritan would do. We only did what our Christian conscience dictated." Jolie climbed up in the wagon.

"But what about my presentation?" Monroe called out.

"I'm sure it was very nice. I'll read about it in the newspaper. You are certainly welcome to come to the schoolhouse. Mama could already be there."

"Yes, but your father could be there also."

Mr. Culburtt pointed at her wagon. "What about those two men?"

"They're going to the meeting with me. You and Mr. Monroe are welcome, and I promise I won't hogtie you."

She slapped the lead lines. Pilgrim and Stranger galloped out of the yard and up the treeless lane. When she reached the top of the rise near the schoolhouse and looked down the other side, the late afternoon sun cast long shadows across the land. Several wagons and carriages were parked in front of the sod schoolhouse.

Jolie drove the big wagon past the building and far into the field behind it. She snubbed Stranger and Pilgrim up to the posts behind the privies and then glanced back at the two men in the wagon.

"Now, Bob and Bill, I'm goin' to leave you back here because if I take you inside, well, you can imagine what could happen. If you lie real still and don't move, I think you'll be safe. Once someone finds out the famous Condor Brothers are back here, they'll want to go down in history, and . . . well, I can't guarantee your safety. Just take little nap and don't make any noise."

Jolie patted the horses as she walked by them. "That goes for you two also."

As she hiked toward the sod building, Ernie Vockney scooted out toward her. "You parked a long ways away, Miss Jolie."

"I expect a crowd, don't you, Mr. Vockney?"

"Did your daddy get home?"

"Yes."

"That's wonderful. I didn't see him with you." He nodded toward the little buildings out back. "Is he . . ."

"He didn't come with me."

"Oh, I heard you talkin' and I figured . . ."

"Sometimes I need to settle Stranger and Pilgrim down." Jolie walked with Mr. Vockney toward the sod schoolhouse. "Daddy and Mama will be coming straight out from Scottsbluff."

"We heard he got arrested."

"Yes, that's true."

"Oh, that's wonderful." Vockney beamed. "I knew he was the right man to send to Lincoln. Our Scottsbluff hero."

Jolie stared at Mr. Vockney's gray eyes. "He was falsely accused, but I'll let him explain."

Mrs. Vockney and the girls waited on the steps. Cart and Emma Meeker sat at their wagon. To their right stood a buckboard with five cowboys. All five pulled their hats off when she approached.

"You the school marm?" a drover with curly red hair asked.

"Yes, I'm Jolie Bowers."

"We heard you was the purdiest girl in Nebraska."

She studied the freckles that peeked through the dirt on his face. "Now who would tell you something like that?"

"Pete Toole." The words came out like a lazy spit. "And he knows the girls."

Jolie bit her lip to keep from giggling. "Eh, I don't think I know Pete."

A blond cowboy who looked no older than Lawson slicked down his greased hair with his hand. "Pete works on the Horseshoe BA, next to the Double O, Miss Jolie."

She glanced at the boy's eyes. "I do know Captain Richardson and Jocko and others on the Double O."

"They ain't more than ten, fifteen miles from our place if there was a road, but there ain't," he announced.

"I'll have you all wait out here just a little while longer while I straighten up the classroom. I'll ring the school bell when you can come in."

"I ain't been in a schoolhouse in a long, long time, Miss Jolie," the red-haired cowboy remarked.

"You ain't been in any kind of house in a long time," one of the others bellowed.

Jolie had Mr. Vockney and Cart Meeker shove the desks against the wall. They carried in the benches from in front of the school. With everything in place, the lanterns trimmed, and the large Nebraska map hanging in front of the room, Jolie strolled outside. The sun was an orange half-circle on the western horizon. The front yard and drive had filled with rigs, horses, and people. Captain Richardson and several men who looked like ranchers huddled behind a black surrey.

"Captain, the school is ready," Jolie announced. "I thought I'd ring the bell when you wanted to begin the meeting."

Richardson pulled his watch from his vest pocket but didn't look at it. "Sort of waitin' for your daddy."

"He stayed in town for the afternoon westbound. Mama was supposed to be on it."

"The westbound went by about thirty minutes ago," one of the other ranchers informed her.

"Then they should be here fairly soon," Jolie said.

"That is, if they let any more through." Richardson pointed to the top of the rise south of the school. Silhouettes of cowboys on horseback dotted Telegraph Road. "We've seen at least one rig turn around and head back."

In the shadows of twilight, Jolie squinted her eyes. "Who's up there?"

"Galen Faxon and his railroad gunmen," Richardson announced.

"What're they doing?" she asked.

A leather-faced, gray-headed man spun his hat in his hands. "That's what we've been wondering."

Jolie tugged at the black lace cuffs on her yellow satin dress sleeve. "Did anyone go ask them?"

"I don't reckon we wanted the shootin' to start before the meetin'," Richardson murmured.

"Shooting?" Jolie snapped. "Nonsense. There will be no shooting around my school. Whose surrey is this?"

A gray-haired man with a Montana crease in the crown of his felt hat cleared his throat. "It's mine, Miss Jolie."

"Would you drive me up there? I want to talk to Mr. Faxon."

"Me? Drive you?" he gasped.

"I'll drive it then." She climbed into the surrey.

"I'll drive you," Captain Richardson offered.

"Captain," the gray-haired man exclaimed, "we need you to run this meeting and help us figure out what to do! Don't get yourself shot."

Richardson tugged his hat down in the front. "If I don't come back, I reckon you'll know what to do."

The captain drove halfway up the rise and then slowed. "Just how close do you intend to get?"

"Right next to Mr. Faxon. He's on the black horse."

"Yeah, I know which one he is. I'm surprised that you do."

Eight cowboys circled the surrey. "Howdy, Miss Jolie," the tall, thin one called out. "We didn't know it was you."

"Miss Jolie." Faxon tipped his hat. "You got a new driver?" He turned to Captain Richardson. "Howdy, Emmett."

"Galen, it's been awhile."

"You said you'd shoot me on sight when we met again."

"I still might," Richardson replied.

"I take it you two know each other," Jolie said.

Faxon sat on his black horse with his right hand resting on the walnut grip of his revolver. "It's a long story neither of us wants to remember."

Richardson shrugged. "We'll leave it at that."

"Did you come up here to see me?" Faxon asked Jolie.

"Folks at the schoolhouse wonder why you're blocking the road."

"We aren't blocking the road, Miss Jolie," one of the cowboys called out. "We're just parked here and watchin'."

"We heard that a meeting was being called to gather the troops against the railroad. This isn't an official visit. We haven't been hired yet, but I wanted to find out what we're goin' to be up against. There are always some things they forget to tell you," Faxon said. "I don't like surprises."

Jolie brushed her hair back out of her eyes. "Mr. Faxon, it sounds like you're planning for a battle." *I forgot my hat. I can't believe I left it at the schoolhouse.*

"Isn't that what Emmett and his bunch are doing?"

She glanced back at the people gathered in front of the school. "No, this is a community meeting to discuss a community problem and seek a workable answer."

"There're a lot of cowboys down there who aren't farmers or ranchers, and they're all packing guns," the tall, thin cowboy pointed out. "I don't reckon they came just to visit and vote."

"There are also women and children down there. Did you notice that?" Jolie snapped. "What kind of man would bring his wife and children if he thought there would be gunfire?"

"I reckon you're right there, Miss Jolie. We really ain't expectin' a ruckus down at the schoolhouse. That's why we're parked up here.

We're just watchin'—that's all," a big man in a brown leather vest offered.

"Then I want you to all come down to the meeting with me," Jolie announced.

"That's crazy, Miss Bowers," the captain growled. "We need a meeting to make some plans—not have hired guns staring over our shoulders."

"Captain, these men aren't much different from your vaqueros and drovers, are they? Both sides might have to put their lives on the line someday soon. I believe they all need to know what they're gambling on. Nobody stays in a poker game without knowing what the pot is. Isn't that right, Mr. Faxon?"

"Do you have any idea what you're suggesting, Miss Jolie?" Galen Faxon replied. "This isn't a schoolyard fight you're trying to break up."

"I'm well aware of the seriousness of the evening, Mr. Faxon. Either take your men back to town, or come join us in the meeting, but lurking up on this hill will only make matters worse. Fear of the unknown often produces foolish acts."

Faxon surveyed his men and then looked at Captain Richardson. "I'm ridin' in, Emmett."

"I figured you would," the rancher murmured. "You know, I can't guarantee ever'one's behavior."

"Nor can I," Faxon replied.

Galen Faxon and his crew sat down on the desks and benches on the south side of the room as the others filed in to the north side. Conversations ceased only for a moment when the gunmen came in, then resumed. Most of the children stayed outside.

Mr. and Mrs. Wells came in and sat on the last available bench. Jolie counted sixteen ranch cowboys, eight ranchers, twenty-one homestead men, and twelve homestead women.

Faxon had seven men with him.

The crowd quieted when Leppy, Chug, Maxwell, and Shakey sauntered in.

"Which side you sittin' on, Verdue?" Faxon called out.

"I reckon we'll sit smack dab in the middle," Leppy said.

"That's a dangerous position."

"So far only Miss Jolie is in the middle, and so I reckon we toss our chips in with hers."

Jolie paced in front of the crowd. "We're just waiting for a few minutes until my father gets here."

"Miss Jolie!" a boy screamed from the schoolyard.

Everyone turned to watch Bullet Wells sprint into the room. "Did you know there are two men hogtied and gagged in your wagon?"

Jolie's hands flew to her face. "Oh, my . . . Bob and Bill. I forgot about them! Leppy, will you, Maxwell, and the boys go get them out of my wagon and bring them in here?"

Leppy scratched the back of his neck. "Do you want us to untie them?"

"By all means, no. Just stack them in the corner for now. I'll explain later."

The four men scooted out the front door of the school.

"How come they're all tied up?" Bullet asked.

"I was late to the meeting and just didn't have time to cook them anything," she blurted out.

Everyone in the building broke out in laughter.

Bill and Bob had just been propped in the corner when Essie burst into the schoolroom. "It's crowded in here," she declared. "And it's stuffy."

"Young Miss Bowers," Captain Richardson said, "I presume your daddy is with you."

"Yep. And so is Mama and Gibs and Lawson, but Lawson was lookin' for April. So I don't reckon we'll see much of him. And Gibs is chasing a porcupine."

While the crowd laughed, Essie scooted over next to Jolie. "Tanner's coming out."

"He is?"

"Yep, he wanted to see what happens. He's with Strath and Landen."

The entrance of Matthew Bowers brought applause from 90 percent of the people in the room. Lissa Bowers held his arm. Many of the children who had been outside now crowded the back entry, peeking into the hot, stuffy classroom.

Captain Richardson quieted the crowd with his hands. "I reckon before we start to discuss any plan of action, we all want to hear a report on Lincoln from Mr. Bowers."

He kissed his wife on the cheek as she released him to the front of the crowd.

Jolie watched her mother's eyes. *She's got her man back. All is well with the world for Lissa Bowers now. Thank You, Lord. I don't think any woman has ever loved a man as deeply as Mama loves Daddy. I can only hope to watch and learn.*

Jolie straightened her father's tie as he turned to address the crowd. Over six feet, he was taller than most in the room, with hair graying at the temples and a thick mustache. Jolie thought he looked the perfect orator.

"I'll be happy to report what I know. Most of what you read in the newspapers was wrong. I'm glad to see the railroad men here. That surprises me though."

"Miss Jolie invited us," the tall cowboy next to Galen Faxon blurted out.

"This isn't official," Faxon reported. "It just seemed like we ought to know what we're bein' hired to do."

"Knowing my daughter," Matthew Bowers continued, "I suppose those two smelly, hogtied men in the back have something to do with Miss Jolie as well?"

"They aggravated me, Daddy," Jolie replied.

"A mistake I'm sure they won't make again. Do you suppose we could sit them up and slip off their gags? That doesn't look too comfortable."

"Only if they promise to behave themselves," she demanded.

Chug sat Bill and Bob up so they leaned against the wall and pulled down their gags.

"She leveled us with her fryin' pan," Bill grumbled.

"Are you goin' to hang us?" Bob gasped.

"Do you need hangin'?" Chug laughed.

"I don't," Bill replied, "but I ain't speakin' for Bob."

"I told you that was an accident," Bob mumbled.

"There isn't a tree for fifty miles; so we won't hang you," Chug replied. "But we might tie a rope around your feet and drag you down the road."

"Shoot, that won't be too bad, Bob. Remember that time I got my foot caught in the stirrup of that tall brown horse we stole? I hung on for miles."

"Until you hit the prickly pear," Bob added.

"Gag them, Chug," Jolie called out.

"We'll be quiet, Miss Jolie," Bill whined.

She nodded, and Matthew Bowers quieted the crowd.

"I was arrested in Lincoln because of a misunderstanding. I tried to prevent violence. That's exactly what I want to accomplish tonight.

"My family moved to Nebraska to homestead. We've only been here a short while, as most of you know. We have no intentions of ever moving again. We came to farm. With the Lord's grace, my wife's ability, and the strong courage of my children, I just might make it as a farmer.

"The captain and some of you others have ranches up in the high country. You're cattlemen, and from all I've heard, very good ones. The railroad has just spent a tremendous amount of money laying tracks out here. They aren't getting a lot of traffic yet. They want to stay in business, just like us homesteaders and you ranchers.

"There has to be a solution that will accomplish that. One thing for sure, no one in this room wants to get shot—not me, not Richardson, not Leppy Verdue, and not Mr. Faxon.

"Things are changing on the prairie. Farming will be different.

It used to be that if a man could feed his family and buy a few supplies, that was all he needed. But now we have farmers' associations, cooperatives, irrigation districts, and shipping to the cities back east.

"The cattle business is different. The open ranges are a thing of the past. Barbed wire is starting to crisscross the land. And since that hard winter five years ago, winter feed has become necessary every place north of Oklahoma.

"Railroads are different. There's not just one railroad. There are many. Most every town will be linked to one, and just like homesteaders, railroad men have families and futures to think about. They have to make a profit or go out of business.

"And justice is different. Twenty years ago, even ten years ago, a man had to be ready to shoulder a gun and stand for what was right. It was the only way to stop injustice and revenge.

"We are a people who can fight. We proved that. We can fight until we die. We all have friends, some even loved ones, who proved that at Antietam . . . and Gettysburg . . . and Missionary Ridge. No one in this room is a coward. Every one of us who came out here knew it's a rough and rugged land. We weren't looking for an easy life."

Jolie scrutinized the faces in the crowd. *Mama's right. When Daddy speaks, everyone stops to listen. It's his deep voice, his confidence, his manner. Mama's watching his every word but thinking about a long walk without the children.*

Tanner Wells and Strath and Landen Yarrow squeezed into the back of the room. *Tanner Wells, you'd better look this way.* He pulled off his hat, stared at her, and winked. *And I know exactly how you feel, Mama.*

Matthew Bowers paced in front of the crowd. "It took courage and strength to move a thousand head of cattle up on the shelf ten years ago and build a ranch in the wilds. Captain, in the past ten years, how many head would you say you lost to drought, cold, disease, and rustlers?"

"Includin' the big freeze of '86-'87?" Richardson asked.

"Yes."

"Over 850 head at least," Richardson reported.

"At a low price of twenty dollars a head, how much does that make, Jolie?" her father asked.

"It's $17,000, Daddy."

"How many in this room can still be in business after losing $17,000 worth of goods?" Mr. Bowers challenged.

Jolie stepped back and looked at Richardson and the ranchers.

Her father continued, "As you know, most of the ranchers are older. Most have no families. The land was too rugged and violent for women and children when they moved here. They sacrificed one dream in order to make another come true."

She studied the men's faces. *Lord, maybe that's what life is about. Sacrificing one dream for a higher one. But do we always know when we've chosen the best one?*

"And it takes courage to homestead western Nebraska," Mr. Bowers said. "Everyone knows the land is better to the east. But the land there is gone. For many of us, this is our last move. There is nowhere else to go.

"Take Cart Meeker over there. Emma, introduce your children to the crowd."

The small woman stood and cleared her throat. "We have four girls—Prissy, Pammie, Patsy, and Peteluma."

"Mr. and Mrs. Meeker, have those cute little girls of yours ever had to go to bed hungry because homesteading was such a struggle?" Matthew Bowers inquired.

Mrs. Meeker covered her mouth with her hands and nodded.

Mr. Meeker cleared his throat. "I aim to see that don't ever happen again."

Jolie tried to catch Emma Meeker's eyes, but the woman's calico bonnet covered them as she stared at the floor. *I just wonder how many in this room have absolutely nowhere to go if this homesteading fails.*

"So don't underestimate the homesteaders' courage." Matthew Bowers pointed to the men against the wall. "And it takes courage to hike into a hostile crowd, like Galen Faxon and the others have done. Mr. Faxon, I read once about an attack on a cattle crew just across the Rio Grande at some place called Mesa Diablo. How many men did you have with you?"

"Eleven, including me."

"How many would you estimate attacked you?"

"Maybe 150, 200. Too many to count."

"How many times were you shot that day?"

"You mean bullets or arrows?" Faxon asked.

"Both."

"Two bullets, one arrow."

"How many of your men survived?"

"Just three of us."

Jolie watched her father and Galen Faxon talk as if there were no other people in the room. *I like Mr. Faxon, Lord. I've never known anyone with such a reputation before. But I like him. He knows who he is. He sees things clearly. He can make split-second decisions. And he remembers what it's like to love and hurt and lose.*

Matthew Bowers slowly surveyed the entire crowd. "Whatever is decided here tonight is not a question of courage. Every man and woman in the room has demonstrated courage."

"Except maybe those two that Jolie hogtied," Essie blurted out.

Jolie glanced back at the two men tied in the corner. *Lord, I clobbered them both but meant them no lasting harm. I wanted to swat them away like annoying flies. Maybe that's wrong. You created them. You don't make mistakes. You must have a plan and a place even for Bob and Bill. As long as it isn't too close to Scottsbluff.*

"Here's my point. We don't have to prove courage tonight. We have to prove compromise. We want to find a way that we can all stay in business and stay alive. So here's my suggestion. I say we have Miss Bowers keep a record of questions brought up at this meeting, that we select some representatives, and that we sit down and resolve as many issues with the railroad as we can."

"We done tried that," one of the homesteaders called out.

"Let's try it again."

"What if the railroad don't want to meet with us?"

Jolie stepped in front of her father. "I know Mr. Culburtt and Mr. Monroe will discuss it. I talked to both of them this afternoon."

"We can talk until we're broke," one of the ranchers grumbled.

"Give us a week," Matthew Bowers implored. "Let's come to a solution by next Sunday."

"Will we have another meeting?" someone called out.

"Yes."

"Let's meet in the afternoon and bring dinner with us," Mrs. Vockney suggested.

"I think that's a wonderful idea," Jolie replied.

"Are me and Bob invited?" Bill hollered.

Jolie was the last one out of the schoolhouse. Tanner was sitting on the front step. She sat down next to him. "Did everyone leave already?"

"I reckon some thought it was late. Others were just happy to be headed home without any shooting."

She slipped her arm around him. "I'm glad you came."

When his arm circled her waist, Jolie felt herself relax.

"Your daddy is quite some speaker."

"Hmmm."

"Hey, and I like Strath Yarrow," Tanner added.

"Hmmm."

"I think I'll stay at my folks' place tonight and go back to the shop early in the mornin'."

"Hmmm."

"Is that all you're goin' to say?"

"I'm just sighing," Jolie murmured.

"I know. . . . It feels good, doesn't it?"

She held onto Tanner's arm. "Before I met you, Tanner Wells, I didn't know how good silence felt."

"I take it that's a compliment."

"Yes, it is. My life can be so hectic some days, and I'm so busy.

Sometimes it's my own fault. Often it's just the things that happen around me. Then I catch a moment like this. A moonlit night. My sweetie sitting next to me. Our hearts visiting without words. And I just want to sit here all night long."

Tanner's voice was deep. Soft. "I reckon we could do that until your mama got worried."

"Daddy would get worried—not Mama. Mama knows how I feel." Jolie laid her head on his shoulder. "What're you thinking about, Tanner Wells?"

"June 14th is a long time away."

Jolie kissed his cheek, then giggled. "You too, huh?"

"Yeah. Whew." He tugged her face close and brushed a kiss across her lips.

"Oh my," she murmured. "Oh my."

Tanner stood up and pulled her to her feet.

"Are we leaving?" she asked.

"I'm listenin' to my head, darlin'. My heart is lost in yours. I reckon you know that."

They walked around behind the schoolhouse arm in arm. "How are you getting to your folks' house?" she asked.

"I figured I'd walk or hitch a ride."

"Hmmm. I suppose I could give you a ride."

"Do you want to hogtie me and toss me in the back?" he laughed.

"If I hogtied you, we'd both be in real trouble."

He helped her up into the wagon and then pulled himself up and plopped down next to her. "You're a lot like your daddy."

"Oh, it must be our mustaches," she giggled.

"Jolie, both you and your daddy shine when you get in front of a crowd."

"I must admit, I like being up front. I hope it's not to show off. I want to know everything that's going on. I want to see every face and expression."

"Jolie, sometimes I worry that you won't be very happy staying at home raising our children."

She threw her arms around his neck and kissed him hard on the lips. When she pulled back, he was smiling.

"Are you still worried?" she whispered.

"Nope."

"Well, you should be," she giggled.

Jolie stared at the bacon that sizzled in the big iron frying pan. The fat swelled to a bubble and exploded with tiny drops of boiling oil, only to swell again in a different location.

I like bacon, because I can see it, touch it, hear it, smell it, and taste it.

She glanced over at a big pot that also sat on the stove. *Mush, on the other hand, is emotionless. Sort of a sensual fast.*

Essie bounded in through the open door. "What're you doin'?"

"Eh, thinking."

"About the mess with the railroad? Daddy says not to worry—that they have all week to figure something out."

"I'm sure Daddy will do it if anyone can."

"You ought to see Max and Mudball!" Essie exclaimed.

Jolie glanced back toward the open door. "What're they doing?"

"They teamed up and are chasing Francis."

"Oh, dear. Poor Francis."

"He's hiding in the privy, and they can't find him."

"Well, this is an exciting morning. Tell everyone that breakfast is ready."

"Mama is hoeing the lower acres."

"Are they dry?"

"Yes, the levee that Lawson and Daddy built really worked."

"What's Daddy doing?" Jolie asked.

"He went to fetch Mama."

"And Lawson?"

"He's hitchin' up Pullman and Leppy. Daddy's going to town to talk to Mr. Culburtt. He said he would take us to school."

"And Gibson?"

"He's restacking the firewood. The windstorm blew it down."

"My, it sounds like everyone is busy."

"Mama said you got home late last night. How late?" Essie probed.

"Everyone was asleep."

"I don't know why it took you so long to close the schoolhouse."

"Some things have to be done right," Jolie mused. "Call them in for breakfast. Then get your hair combed."

"Do you think this week will be as busy as last week?"

"I hope not. Did you study for the spelling test?"

"Spelling test? We have spelling tests on Fridays, and we didn't have school on Friday."

"So that means the test is today."

"You didn't tell me that," Essie complained.

"I was hoping your conscience would tell you that."

"C-O-N-S-C-I-E-N-C-E. I did remember that one." Essie grinned.

The Vockney girls were waiting at the schoolhouse when Mr. Bowers pulled up.

"Where's Lawson?" April asked.

"Mama needed him to help hoe since Daddy had to go to town," Jolie reported.

"You mean he isn't coming to school today at all?"

"I don't believe so."

"That's a fine shinley," April moaned. "I had important news to tell him."

"Would you like for me to tell him?"

"No!" April giggled.

Lawson was the only student of the twenty-two who was absent. May Vockney was standing and spelling compromise when someone knocked on the schoolhouse door. Everyone stopped and stared.

"Gibson, would you take care of that." She turned back to the dark-haired girl. "Go ahead, May."

"C-O-M—"

"Shakey Torrington wants to see you," Gibs called out.

"Tell him to wait right there, and I'll visit with him at recess. Go ahead, May."

"C-O-M-P—"

"Shakey said he can't wait. He's on his way to Missouri."

"I'll be right there as soon as May finishes her word. One more time, May."

"C-O-M-P-R—"

Shakey Torrington stuck his head in the classroom. "Are you real busy, Miss Jolie?"

"I believe we were compromising," Jolie murmured.

"—O-M-I-S-E!" May curtseyed and sat down at the desk she shared with June.

"Are you spellin'?" Shakey asked, hat in hand.

"Yes, we are. Would you like to join us?"

"Spellin'?"

"Yes."

"No, I don't reckon I'm too good with spellin'."

"Shakey, what did you need?"

"I need to talk to you, Miss Jolie."

"We'll have recess as soon as I finish with the spelling. Can we talk then?"

"I'm going to Missouri," he murmured.

"Do you have family there, Shakey?"

"My big sis is there and her family. I thought I'd see how they was doin'."

"That's nice." Jolie glanced at the children. "Prissy, how about you spelling cooperative? That was another word we heard last night."

The red-haired girl stood and licked her lips.

"Her husband's brother is a preacher, you know."

"C-O—"

"That's nice, Shakey. He'll be good to talk to," Jolie encouraged.

"Yep. That's what I'm thinkin'. I think I'm on the right track, Miss Jolie."

"—O-O—"

"Yes, you are, Shakey. Just two O's, Prissy."

"Thanks for takin' me to church with you."

"You are more than welcome, Shakey."

"I was just backin' up, Miss Jolie," Prissy explained.

"Well, very good. Please continue."

Shakey leaned against the doorframe. "You know what made me have the nerve to pray?"

"No. What was it?"

"I said to myself, if Miss Jolie ain't gave up on me, maybe the Lord hasn't either."

"—P-E-R—"

"No, He hasn't. That's an important lesson. He never rejects a repentant heart."

"—A-T-I-V-E."

"I'm goin' now, Miss Jolie."

"That was very good, Prissy. The Lord bless you, Shakey Torrington."

"Good-bye, Miss Jolie."

There were giggles and a chorus of "Good-bye, Shakey" in reply.

It was just before lunch, and Jolie was reading Melville to the class. Essie was playing the part of Captain Ahab, and Bullet Wells was wallowing on the floor imitating a whale when there was another bang at the door. Mary Vockney ran back and peeked out.

"It's Phil and Bog!" she called out.

Jolie stared toward the back of the room.

"You know, the ones you flattened with the fryin' pan," Mary reported.

"Bill and Bob?"

"Yep, it's them."

"Have them come in."

Bob led the way. Both carried hats in hand.

"What can I do for you two?" she asked them.

"We need a note, Miss Jolie."

"What kind of note?"

"The sheriff said he wouldn't put us in jail if we told you we was sorry and got you to sign a note saying we did it," Bob announced.

"Oh, I see, and so you rode all the way out here to apologize?"

Bill glanced over at Bob. "He jist said we had to say we was sorry."

"Are you?" she challenged.

"Are we what?" Bill asked.

"Are you sorry?"

"Yes, ma'am." Bob nodded.

"What're you sorry about?" April Vockney asked.

"I'm sorry we frightened Miss Jolie and . . . and sorry I grabbed her—"

"Eh—umpth," Jolie said.

"Sorry I grabbed her 'eh—umpth,'" Bob continued.

"I'm sorry I missed her cookin' that ham and potatoes. All we got at the jail was mush," Bill reported. He glanced over at Bullet Wells. "What's the boy doin' on the floor, Miss Jolie?"

"It's a charade."

Bill glanced at Bob in near panic. "Hope you learned your lesson, son. But I reckon Miss Jolie will give you a note too."

Essie was cleaning the slate board, and Jolie was sweeping the front steps when Matthew Bowers returned.

"I trust you haven't been waiting after school too long," he said.

"No, Daddy. I had time to get everything ready for tomorrow." Jolie waited for Essie and then locked the door.

"Did Gibs walk home?"

"Leppy, Chug, and Maxwell came by and gave him a ride."

"I'm surprised a certain young lady didn't bum a ride with Mr. Verdue."

"Ladies don't ride double in the saddle with men," Essie mumbled.

"Jolie wouldn't let you?" he grinned.

"No, and I purtneer pitched a fit."

"How was the meeting in town, Daddy?" Jolie asked.

"We got quite a bit done, darlin'. Strath Yarrow knows a lot about the law. He helped us with papers for a farmers' and shippers' cooperative. I think that might be something that will work for us."

"Did Mr. Culburtt think that was the right thing to do?"

"Culburtt doesn't want trouble any more than we do. But he's not in charge. He said this man Monroe was the one to talk to. Monroe's the one who hires the gunmen. But Monroe isn't about to address a hostile group."

"It wasn't a hostile group last night," Jolie remarked.

"That's what I tried to tell Culburtt. I believe he'll meet with us, but we really need Monroe there. I just need him to see our proposal and talk with some of the folks. Both sides forget that we're dealing with ordinary people."

"I think I can get Mr. Monroe to the meeting, Daddy," Jolie declared.

"How're you goin' to do that, darlin'?"

"Do you think you could talk Mr. Adair at the newspaper into printing us some handbills?"

"Perhaps. He did want me to give him an interview. What did you have in mind?"

"A celebration," Jolie replied.

Eight

"Another ham and two more fried chickens just arrived," Essie hollered. She and Mary Vockney sprinted to the front steps of the schoolhouse. "There's a hominy casserole, cold mustard pickles, suet pudding, a Dutch meatloaf, pickled onions, a roast leg of antelope, and fracadeller. . . . What's fracadeller?"

Jolie peeked under a linen napkin at a flat dish. "It looks like Danish meatballs. Who brought it?"

"Mrs. Hansen."

"Set it over on the woodstove," Jolie directed. "I would rather know which people arrive than what food they're bringing."

Mary Vockney reached down and pulled a pebble out from between her toes. "Why?"

"It was the Petersons, Grandma Marie, Mrs. Fleister, the Hansens, the McCormicks, and Nadella Ripon," Essie reported. "They drove a buckboard with a gray mule and a donkey."

"I'm surprised. They're townspeople. But I'm glad they're here," Jolie said.

"They heard you ask for prayer in church this mornin'; so they said they would come out and pray for you here."

"That part is wonderful."

"Mr. Peterson said he hadn't seen any fireworks since the Fourth of July anyway," Essie said.

"Are we goin' to have fireworks, Miss Jolie?" Mary asked.

"I believe that was a metaphor."

Mary turned to Essie. "Does that mean yes or no?"

Essie shrugged. "I think it means no, but who can tell? Chester said he was planning some surprises."

Jolie jerked around. "Oh, he did?"

"Yeah, but he doesn't always do what he says." Essie peeked under another linen towel. "What's in this white gravy, Jolie?"

"I believe that's calves' brains."

Essie's mouth dropped open, and she stared at Mary, who made a face. "I'm glad I left Francis at home," Essie moaned.

"Gibs said there are too many people to all fit into the building this week," Mary Vockney said.

"Then it's a good thing it's a nice day outside."

"It's kind of cloudy to the west," Mary observed. "Daddy said it could rain by dark."

Jolie clomped out to the front porch. Kids swarmed near the swing. Cowboys and ranchers parked to the north, homesteaders right in front of the school, and railroad men to the south toward the tracks.

Jolie watched as her mother glided through the crowd and up to her. "Do you have a plan for this feast, darlin'?"

"We'll put all the food inside. Then we can come in and serve ourselves," Jolie declared. "We'll encourage people to eat outside. However, I do wish they wouldn't clump together in their own little circles of friends."

"Do you need some help getting it organized?" Lissa Bowers asked her eldest daughter.

"What do you think?"

"I'll help," April Vockney offered.

"April and I will take care of it, Mama."

"Thank you, honey. I knew you would. Say, have you seen—"

"Daddy's over by Mr. Culburtt and the railroad men." Jolie pointed.

"Is it that obvious?" Lissa Bowers asked.

"Yes, Mama. You are quite predictable."

"It's pathetic, isn't it?"

"It's wonderful." Jolie glanced around the crowd. "Have you seen—"

"He's out back helping his father get Bullet."

"What's happened to Bullet?"

"He got his foot stuck in the privy," Lissa Bowers reported.

"He what?"

"Don't ask."

"Go on, Mama—hang onto your man."

Jolie watched her mother slip through the crowd. She was the only woman in the crowd without a hat or bonnet and the only one over twelve in the county who wore a braid.

Lord, I hope Mama never changes. Okay, now, Jolie Bowers, you have some work to do.

"April, get May and June to help. You circulate among the homesteaders and the townspeople. Tell them to bring any food they brought to share into the school. Essie, you and Mary talk to Leppy and the cowboys and ranchers. Make sure you tell the ones that didn't bring anything that there will be plenty of food for everyone."

"Where are you goin'?" Essie asked.

"To the railroad men."

"Are they eating with us?" Mary pressed.

"Of course they are."

Jolie marched across the yard, stopping to visit as she approached the men huddled on the south side of the schoolhouse.

Galen Faxon pulled off his hat. "Looks like everyone in the Nebraska panhandle is here, Miss Jolie."

"There aren't too many social events. I suppose this is as good an excuse as any to get together."

"Miss Jolie, Mr. Culburtt said he was bringin' our share of food," the thin cowboy said. "We ain't freeloadin'."

"That's nice, but there'll be quite a bit without it. Homestead women do know how to cook."

The tall man beamed. "Yes, ma'am, and some of them ain't half bad-lookin' neither."

Jolie shook her head and grinned. "Are you boys checking out the girls?"

"Ain't none of them can hold a candle to you, Miss Jolie," the big man with the brown vest hooted.

"You boys are way too kind. I'll ring the school bell when it's time to eat. Is it really necessary to wear your guns?"

Faxon pointed to the other side of the schoolhouse. "As long as they have theirs on, I reckon it is."

"What kind of food you got over there?" the thin cowboy asked.

"You mean, besides venison, buffalo, chicken, hams, chops, and roast?"

"Yeah, what else?"

"Dumplings, drop biscuits, corn meal griddlecakes, scrapple, porcupine rice, ham loaf with pecans, Russian fluff, stuffed prunes, corn pudding, chicory salad, white fruitcake, chess pie, Platte River rum pie, cherry winks, spiced Seckel pears. . . . Should I go on?" she grinned.

The thin cowboy licked his lips. "Miss Jolie, I don't reckon we could do this ever' week, do you?"

"No, I'm afraid not. Is Mr. Culburtt bringing Mr. Monroe?" she asked.

"That's what I heard," Faxon reported. "Davenport and his railroad guards were goin' to bring them out. That Monroe is a very nervous little man."

"It looks like a whole parade of folks is still comin'. Telegraph Road is crowded almost back to town," the thin cowboy said. "Do you reckon anything important will happen?"

"I know one thing: This might be the biggest meal in the history of the Nebraska panhandle." Jolie smiled.

She glided back to the schoolhouse and placed the food on separate tables and desks as it was brought indoors. It was thirty minutes before the flow of food slowed. She slipped a pan of steamed carrot and potato pudding on the woodstove and then stepped out on the porch.

"Look at all the people, Jolie," Essie said.

Jolie shook her head. "I'm amazed. Have you seen—"

"Tanner's helpin' his mama with Chester."

"What's wrong with Bullet now?" Jolie asked.

"He got his hand caught in the pickled watermelon rind jar."

"Hmmm . . . Bullet seems to be having a rough day."

"Did you hear what happened to him and the boiled red potato salad?" Essie smirked.

"I'm afraid to ask."

"Let me say that it would be better if you didn't eat any potato salad."

Tanner grabbed her from behind. "Hi, darlin'."

Jolie tugged away with a smile. "I hear little brother has kept you busy."

Tanner patted her hand. "Yes, he's spinnin' out of control today. Sorry about the buttermilk rhubarb pie."

"The what?" Jolie asked.

"Eh, never mind. When are we gettin' this thing goin'?" Tanner asked.

"Mr. Culburtt and some others are bringing out some food. We should wait for them."

"What do you want to do while we wait?" he asked.

Jolie clutched his arm. "How about you and me takin' a team to Scott's Bluff and hiking to the top with a knapsack supper and sitting on the bluff to watch the sun go down?" she suggested.

"Really?" he gasped.

"You asked what I'd like to do. That would be it."

"Just you and me?"

"All alone."

"You know, darlin'," he said, "it could be dangerous tryin' to hike down Scott's Bluff after dark."

"We might have to wrap blankets around our shoulders and stay up there until morning," she replied.

"Now that could be really dangerous." He winked.

"My, you are a fearful man, Tanner Wells. It's a good thing I'd be along to protect you."

"Now, Miss Jolie, what're we really goin' to do?" he laughed.

"Visit with folks." She tugged his arm and led him through the crowd.

A young lady wearing a blue calico bonnet giggled as Tanner and Jolie approached.

"Celia . . . and Maxwell. I'm glad you both are here," Jolie greeted them.

"Did you know that my Max once met Wyatt Earp and Stuart Brannon on the same day?" Celia asked.

"I don't remember that your Max ever told me that."

"It's true, Miss Jolie," Maxwell said. "I was down in Prescott, Arizona, at the time."

"I trust you didn't call them both out at the same time," Jolie laughed.

Maxwell Dix pulled off his hat and smiled. "No, ma'am. I ain't nearly as dumb as I look."

Celia combed his long blond hair back over his ear with her fingers. "Max, honey, you look wonderful."

Jolie tilted her head and smiled. When she scooted by Maxwell, she whispered, "You treat her good, Maxwell Dix, or you'll answer to me."

"Yeah, I sort of figured that," he whispered back.

"Figured what, honey?" Celia asked.

"Oh, Miss Jolie said I need to eat some vegetables today, or she wouldn't let me have any pie."

"But I baked a sourdough rhubarb pie just for you."

Gibs trotted up. "Tanner, did you find me a lever for my Henry?"

"Yep, it's a used one, but it will be fine as soon as I heat and straighten it."

"Wow, that's great. Maybe I'll be able to hunt with it this fall. Jolie, have you seen Lawson?" Gibs asked.

"He was in the schoolhouse with April."

"I'll bet he's checkin' out the desserts," Gibs commented.

Jolie squeezed Tanner's arm. "That might very well be true."

"Maybe I'd better keep an eye on him," Gibs suggested.

"You might be more right than you know," Jolie chuckled.

They sauntered by the Meades, the Harrisons, and the Carpenters—all sprawled on blankets that covered the brownish yellow dirt. Two men sat on canvas camp stools in front of a team of mules.

"Luke and Raymond, I didn't expect to see you two this far from the store," Jolie said.

Luke tugged off his hat. "Afternoon, Miss Jolie . . . Tanner. Ain't hardly anyone left in town."

"We ain't takin' sides; so don't go linin' us up. We just came to watch," Raymond insisted.

"And eat," Luke added.

"There's only one side, boys," Tanner announced.

"There is?"

Tanner hugged her shoulders. "Can you two imagine anyone in their right mind opposin' Jolie Bowers?"

"Nope. But I ain't sure all of 'em here is in their right mind." Luke shot a plug to the dirt and wiped his mouth with the back of his hand.

"You have a good point, Luke."

"Say, Miss Jolie, do you know the name of that fine-lookin' lady over by the small buggy?"

Jolie glanced through the crowd at a large woman in a long black dress. "Do you mean Mrs. Sitmore?"

"Is she wearin' black because she's a widow?"

"Yes, she is."

"Mmmm," Luke mumbled. "What a fine vision of feminine loveliness."

Jolie prodded Tanner on through the crowd. "Don't say it," she whispered between clenched teeth.

"I didn't say a thing," Tanner responded. "But I don't reckon Mrs. Ophelia Sitmore has been called a fine vision of feminine loveliness for quite a spell."

Leppy Verdue signaled her over. "Miss Jolie, Tanner. Say, have you two seen Miss Essie?"

"I think she's guarding the food from flies and Bullet Wells. Are you looking for her?"

"Yes, I need to talk to that little darlin'. She's been tellin' everyone that we're getting married someday."

"Is that cooling off your reception with the other ladies?" Jolie laughed.

"It doesn't help. Now you know how much I like li'l sis. She's just like a—"

"Little sister?"

"Exactly."

"I'll try to keep her occupied," Jolie offered.

"Thank you. I'd appreciate that."

They strolled toward Captain Richardson and the other ranchers, but Mrs. Meynarde stopped Jolie with the polished hickory point of her blue parasol.

"Jolie, dear, may I have a word with you?"

"Do you want me to leave?" Tanner asked.

"Of course not," Jolie insisted. "Mrs. Meynarde, you don't mind if my honey stays, do you?"

The gray-haired, short, thick woman smiled. "Of course not. Honey can stay. I just wanted to know how well you know Mr. LaPage."

"Chug? Why, I met him the day we moved to Nebraska. So he's been a friend as long as anyone around here."

"I'm glad to hear that," Mrs. Meynarde said.

"Why do you ask?" Tanner quizzed.

She tipped her straw hat as she smiled at him. "Honey, Mr.

Meynarde is thinkin' about hirin' Mr. LaPage to work at the bank."

"Chug? Work at the bank?" Jolie repeated.

"Nathaniel thinks he'll be a natural at guarding transfers and even serving papers on delinquent loans."

"Mrs. Meynarde, I would not hesitate to let Chug guard my bank account," Jolie declared. "If I had a bank account."

"That's all I need to know."

"Where is Chug?" Jolie asked.

"He and Nathaniel are over discussing the plans for a new bank building. Thanks, Jolie and . . . eh . . . Honey. I feel better now."

The banker's wife scooted between a white horse and the McMasters sisters.

"Chug, the banker?" Tanner mused. "I can't see that."

"I can. Especially if he shaves and gets a haircut."

Mrs. Henrietta Fleister took Jolie's arm and led them both to the edge of the roadway. "That poor boy has been through so much."

"Landen?" Jolie asked.

"No, his father, Strath Yarrow. I've had him over for supper almost every night this week."

"Did you find him a wife yet?" Tanner asked.

Mrs. Fleister stared at him for a moment. "Just like a man to ask such a question."

Jolie slipped her arm into Mrs. Fleister's. "Mildred, did your niece in Cheyenne ever marry that older man you were worried about? You mentioned your concern at the women's prayer time."

Mrs. Fleister's eyes widened. She patted Jolie's hand. "You know, dear, he wasn't right for her. Why, I was just telling her last night that whole escapade was a learning experience which made her better prepared for the next step in her life."

Jolie held on, but her eyes searched the crowd. "She's here?"

"Yes, dear girl. She was rather despondent and wanted to come visit Auntie Mildred; so naturally I sent the train fare."

"Oh, of course. You're so thoughtful that way." Jolie squeezed her arm. "Did they hit it off?"

Mrs. Fleister's eyes gleamed. "I believe so. Much better than he did with the Peppermill girl."

"Florence?" Jolie asked.

"No, Daisy."

"She's very cute."

"In a farm girl sort of way," Mrs. Fleister agreed. "The real cutie was Sarah McGill, of course."

Jolie brushed a grass stem from Mrs. Fleister's dress. "But Sarah is so tall."

"Precisely what I thought. And she does have that slightly annoying giggle. But who am I to say?" Mrs. Fleister straightened her straw hat.

"You're a very good judge of character."

"Thank you, dear. I try to be of help where I can." She studied the rolling clouds. "I do trust the good Lord will have the decency to hold back the rain until after I'm home."

"He has a habit of doing whatever He wants," Jolie replied.

"Yes, you're right. Quite perturbing at times, I might add." Mildred Fleister laid a ringed hand on Tanner's coat sleeve. "Young Mr. Wells, I made a fabulous green tomato pie. I know you'll want to try it."

He nodded as Jolie towed him down to a long string of picketed horses.

"Now why was it wrong for me to ask if she had poor Strath married off?"

"It's not what you ask. It's how you ask it."

"Do I really have to eat some of her green tomato pie?"

"Stay at the back of the line. Perhaps it will be gone by the time you get there."

Jocko Martinez and two other vaqueros waved her over to the ranch wagon.

"Miss Jolie, where would you like this?" Jocko pointed to a boulder-sized object under a canvas in the back of the wagon.

"What is it?"

"A whole hog," Jocko replied.

Jolie stood on her tiptoes and tried to peek into the wagon. "A hog?"

"Yep, it's our contribution," Martinez explained. "We dug a pit and cooked it for two days in green willows."

"A whole hog?" Jolie gasped again.

"This is a big doin's."

"Can you carry it?" she asked.

"It's on a wood pallet."

"Drive the wagon up to the front of the school. We'll put it right inside the door. I trust that when it's time to eat, one of you will carve it for us. I don't believe I've ever carved a whole hog."

Tanner released her hand. "I'll go with them."

"I'll be right there," Jolie said.

She tramped over to the tall buckskin horse and the man standing next to it. "Sheriff Riley, I didn't expect you out here."

"If there's goin' to be trouble, I reckon it will be out here today—not in town."

She turned to the man standing next to him. "There isn't goin' to be any trouble, is there, Captain Richardson?"

"It will be a long day, Miss Jolie, but it seems to be shaping up fine so far."

"Thank you for the roast pig."

"Thank Jocko. He and the boys decided on it. That wild hog wandered up onto the plateau durin' that big storm the other day. No one came to claim him, and we didn't have anywhere to keep him."

Jolie hiked back to the schoolhouse. Clouds filled up the entire sky.

Lord, this would not be a good day for a rain. Let me rephrase that. I don't want to sound as bossy as Mrs. Fleister. Lord, is this a good day for rain? If so, bring it on.

She and Tanner stood staring at the big cooked hog when Matthew and Lissa Bowers came in.

"Darlin', perhaps we can start eating," Mr. Bowers suggested.

"Mr. Culburtt is on his way out with a few more things. I hate to start before he gets here."

"Will the vice president be with him?" Lissa Bowers asked.

"I assume that. Mr. Culburtt said he was having a difficult time getting Mr. Monroe to commit."

"To being here?" Matthew Bowers asked. "Or to our agreement?"

"Both, I believe," Jolie replied.

Greg Wells and May Vockney trotted into the schoolroom. "Tanner, have you seen Bullet?" Greg asked.

"Eh, no, is he missing?"

"I'm not sure anyone misses him, but Mama wanted him for something," Greg replied.

"Did you check the privy?" Tanner asked.

"Yep. No one's in there."

"You mean, you opened the door and didn't see anyone?"

"Eh," Greg mumbled, "you're right. I should double check."

Strath Yarrow meandered in as Greg and May left.

"You've got to hide me, Miss Jolie," Strath said urgently.

"Mrs. Fleister?"

"No," he said. "I'm getting along fine with Mildred. But do you know a lady named Nadella?"

"Oh, my . . . Nadella Ripon spotted you?" Jolie gasped.

"Yes. What do you know about her?"

Jolie shook her head. "Her name tells it all."

Tanner rocked back on his heels "Say, is she the one that—"

"Careful, Tanner Wells," Jolie cautioned. "Don't you go saying bad things about little Nadella."

"No one on earth ever called Nadella Ripon little," Tanner mused.

"Except for her size and the twitch in her right eye, Nadella is a very nice girl," Jolie declared. "I've heard she can sing quite well. Daddy said she can sing both tenor and bass."

Strath glanced around the schoolroom. "Just the same, I believe I'll study your maps."

"We only have the one—of Nebraska."

"Just the one I wanted to study," Strath declared.

"Don't you think you're over-concerned about Nadella?"

"Let him alone, darlin'," Tanner cautioned. "A man's drive for self-preservation is powerful."

"You two are exaggerating the situation," Jolie insisted.

"I'd rather face Galen Faxon in a dark alley than Nadella Ripon," Tanner murmured.

Gibs raced through the front door. "There's a fight. Some of the cowboys got in a fistfight with the railroad men! I don't know where Sheriff Riley is. Do you think I should try to break it up?"

Jolie rushed outside. A hundred or more people clustered at the road in front of the schoolhouse. Several men rolled in the dirt, pounding each other.

Some of the crowd cheered.

Some cowered.

Most gawked.

Jolie raced toward the commotion. She spied two men watching from behind the picket line of mules. "Luke . . . Raymond, where's Sheriff Riley?"

"He went down to the tracks," Luke said.

"Why?"

"There's a boy stuck in the railroad ties," Raymond reported.

"Stuck?" Jolie repeated.

"Yep," Luke replied. "He was screamin' and hollerin' before this fight broke out."

"Was it Bullet?" Tanner called out.

"It's the one that got stuck in the privy," Raymond answered. "Your mama and daddy went down there too, Miss Jolie. Then these old boys got to callin' names, but they ain't pulled their pistols yet."

"I'll go check on Bullet," Tanner cried. He sprinted toward the railroad tracks.

Jolie focused on the four men slugging it out in the dirt. "What is this all about?"

"It's been boilin' up," Jocko Martinez told her. "I don't think they could hold back any longer."

"That's preposterous," Jolie fumed. "It simply has to stop now." She looked around the crowd. "Jocko, do you have a shotgun in your wagon?"

"Yep." He pulled out a short double-barreled Greener. "Which side are you goin' to shoot?"

"Both, of course." She grabbed the gun.

"What're you goin' to do, Miss Jolie?" Jocko asked.

"Like a good schoolteacher, I'll teach manners and character development," she mumbled.

Jolie hiked past the crowd toward the four battling men covered with blood, sweat, and dirt.

A blast in the sky from the shotgun silenced the crowd and froze the combatants. Those not at the railroad tracks scurried to the roadside. One of the men stood up.

"Woman, what in blazes do you think you're doin'?" he growled.

"There will be no fighting on my schoolyard."

"Do you think I'll listen to some half-growed schoolteacher?"

Jolie stepped up and slammed the warm muzzle of the shotgun against his temple. "No, but you'll listen to the ten-gauge shell in this shotgun."

Gibs pushed his way through the crowd, his Winchester model 1890 at his side. "You want me to disarm them, Jolie?"

One of the men on his hands and knees in the dirt reached for his holstered revolver. "No kid is goin' to . . ."

Gibs pumped his rifle and shoved it in the man's ear.

"Are you goin' to cover me with a .22?" the man barked.

"Jolie, do you think a .22 bullet would go clean through his head and out the other ear, or would it get stuck in his brain?" Gibs asked.

She glanced down at the man. "I don't think it will find much resistance in that one's brain. Who is going to disarm these other two men for me?"

Nadella Ripon blustered through the crowd. "Well, isn't this a fine shinley?" she hollered. "Not one man standin' here to stop a fight. Don't worry, honey, I'll grab their pistols. This is the work of demon alcohol, and we in the Temperance League will not tolerate it."

"I'll help Nadella," Pearl Anderson called out. "She's right. We must make our stand."

Minnie Clover and Mary Tarnes pushed their way into the circle with Pearl and Nadella.

A third man rolled to his feet. "I ain't givin' my gun up to no woman."

Nadella's boot heel crashed into the man's toe, and most of her 275 pounds ground into his foot. His gun was easily removed amidst his screams.

"Ladies, take these men to the horse trough and wash them up," Jolie ordered. "I will not have anyone that messy eating in my schoolyard."

"What if they don't want to go?" Nadella asked.

"Shoot them, of course."

"I was hopin' you'd say that. Shall we kill them outright or just maim them?"

"Maiming would be preferred," Jolie said.

Nadella and a dozen other women marched the grumbling men toward the water trough.

The distant blast of a train whistle made the rest of the crowd spin around toward the railroad tracks.

"There isn't any train this time of day," Gibs said.

"It must be Culburtt and Monroe. I assumed they were bringing a buggy. Is Bullet still caught in the tracks?" Jolie led the crowd south where several men yanked at a twelve-year-old boy who was stuck halfway under a railroad tie in the middle of the tracks.

Mr. Bowers and Mr. Wells had their coats off and shirtsleeves rolled up. On their hands and knees, they tugged at Bullet's shoulders while Tanner and Sheriff Riley tried to shove his feet. Lissa Bowers held the sobbing Mrs. Wells.

"What happened?" Jolie asked.

Essie and Leppy Verdue scooted up to her side. "Portie Tidwell dared Chester to crawl under that railroad tie."

"I didn't think he'd try it," Portie bellowed.

Essie stared down the railroad track. "I think a train is comin'. Jolie, what was that gunshot?"

"I had to break up a fight," she reported.

"Were they fightin' over you?" Essie asked.

"No, they weren't."

Matthew Bowers glanced up. "Jolie, you and Mama have to stop that train. You've done it before."

"Daddy, I'm sick and tired of this. Get away from Bullet. Tanner, Mr. Wells, Sheriff Riley . . . please stand back."

"What?" Tanner puffed.

"Trust me. Tanner, get your father back."

"The train is getting closer," Mr. Wells warned.

"Then hurry. Get back. Everyone seems to be intent on messing up my day," Jolie fumed. "I just won't have it. This is the last straw."

"My baby!" Mrs. Wells sobbed.

Jolie spun around as the men cleared the tracks. "Mrs. Wells, your Chester is a pill. He is spoiled rotten, without an once of self-control, and seemingly without conscience. I have no doubt he deserves to be run over by the train."

"Jolie Lorita!" Lissa Bowers snapped.

"However, the grace of God is sufficient for all of us. None of us get what we deserve." She turned toward Bullet. "Chester Wells, get out from under there right now, or you will be last in line at the potluck. Do you hear me?"

Tanner stepped back to the tracks. "He's really stuck, Jolie."

"Do I get to be first in line?" Bullet asked.

"Tenth," Jolie replied.

"Third?"

"Sixth."

"Fifth?" Bullet bartered.

"Only if you are out of there when I count to three. One . . . two . . ."

Chester Wells scampered out from under the railroad tie and raced toward the schoolhouse shouting, "Stand back. I get to be fifth in line."

The entire crowd stood by the railroad tracks as the train slowed to a spark-flying, screeching, steaming stop. Behind the coal car were two passenger cars, a freight car, and a caboose. The freight car door opened first. Six armed gunmen appeared at the door.

A dozen men in the crowd dropped their hands to their revolvers. Leppy Verdue, Maxwell Dix, and Chug LaPage shielded the Bowers family.

Jolie stomped around them to the freight car. "I've had enough of this, Mr. Davenport. It's time to eat. Put down your guns and wash up."

The door to the Pullman car opened. The crutches-wielding Edward Culburtt was helped down. "Miss Bowers, is this a hostile crowd?"

"Just hungry, Mr. Culburtt."

Mr. Hubert R. Monroe peeked out. "I say, there are more people here than I expected."

Jolie stepped up next to the railroad men and turned to the crowd. "Listen, everyone . . . this is Mr. Monroe. He's a vice president of the railroad."

Loud jeers roared through the crowd.

Jolie held up her hands. "Wait. Mr. Monroe has a speech to make and a very important presentation. Don't you?"

"Eh, yes. Quite so."

"Is the railroad goin' to lower them rates?" someone shouted.

The crowd released thunderous cheers.

"I say, that's not what I have to announce," Monroe tried to shout above the crowd noise.

"Don't worry, you can explain that later." Jolie smiled.

"How?" Monroe asked.

"I'm sure you'll think of something while we eat."

"I say," Culburtt hollered up to the men in the freight car, "don't forget to unload the pheasants and the corn."

"Pheasants?"

"Mr. Monroe brought down twenty-four curried Hungarian pheasants for the potluck."

"Where did he get curried Hungarian pheasants?"

"You don't want to know," Culburtt replied. "But he also brought ten watermelons and an ear of corn six feet long."

"Six feet!"

"It's a cake actually." Monroe beamed. "There's a bakery up in the Black Hills that makes enormous specialty cakes. I had one made like an ear of corn. Corn is the crop of the future for western Nebraska."

Jolie helped Mr. Culburtt navigate down off the railway embankment. "He's kidding, isn't he?" she whispered.

"I'm afraid not," Culburtt mumbled. "It's actually quite grotesque."

Within minutes the food was stacked in the schoolhouse, and the crowd circled the steps. Jolie rang the school bell, and everyone quieted down.

"This is a historic day. I believe it's the biggest meal ever served in our county. Thanks to all who made it possible. After Mr. Matthew Bowers says the blessing, we will eat. After that, there will be speeches and discussions. Then we will share in the world's largest corn-shaped cake.

"Mr. Hubert T. Monroe, as our special guest, will be first in line. Then Mr. and Mrs. Bowers, Mr. Culburtt . . . and Bullet Wells. There's more food than most will ever see in one place in a lifetime. So don't worry, everyone will have enough."

Jolie carried her plate through the crowd. Most people settled in families and groups of four to ten on blankets, wagons, and buggies.

Tanner sat with Strath Yarrow and Landen. "Come sit with us, darlin'," he called out.

"I need to check on everyone," she replied.

"Do you have to play hostess to this entire horde?" Strath asked.

"I don't have to. That is, no one requires it. But I will. It's what I do. I suppose I really can't help myself."

"Miss Jolie, this is the best cornbread I ever ate in my life. Who made it?"

Strath mussed his son's hair. "Landen, Miss Jolie had lots of different cornbread to—"

"Larryn Edgemont made that one," Jolie replied.

"Which one is she?" Landen asked.

"The lady in the blue dress with the stunning curly black hair."

"Is she married?" Landen asked.

"Her husband died about a year ago. She and her daughter homestead on the other side of the river, toward Gering, I am told."

"How old is she?" Landen asked.

"Larryn?"

"No," the boy giggled. "The daughter."

"I believe she's eight."

"Strath, did you hear . . ."

Strath Yarrow laughed and shook his head. "Between Landen and Mrs. Fleister, I will have a busy social life in Nebraska."

"She makes good cornbread, Daddy," Landen said.

"That's a crucial attribute."

"Daddy?" Jolie teased.

"When he gets serious, an occasional 'Daddy' slips out," Strath reported.

"When you're ready for introductions to Larryn, let me know," Jolie offered. She glanced around the crowd. "Tanner, your mother and Mr. Monroe have been chatting for half an hour. She's usually so shy in a crowd."

"My Uncle Rex served in the army with Mr. Monroe, in the

Tenth Indiana Volunteers. They were in that Confederate prison camp together."

"I've never heard you mention Uncle Rex," Jolie remarked.

"He died on the steamboat that exploded bringin' the prisoners home right after the war."

"Oh, dear. No wonder they're visiting."

"Your daddy and Mr. Culburtt have been goin' at it," Tanner reported.

"Good. If there's a solution to all this, those two will figure it out."

Jolie spied movement behind the sod schoolhouse. She stole around the building, still carrying her plate of food.

April Vockney giggled.

Lawson Bowers blushed. "Hi, Jolie. Eh . . . Miss April was just showing me her, eh, potato salad."

"Yes, I imagine she was."

"Lawson was bein' good, Miss Jolie."

"Oh?"

"Real good," April giggled.

"Why don't you two stay out front with the others? Maybe someone else will want to see April's potato salad."

"Yes, ma'am," April replied.

Jolie watched them move back around into the crowd. *Lord, I'm not their mother. Maybe I should just let them alone. Why do I have to mother everyone? I trust Lawson. Maybe not April . . . but that's only because she's like me.*

"Psst! Miss Jolie!"

She turned toward the back of the schoolhouse.

"Bob, is that you?"

"Me and Bill is back here."

She hiked around. They stared at her plate of food.

"Miss Jolie, could you bring us a plate of food?"

"Two plates, Bob. We both need one."

"That's what I meant, Bill."

"Well, you didn't say it that way."

"She knew what I meant, didn't you, Miss Jolie?"

"Boys, why don't you clean up and go help yourself?"

"Miss Jolie, they talked about hangin' us last week. I don't reckon we should be seen."

"Nonsense. You two go over to the trough and scrub your hands and faces until they're pink, and I'll escort you in to the food myself."

"You will? Did you hear that, Bob?"

"How do we know she ain't funnin' us? Then we scrubbed up for nothin', Bill."

"Are you funnin' us?" Bill asked.

"No, I meant every word, and you know I've never lied to you."

"You clobbered us with a fryin' pan," Bob whined.

"But she didn't lie to us. I'll scrub up, Miss Jolie. You come back and get us," Bill said. "'Cause I surely want a piece of that big yella cake."

"Isn't that the most monstrous ear of corn you've ever seen?" Jolie commented.

"Corn?" Bill questioned. "I thought it was a banana."

When Jolie returned to the front of the school, she spied Celia Delaney forking a bite of boiled raisin cake into Maxwell Dix's mouth. Lissa Bowers stepped up beside Jolie. "Well, darlin', this is quite a party you staged."

"It isn't my party, Mama."

"Jolie Lorita, shall I take a vote and ask this crowd whose party it is?"

"Mama, why am I that way? Why do I always have to be in charge?"

"Don't worry about it, darlin', until someone complains. You're the perfect hostess, beautiful and efficient."

"You always make me feel good about myself."

"That's a mama's job. Have you seen Lawson and Gibs?"

"Gibs is out there next to the road with Sheriff Riley. The sheriff gave him a deputy badge."

"Oh my. Little brother is in heaven. How about Lawson?"

"I think he's in heaven too. He and April are right over by that . . ." Jolie glanced at the surrey and then back at the schoolhouse. "I'm not sure where Lawson is, but he's happy wherever he is."

"Yes, his April hardly leaves his side."

"She reminds me of Melissa Pritchett."

"Me? Why, look, I'm over fifty feet away from your father."

"I'm proud of you."

"Yes, I'm the epitome of self-control. He sent me to fetch him a plate of supper."

"I'll get it for him if you have something else to do."

"Darlin', go sit down. You have a man out there pinin' for you."

"Jolie!"

She looked around to see Lawson at the side of the school.

"Jolie, Bill and Bob need to see you," Lawson called out.

Mrs. Bowers shook her head. "I see all sorts of men need Miss Jolie!"

"Put my plate on my desk, Mama." Jolie scurried over to April and Lawson.

"We heard a commotion, Miss Jolie," April explained, "and wanted to check it out."

"Yes, well, Lawson, you and April go back there and see if Stranger and Pilgrim are all right."

"Is somethin' wrong with them?" he asked.

"No."

He raised his eyebrows. "Oh! Really, Jolie?"

"Go on." She motioned to them. "And be good."

April nodded her head. "Lawson is really good, Miss Jolie."

Jolie watched them disappear behind the rigs. *You've told me that before, April Vockney. Lord, You watch them. I have other chores tonight.*

With hats in hand, Bob and Bill Condor loitered at the back of the schoolhouse.

"We combed our hair too, Miss Jolie," Bill said.

"I see that. You boys could be right handsome if you had your hair cut and washed and took a bath and put on your good clothes."

"These are our good clothes. Ain't they, Bob?"

"These are our only clothes, Bill."

"That's what I meant."

She offered one arm to Bill, the other to his brother. Both grinning cowboys strolled with her to the front of the schoolhouse.

"Shoot, I don't think anyone even knows we're here, Bob."

"What if we get challenged?" Bob asked her.

"Tell them you're guests of Jolie Bowers."

"Yes, ma'am. Ain't this a fine shinley, Bob? Last week she hit us on the head with a fryin' pan and hogtied us. This week she leads us to the feed trough."

"Kind of reminds you of Mama. Don't it, Bill?"

"That was just what I was thinkin'."

Jolie shoved the men inside the schoolhouse. "Boys, help yourselves. Just remember to use a fork, knife, or spoon. Don't eat with your fingers, and don't lick your plate."

"She does sound like Mama!" Bill remarked.

Clouds continued to stack up, and the temperature dropped enough that some of the quilts and blankets now covered shoulders instead of merely cradling dinner. Jolie rounded up her mother and father, Mr. Culburtt, Mr. Monroe, Strath Yarrow, and Sheriff Riley and brought them to the steps of the schoolhouse. Then she rang the bell.

Exactly 317 men, women, and children, nine dogs, and one peacock crowded in front of the stairs.

Jolie funneled her hands to her face, which felt warm, sweaty; her fingers felt cold. "We're going to proceed with our meeting. We really have two purposes. There will be a presentation. Then . . . we will hear a report on the negotiations with the railroad."

It was difficult to distinguish if the roar from the crowd contained cheers or jeers.

"My word," Monroe mumbled, "you will allow me to exit before they get riled up, won't you? Perhaps I should have Davenport and some of them up here with me."

"How do you know they'll be riled up?" Jolie queried. "They might like the way you negotiated."

Monroe's eyes widened. "But . . . I—I . . . I didn't . . ."

"Sure you did. You forged a history-making alliance, and you'll get credit for it too," Jolie insisted.

She turned back to the crowd and held up her hand until they quieted. "Let me introduce the guests. This is Mr. Hubert R. Monroe, vice president of the railroad."

Boos followed.

"How many of you have the nerve to hike into a railroad meeting at the train yard in Omaha?" Jolie challenged. "Not many, I suspect. Yet here is Mr. Monroe, a brave, reasonable man."

"Or a dadgum fool," someone shouted.

Jolie put her hand on the shoulder of the man with the crutches. "I believe you all know Mr. Culburtt, the district superintendent of the railroad."

The jeers lessened. Applause was scattered.

She moved to the lawman. "I've asked Sheriff Riley to be here to make sure none of you are inclined to violence. Mr. Gibson Bowers is one of his deputies today. And I believe some of the ladies from the Temperance Union are also helping keep the peace."

"Who's the boy on the roof?" someone yelled.

Jolie turned around. Dark gray clouds huddled over the tattered cedar shingles, but she didn't see anyone. "That must be young Mr. Wells, one of my more energetic students. Are you stuck, Bullet?" she hollered.

"Nope, Miss Jolie," a voice shouted back down.

She faced the people. "This is Mr. Strath Yarrow, recently of Chicago, but soon to be a homesteading neighbor of ours. He is an attorney. He drew up some legal papers for us. He served as legal advisor to the negotiations, to make sure all was done in a proper fashion."

"And, of course, you all know my mama and daddy." She drew attention to the couple holding hands.

When Matthew Bowers waved his hand at the crowd, the cheers rolled up like waves breaking on the shore.

"Bowers, did you beat the railroad back down?" a man shouted.

"We'll take them on like you did in Lincoln. We got guns," another hollered.

Jolie grabbed Mr. Monroe's arm to keep him from bolting off the school steps. "Be courageous, Mr. Monroe," she whispered. "This is your moment to shine."

"My word, where is Galen Faxon and his bunch when I need them?"

"Sitting right out there next to the road," she replied. "I told them to stay behind the crowd. It will be fine. You wait and see."

Mr. Bowers quieted the crowd. "I believe we do have some good news to share with you about the negotiations. However, Mr. Monroe has a presentation to make before that. I expect you to be gracious because this involves three beautiful Bowers ladies." He turned to the man in the three-piece suit. "Mr. Monroe."

Monroe pulled out a beige piece of paper from his vest pocket and unfolded it. Then he cleared his throat.

"I can't hear him," someone shouted.

"He ain't said nothin' yet," another explained.

"Ladies and gentlemen, boys and girls, I am here today to express the railroad's deep gratitude to two of your citizens."

"Three," Jolie corrected.

"Three?" he murmured.

"My sister Essie was with us too."

"To three of your citizens. It does not have to do with railroading, or farming, or ranching. It deals with human decency and dauntless courage. Last week a thunderstorm washed out the railroad tracks just west of here. That fact was unknown to the engineer and crew of the 1021. These two ladies, eh, three ladies risked their very lives in order to save the train.

"Frankly, there are not many who would jeopardize themselves for others, and not too many in this crowd willing to do that for the railroad."

"You got that right, mister," a man yelled.

"The railroad and seventy-three passengers and crew owe a great debt to these ladies. I have a presentation to make to Mrs. Matthew Bowers, Jolie Lorita Bowers, and . . ." He turned to Jolie.

"Essie Cinnia Bowers."

Essie moved up onto the porch next to Jolie. "You can call me Estelle."

"And Estelle Cinnia Bowers," Mr. Monroe continued.

Lissa, Jolie, and Essie scooted together on the step in front of the men. The crowd broke into applause.

Lissa Bowers reached back. Jolie saw her father grab her hand. Daddy loves to be up front, and it scares Mama to death. She'd rather stop a stampede of wild horses than stand up here when people applaud.

Matthew Bowers finally raised his hands. The clapping died out.

Monroe unrolled a document. "On behalf of a grateful railroad, we would like to give to Melissa, Jolie, and Estelle Bowers this certificate of appreciation and—"

"They save your tail, and you give them a lousy piece of paper?" someone yelled.

"Wait!" Monroe raised his voice to a shout. "There's more. From the foremost company of ready-built houses in Chicago, we are going to present the Bowers family with a deluxe, two-story model home."

The crowd was silent.

"A house?" Essie mumbled.

"What good is a house in Chicago?" someone yelled.

Strath Yarrow raised his hands. "Let me explain since I'm buying one too. These are house kits with all the boards cut to size and some of the walls already constructed. It comes complete with windows, doors, and chimney. It's sent out on the train and can be constructed in two weeks."

"We get a real house?" Essie said.

Jolie glanced back at her father. His shoulders slumped; his natural smile melted. *Oh, Daddy, Daddy, Daddy, they are stealing your dream of building Mama her house. That's not right.*

Lissa Bowers covered her mouth with her hands and rocked back on her heels.

The crowd cheered again.

Jolie poked her mother and pointed back at Daddy. One glance made Lissa's expression change. She held up her hands.

"Mr. Monroe, the generosity of the railroad is overwhelming, but I'm afraid we must decline your offer," Lissa Bowers announced.

"We will?" Essie squawked.

"You see, my Matthew is in the process of building me a home. We have no need for two," Lissa explained.

"Besides," Jolie chimed in, "it would seem to some to be a compromising position for a homesteader to accept such a generous gift. We're very grateful for your offer, but we cannot accept it."

"But—but—what am I going to do with it?" Monroe gasped.

A loud crash silenced the crowd, and Bill Condor staggered out of the schoolhouse onto the porch. "A kid just fell through the ceilin'!" he mumbled.

"Chester?" Essie yelled.

"He's okay. The yellow cake broke his fall," Bill reported. "But you got a hole in your roof, Miss Jolie."

"A new school!" Jolie waved her arms. "Mr. Monroe, we would like to accept the two-story house to be built right on this site and used for a new school!"

The crowd broke into loud cheers.

Jolie stepped over. "Mr. Monroe, they're cheering for you."

He pulled off his top hat and held it in front of him. "Really?"

"Yes, that was quite a generous offer."

Monroe stood straight up. "Yes, I believe they are. I don't think I've ever been cheered like this before."

"It feels good, doesn't it?" she prodded.

"Quite right."

"Wait until they hear your stand on the new rate proposal. They will cheer even louder."

"You don't say?" Monroe spun around to Culburtt. "What is my stand on the proposal?"

Mr. Culburtt shoved a paper into his hand.

Matthew Bowers stepped forward. His smile had returned, and Lissa Bowers clutched his arm. "That is a wonderful offer, Mr. Monroe. The whole community is grateful. Now let me present you with our proposal. I'll be glad to discuss the details with any of you. Here's the outline of what is being proposed. Two associations will be formed. One will be a cattlemen's, the other a farmers' alliance corporation. Mr. Yarrow will file those papers this week. Both associations will coordinate their respective business for buying and selling in such a way as to command the lowest prices for products we purchase and the highest prices for our goods. Together we will form a Shipping Cooperative that will work with the railroad to insure coordinated filling of entire trains at one location, thus assuring the lowest possible rate."

"What did the railroad promise?" Cart Meeker yelled.

"They agreed to a minimum shipping fee for three years, with increases tied to product prices. In other words, a minimum cost, unless prices go up, in which case their fee will increase accordingly."

Monroe turned to Culburtt. "I can't agree to that."

But his voice was drowned by the cheers of the crowd.

"Listen to them, Mr. Monroe," Jolie offered. "You're a hero."

"But . . . but . . . but . . ."

"Mr. Monroe, how often have you gotten to be the hero?" she challenged.

Mrs. Wells scooted up the steps and gave Mr. Monroe a big hug. "Well done, Hubert. Very courageous. Rex would be so proud of you. Just like you were proud of him at Chickamauga."

"Yes . . . well . . . perhaps . . . perhaps that is the solution," he stuttered.

The crowd buzzed with enthusiasm as the meeting continued. Jolie saw Galen Faxon and his crew mount up, tip their hats, and ride toward Scottsbluff. The throng didn't dissipate until after dark when it started to sprinkle. Tanner, Leppy, and Lawson climbed to the roof and fastened a temporary tarpaulin on the schoolhouse roof.

The cowboys and ranchers rode north to the plateau. Jocko and the boys toted half a roasted hog.

The railroaders boarded the train and chugged east.

The homesteaders hurried to get home before the roads slicked up.

And the townspeople raced the rain west.

Jolie sent her family home in the little wagon and kept Pilgrim and Stranger for herself. She straightened the desks and swept yellow cake crumbs into the dustpan.

"Lord, it turned out to be a marvelous evening. What a feast— a feast of food, and ideas, and plans, and new friends, and a future for all of us. You have been very, very generous, and I am grateful."

"Amen, Miss Jolie."

She moved to the slate board and peeked behind her desk at a man prostrate on the wooden floor.

"Bill?"

Bill Condor lay on his back. "I reckon I ate too much, Miss Jolie. If you'll help me to my feet, I'll leave now."

"You can stay there until I get things cleaned up."

"I ate four of them little chickens," he reported.

"Chickens? They were curried Hungarian pheasants."

"If they fed 'em corn, they wouldn't be hungry. I wonder if that meat was a little rank. They almost tasted sweet."

"I suppose you tried some of the cake?"

Bill groaned and rolled over on his side. "Yes, ma'am. Your little sis cut me a piece the size of a pie, and I felt obligated to eat it. It was quite tasty, especially the crunchy part."

Jolie continued to straighten the desks. *I will not ask him about the crunchy part.*

"Where is Bob?"

"He went to the privy a long time ago. He either fell in or fell asleep, I reckon. He ate that entire green tomato pie."

Jolie stood at the open school door and gazed into the dark night. "Bill, it's rainin' bad out there. Where are you and Bob goin' to spend the night?"

"We'll probably jist sleep under the railroad bridge up there. The water stands in pools a little, but you can't feel the rain."

"Bill, you listen to me. I'd have you come stay in our barn, but Leppy, Chug, and Maxwell invited some friends over, and I think there's a dozen men out there. Strath Yarrow and Landen are in the house; so I just don't have anyplace to put you."

"It's okay, Miss Jolie. Me and Bob's been sleepin' out since Christmas." He sat up. "Course, I don't remember which Christmas."

"Bill, I'm worried about that temporary roof they put on this building. What if it blows off in the night? It will ruin books and papers. Do you think you and Bob could sleep in here and watch the roof for me?"

"You mean, inside the schoolhouse?"

"And guard it for me. If everything is neat and dry and in place in the morning, I'll cook you some breakfast."

"Eggs and ham and some little peppers?"

"Yes."

"We'll do it, Miss Jolie. I reckon it will take until mornin' before I can eat again anyway."

Jolie held her black parasol over her head as she ran out into the dark schoolyard to the team. Rain splashed her face. *Lord, it's a cold rain at the wrong time of the year for the crops, but that's Your department. It was a wonderful day. And I accept the rain as well as the other miracles.*

She pulled herself up into the wagon and plopped down on the wet wooden seat. She heard a noise in the back of the wagon.

"Bullet Wells, if you're back there, so help me, I'll hogtie you and drag you home in the mud."

"How about Bullet's oldest brother?" the deep voice said.

"Tanner!"

He crawled up on the seat next to her and dragged the canvas tarp around their shoulders.

"I thought you went home."

"I got to talkin' to Captain Richardson and missed my ride."

Jolie slapped the lead lines, and the rig splashed out into the dark roadway. "Do you expect me to believe that?"

He reached over and kissed her ear with very cold lips. "Nope."

"I'm glad you waited, honey."

"Did you ever notice how much work it takes for you and me to be alone?" he replied.

She let out a deep sigh. "Yes, I did notice that." Jolie could hear the mud trail up from the wheels as they crested the hill and dipped down toward the railroad bridge.

Tanner kissed her ear again. This time his lips felt warmer.

Jolie wrapped the lead line around her wrists. When they approached the underpass at the railroad, she threw herself back. Stranger and Pilgrim slid to a stop under the bridge.

"What are you doin'?" Tanner asked.

"The road is too slick for Stranger and Pilgrim. I thought we'd better wait here. I hear it's dry under this bridge."

"Those two big horses can go anywhere in this county, day or night, under any conditions. Do you expect me to believe that story of yours?"

"Nope." She leaned over and kissed his cheek.

Her lips were very warm.

"How long do you aim to park here?" he asked.

"Oh, just until it stops rainin' so hard."

"That could be half the night, darlin'."

Jolie sighed and laid her head on his chest. "I know."

For a list of other books
by this author
write:
Stephen Bly
Winchester, Idaho 83555
or check out his website:
www.blybooks.com